B] MATCHMAKER

BY SIERRA CARTWRIGHT

DEDICATION

Producing a book takes a team. And I am profoundly grateful for the help I've received along the way.

A very special thank-you to Lexi Blake and Cherise Sinclair, who encouraged me to go for it. Cherise, you've been encouraging me for years. Thank you. And Lexi, not only did you say go for it, you provided advice and resources for which I will always be grateful.

Chloe Vale, YOU are spectacular and valued.

Shannon Hunt, at Once Upon an Alpha, you're amazing! Thank you for being on my team.

Miss Whit—for everything. For you.

Angie, you help keep it all glued together.

Shari Slade—Hey, Girl, I don't know what I would

do without you.

Skye Warren, you are valued more than you will ever know.

Bev, every day, you're there. Thanks for the insight, the support, the encouragement. You really are Bad Ass.

And to my crack editorial team: Nicki, Jennifer, MT, BAB, ELF. Your hard work is valued.

Julie and Ian Kirby, you are so inspiring. I love your love.

Kallypso Masters, you are a heroine among heroines. Thank you!

This also goes out to some special friends from KallyCon: Laura, Carmen, Kim, Alissa, Barb, Darlene, Shawn, Sandie and her wonderful hero John, Lilith, Chloe, Marion, Sue, Dawn, Jennifer and Noel, Melissa, April, Ilene and Jeff, Chayo, Lib, Saya, Sylvie, Deb, Marion, Angelique, Kimi.

And for Crystal and Tony—I appreciate your endless patience with my questions, your great humor, and your kind perspective.

CHAPTER ONE

Rafe Sterling strode through the door of his downtown Houston office and into a Monday morning predawn ambush.

To make matters worse, his shoulder hurt from where he'd landed on it during a bicycle race the previous day, he'd slept badly, and he hadn't had a single cup of coffee.

Three women stood with their backs to the window, a terrifying army in silk and stilettos.

His mother, Rebecca, had her arms folded across her chest, wearing resolve like armor. His sister, Arianna, was in the middle, and she squirmed under his scrutiny. *Good.* At best, she was a reluctant accomplice.

The third woman, all the way on the right, he'd never met.

Her well-defined cheekbones were striking, and her lips were painted a wicked shade of fuck-me red. She wore her long brunette hair loose, the locks flowing around her shoulders. But it was the way she studied him, with total focus, that riveted his attention. Her eyes were a startling shade, not hazel but deeper, like gold. For a moment—a fascinating, unwanted, and mercifully brief flash of time—he imagined them swimming with tears of submission.

He cleared his throat, and she broke their connection by glancing toward the floor.

Fuck. Her gesture arrowed through his gut. For the first time in years—since Emma—he was captivated.

Rafe shook his head. He had no patience for relationships, not even with a woman who wore a skirt that hugged her enticing curves.

"Rafe, darling!" His mother broke ranks and took a couple of steps toward him.

Galvanized, he closed his office door behind him. Better to meet the battle head-on so he could get on with his day. "Morning, ladies."

He crossed the room to drop an obligatory kiss on his mother's cheek, then he noticed a pile of folders on his desk. Something to do with the visit from the unnamed woman, no doubt.

With distrust, he flicked another glance in her

direction. Who the hell was she? "To what do I owe the pleasure of your company?" Rafe eased into his leather executive chair.

His mother took a seat across from him and skipped any further pretense of pleasantries. "You need a wife."

"Ah." He slid the manila menaces to the edge of the desk and resisted—barely—the urge to knock them into the waiting trash can. "Understood. Now this is the part of the confrontation where I tell you I will find a bride when I'm damn well ready. Thank you for your time and concern." He attempted a smile. Judging by his mother's wince, the curl of his lips was closer to a snarl. "I'm sure you can show yourselves out."

"Don't be rude, Rafael Barron Sterling."

He quirked an eyebrow. His mother hadn't used his full name since he was in college.

"Your father is planning to marry Elizabeth."

Rafe opened his mouth, then closed it without speaking. He didn't need to state the obvious. His parents were still married.

"It's imperative we make you the CEO of Sterling Worldwide. This madness must stop at once," Rebecca finished.

"Mother—"

"He bought her a forty-thousand-dollar ring. I saw a picture of it in his email. Gaudy. He has terrible judgment and even worse taste." She shoved the manila folders back to the center of the desk.

Because of Theodore's unstable behavior, his

mother suspected her husband had the early stages of dementia. His physician disagreed, saying that Theodore was at an age where he'd acquired vast wealth and wanted to enjoy it. The motorcycles he couldn't ride and the yacht that needed a crew were proof of that, as were the classic Rolls Royce, a chauffeur, a château in France, and a twenty-three-year-old mistress to enjoy it with.

Rafe suspected that both his mother and the doctor were partially correct. Theodore had never wanted any part in Sterling Worldwide. He'd been the unexpected and much pampered late-in-life and third-born child of Barron and Penelope Sterling. His parents had believed Theodore to be nothing less than a gift from God, and they'd treated him as such, indulging his every whim, allowing him to travel the world from a young age, buying him gifts that had been denied to his siblings. He'd also bypassed the boarding schools that the other Sterling children had attended. But his parents had insisted on a college education. They'd made a sizable donation to the university's foundation to ensure he received passing grades. Surprising everyone, including himself, he'd excelled in business school.

When his older brother, Barron Sterling, Jr., had been killed in a hunting accident, Theodore had been thrust into the unwelcome role as heir and CEO of a worldwide hotel empire. He hadn't known that his much more qualified sister couldn't inherit the business. He'd hired attorneys, but in the end, the terms were absolute. Theodore had lost his freedom and his jet-setting lifestyle. Within weeks of his brother's burial, he was married to the formidable Rebecca, a woman his mother had selected.

Now that Rafe had proven himself competent as the conglomerate's Chief Financial Officer, Theodore had run away from his day-to-day responsibilities in favor of living the life he'd imagined.

Unaware or uncaring that her son hadn't responded, Rebecca continued. "Ms. Malloy"—she pointed to the brunette—"has compiled a list of suitable candidates for your consideration."

"Candidates?"

"To become your wife," Ms. Malloy clarified, taking over the meeting. She crossed the room toward him, her hips swaying and her peep-toe shoes sounding a tattoo that did evil things to his libido.

When she stopped near his desk, her scent reached him, lilacs and summer, a contrast to the darkness that hovered over his life.

"The list has been narrowed to five finalists for your consideration." Obviously she had no clue she was rearranging his brain cells. "Each of the ladies is qualified to be your wife. Of course, for your privacy, they only know certain things about you. A general description, the fact that you're an executive, that you live in Houston. The women have been interviewed and prescreened. We have nondisclosures on record, so any exchange of information will be confidential. Because time is of the essence, a mixer on Thursday or Friday would be most expeditious. If you prefer, we can arrange casual meetings, coffee or breakfast, perhaps lunch as you narrow your selection to three. From there we will be happy to set up dinners. That way you can get to know her before actual social events. We can make it appear like a whirlwind romance and—"

"Stop." He held up a hand and trapped her gaze. "Who the fuck are you?"

"I didn't realize that you weren't aware…" She glanced toward his mother, but Rebecca looked down to pluck a piece of lint from her skirt

Recovering, the brunette smiled. The gesture was quick, practiced, and polished—meant to impart confidence without being too familiar.

Irrationally, it—she—irritated the hell out of him.

"I beg your pardon. I'm Hope Malloy." She extended her hand. "It's a pleasure to meet you, Mr. Sterling."

He ignored her gesture. "I asked you a question."

As she dropped her arm, her smile vanished. When she spoke, her tone was more formal. "I own The Prestige Group. Celeste Fallon recommended my team to your mother."

"Team of…what?"

"We are an elite matchmaking service for the world's wealthiest, most discerning individuals. We understand that it's difficult for men such as yourself to meet appropriate—"

"You're a *matchmaker*? You stick your nose in

other people's business for a living?" Stunned, Rafe swung his gaze toward his mother. "What the hell are you thinking?"

"Watch your tone."

"You've got thirty seconds before I throw all of you out."

"I know this is a shock, so I'll forgive your bad manners. Prestige will be discreet on this search. No one needs to know it's happening."

He stood and slammed his palms flat on the desk surface. "You hired them to find me a *wife*?" The killer-heeled woman was here to marry him off to some nameless woman to safeguard the Sterling empire?

"Celeste has assured me that Ms. Malloy is the best."

Of that, he had no doubt. Fallon and Associates was one of the world's most exclusive crisis management firms. For more than a hundred and fifty years, they'd specialized in high-profile cases, restoring reputations, saving careers, ensuring people never talked. Like Sterling Worldwide, the Fallons had also kept the business private, and all owners had been related to the founder, Walter Fallon—who'd been part of a secret society at the University of Virginia with Rafe's great-great-great-great-grandfather, John.

Along with five other young men who'd been in the same organization, John and Walter had become lifelong friends. Over the years, the Sterlings and Fallons had helped each other numerous times, including earlier in the year when Theodore and Lillibet had been caught in the first-class toilet of a commercial aircraft.

Thanks to Fallon and Associates, the investigation had gone away, and Celeste had managed to kill the story before a prominent East Coast newspaper could get anyone to verify the distasteful rumors.

As it was, only one blog had run the story, under the headline, *Little Girl and her Teddy Join the Mile High Club!* The teaser, as vile as it was provocative, had been a clever play on his father's name and the ridiculous age difference between the lovers.

A week later, the website had vanished.

"Ms. Malloy has done a fine job. At this rate, we can announce your engagement within a few weeks."

"Goodbye."

Undaunted, his mother went on. "It's a matter of time before your father causes a disaster we can't recover from." Even though anger strung her words together, she didn't raise her voice. As always, Rebecca was the picture of calm, focused resolve. "You're over thirty. If you had done your duty years ago, we wouldn't be facing this situation now."

He winced at the truth of the accusation. Ever since Rafe was a child, his mother had been clear about his obligations. But to him, love equaled drama, and he despised both.

"You need to be sensible." She brought her index fingers together and studied him.

Arianna joined them. "I know you don't like

people meddling in your life, but—"

"Meddling?" He'd had enough. "You call this *meddling*?"

"Things are going to get worse, not better, with Dad and his—" Arianna caught her bottom lip with her teeth. "With Elizabeth."

Every day, Rafe hoped his father would return to Houston and his office, but since his dad and Lillibet, as he called her, had been ensconced in their St. Pete's Beach love nest for two weeks, that didn't seem imminent.

Rafe sighed. "I know you're concerned, and I understand it." More than ready to get out of this mess, he said, "I'll talk to him again."

"You've done so numerous times," Rebecca pointed out.

Dozens. Maybe more. "If necessary, I'll fly out there."

"What if it doesn't work?" Rebecca asked in a chilled tone. "This cannot continue. You're a smart man, Rafe. You know how delicate this situation is. Let's not make it any more complicated than it needs to be."

Possible scenarios lined up in his mind and fired across his brain in a burst of nightmares, each worse than the last. Theodore asking for a divorce. His mother being awarded half of the company and the courts being involved in the painstaking divisions. It could drag on for years while his father played with his mistress. In a worst-case situation, Theodore might, indeed, commit bigamy, which would create a public relations quagmire that Sterling Worldwide might not recover from.

Rafe pinched the bridge of his nose.

"Noah stopped by the house Friday evening," Rebecca said. "Your father isn't returning calls. I understand from his assistant that Noah's been dropping by the executive office every day. She's been making excuses, but she isn't convinced he believes her."

Rafe struggled to hold his temper in check. His cousin, Noah Richardson, son of Rafe's aunt, Victoria Sterling-Richardson, believed he had grounds to challenge Rafe's position as heir apparent. According to the archaic terms of the trust, succession went to male descendants in birth order. Even then, the heir was required to be married.

Noah ran one of the divisions, was a multimillionaire in his own right, and he believed he was the rightful heir since Rebecca and Theodore hadn't been married when Barron, Jr., had been killed. Noah itched to break up the corporation and sell it off, a philosophy Rafe was against. Noah had threatened to see Rafe in court numerous times. Rafe had responded that any challenge should have come a generation ago. But because Noah was married with children, there was a chance, however slight, that he might prevail in a court case. Even if the decision was in Rafe's favor, the litigation could drag on for months, even years. The financial cost could be devastating.

"I'm sorry." Arianna wrung her hands. "I hate

this, and I didn't want to be part of it. It's awful that we have to coerce you into doing something you're not ready to do."

He believed her. Unlike him, she was a romantic, a dreamer shattered by her second divorce.

"Arianna and I will leave you to it." Rebecca stood.

"I haven't agreed to anything." He refused to be railroaded.

"You'll do what you need to." His mother wasn't backing down.

She closed the door with a decisive *click*, sealing him in with the enemy. Hope was a beautiful, seductive temptress, but the enemy, nonetheless.

"You're a matchmaker."

"It's an honorable profession."

"Is it? Much like operating an escort service. I hire you. I will end up paying to fuck a woman, one who's interchangeable with any number of other *candidates*."

"That's as insulting as it is crass." She set her chin and didn't sever the connection of their gazes, meeting the heat of his anger with cool, aloof professionalism.

He wanted to shake it from her, strip her bare, discover what lay beneath the surface to leave nothing but aching, pulsing honesty between them.

Either not noticing the tension or ignoring it, she continued. "Throughout history, families arranged marriages all the time. In parts of the world, it still goes on. Today, there's a bigger need for my services than ever before. I have clients all over the world, from all sorts of backgrounds and of all ages. Often, men in your position don't have time to meet women in the traditional way. You're far too busy, important, insulated."

"Spare me the sales pitch."

"It makes sense to select someone I've interviewed, a woman who suits the needs of a man such as you. A woman of the right temperament, with the same interests, goals, morals, outlook, political leanings, religious preferences. A woman who understands what is expected of her and is willing to assume those responsibilities."

"A business arrangement."

"If you like."

Rafe took his seat and left her standing. It was undoubtedly rude, but justified. His mother had hired Prestige, but Hope had been part of the early-morning intervention. She could have refused, but she hadn't. That made her complicit. "So that's what's in here?" He flicked a glance at the folders. "A money-hungry bride-to-be—I beg your pardon, *candidate*—who understands what she's getting herself into?"

"These women all deserve your respect."

"And an expensive engagement ring?" He leaned back. "Why should I trust you?"

"Five years of success. Thirty-seven marriages."

"Divorces?"

"Two."

"Much better than the national average. Yet five

years in business means your experiment hasn't made it to the seven-year itch yet."

"Whether that exists or not is a matter of debate. There's a study that suggests there's a four-year itch as well as a seven-year one. Oh, and a three-year one. And most couples who divorce tend to do so after a decade. So that means there's a twelve-year flameout as well." She lifted one delicate shoulder in a half shrug. "Whatever your bias, you can find a study to support it. The truth is, each individual is unique, and so are their relationships. People divorce for a lot of reasons and after any length of time."

"Fair enough."

"There are, however, a number of factors that enhance chances for success. I call them the Three C's — compatibility, chemistry, and commitment."

"Define success."

She tipped her head to one side. "I suppose that's in the eye of the beholder."

"Take my parents. They've been victims of wedded bliss for thirty-three years."

"There are financial and legal benefits for people who are married."

She'd sidestepped his point neatly.

"Couples who are wed, versus those who cohabitate, tend to live longer."

"Or perhaps it only seems that way."

She smiled, and it transformed her features, making her no longer standoffish and professional, but warm and inviting. No wonder lemmings turned to her for matrimonial advice. "Have you always been a cynic, Mr. Sterling?"

"About marriage?" *Not always*. But the few illusions he'd held had been shattered. "Can you blame me?"

"You can't think of any positive examples?"

"Like my sister? She's twenty-seven and going through her second divorce, and this one is more gruesome and costly than the first. My best friend and college roommate, Griffin Lahey? His wife of three years just walked out, dumped him, ripped apart their future, and took away their son. For the final knife in his heart, she's suing for half of his estate because she met an artist who she fancies and wants to move to Paris with him. Noah's parents live on separate continents. My grandmother had to be coaxed into attending my grandfather's funeral. I'm told she was drunk at the time, and not from grief. On the morning he was to be buried, legend has it that she knocked back an entire bottle of champagne...from the private reserve he had saved for special occasions. So, no, I'm not anxious to stick my neck in the matrimonial noose."

"You asked why you should trust me. You shouldn't. You have no reason to, yet. I could give you references from satisfied customers. I could reassure you that I've signed a nondisclosure. Or that Celeste Fallon believes in me. But none of that means anything. You need results. If the potential women I've matched you with don't suit your needs, I'll give you another five. Or fire me and I'll refund your mother's fee."

"Fee?" He narrowed his eyes. "How much do you charge?"

"I'm expensive, Mr. Sterling."

"Ten thousand dollars? Twenty?" When she didn't react, he tried again. "More than that?"

"A hundred thousand."

"Shit." People were willing to pay a hundred grand to meet someone? If it worked out, he'd have the honor of shelling out thousands more for baubles to go along with it? Then, when the shine wore off, she'd keep them *and* half his fortune?

"I'm worth every penny."

"That's pretty confident."

"I am." She folded her arms across her chest. "I work hard to ensure I satisfy my clients."

He glanced at the top folder as if it were rabid. "How did you choose these particular women?"

"In normal circumstances, I meet with a gentleman so I can get a sense about him. Then he fills in a questionnaire. It's rather detailed. Fourteen pages of likes, dislikes, things that worked in previous relationships. Things that didn't."

"Go on."

"Expectations around traditions are important as are roles in the relationship. To some, religion is important. I find out if he wants children. If so, how many? Will he want them raised in a particular religion? Where does he plan to live? In the US or abroad? Will the children attend private school? Boarding school? Will a nanny be hired? A housekeeper? After I've reviewed that, I have a second meeting with him for further clarification."

"And they need you for this?"

"Most of the men I work with don't have the opportunity to meet women they might be serious about marrying. They've often focused their attention on their careers or education. Some of them are famous, but they don't want to settle down with a woman they've met on the road or someone who's been part of their fan club."

"And where do you find the women who are anxious to throw themselves at the feet of these rich men?"

"I belong to a number of organizations, and I'm active in Houston's art and business communities. It may surprise you, but I'm often invited to high-society events. I've seen you at a few."

Rafe regarded her again. "We haven't met." He would have remembered. Her eyes, her voice, the sweet curve of her hips, the way her legs went on forever in those shoes. Yeah. He would have remembered.

"No. I spend most of my time talking with women. Part of my value is that I've met all the candidates, interviewed them, watched them interact at social events." She nudged a folder toward him. "Try me."

"Have a seat." Rafe wondered at his sudden offer of hospitality. He didn't need Hope and her lilac-and-silk scent in his office while he looked through the files.

She sat opposite him, her movements delicate.

Her skirt rode up her bare thighs, just a bit. He imagined skimming his fingers across her smooth skin while she gasped, then yanking down her panties, curving his fingers into the hot flesh of her ass cheeks.

Christ. He'd spent all Saturday working on next quarter's business plan. In the previous day's bike race against some of his friends, he'd pushed too fast, too hard, on a grueling part of the course and crashed. He'd had a shot of Crown before going to bed but skipped taking anything else for the pain. He'd slept like hell, and he'd spent too long working out cramps in the shower to even think about masturbating.

Now, he wished he had taken the edge off.

It had been over a month since he'd visited the Retreat, a BDSM club in a historic warehouse on Buffalo Bayou in downtown Houston, and even longer since he'd enjoyed the singular pleasure of playing with a sub at the discreet second-story Quarter in New Orleans. Of course being this close to an attractive female after such an intense drought would give him an erection. *Shit.* He couldn't force himself to believe his own fucking lie. Every day, he was surrounded by beautiful women. He wanted Hope. With her ass upturned, listening to her frantic breaths as she waited for his belt...waited for his touch. It was more than the sound of her voice or the innocent-yet-provocative shoes, it was carnal desire. Lust. The last time he was gripped by its power, he'd been in college and far more helpless than he was now.

He imprisoned his thoughts and focused on the task in front of him.

Picking up the first file, he flipped it open.

The top page had a name, a picture, and the vital statistics of a beautiful twenty-four-year-old blonde. She was a UT Austin graduate, a pageant winner who flashed a tiara-worthy smile and worked as a fundraiser for underprivileged schools.

In every way, on paper, she should interest him. She was attractive, knew how to handle herself in public, and she had philanthropic inclinations.

Naturally his mother would approve. And yet… He felt nothing—less than nothing. He was uninspired and disinterested. The hard-on he'd been sporting vanished. He glanced up at Hope Malloy. "You said chemistry matters?"

"She doesn't appeal to you?"

"Not in the least."

"Perhaps you'll have better luck with another choice?"

He didn't.

After perusing the second picture, he glanced back at Hope.

"Nothing?"

"No."

"It's possible the attraction would develop after you meet someone. Her choice of conversation, the way she moves or looks at you." She shifted. "Pheromones."

Those, he was starting to believe in. Keeping his

mind on the folders, he said, "I see. My mother hopes I will select a bride, whether I want to fuck her or not?"

Hot pink scorched Hope's cheekbones before she recovered. "So, you would rather have a spine-tingling attraction to someone who consumes you?"

"No." He'd had that. Once. With Emma, in college. He'd been crazy enough about her that he'd bought her a stunning ring.

He had been invited to join her family for Christmas brunch, and he'd intended to propose then. Unbeknownst to him, Emma had been so intent on getting married that she'd been juggling dates with three different men. One of them had popped the question on Christmas Eve in front of the tree's twinkling lights.

When she'd called to let him know, she wasn't apologetic. She reminded him she wanted a wedding as a college graduation present, and Aaron had offered her just that. It was nothing personal. She would have been happy marrying any of them.

Rafe had hit the local bar near a shopping center. When he left, there'd been a red kettle set up outside. A man nearby was ringing a bell and asking for charitable donations. Rafe stuffed her ring through the slot and accepted the candy the bell ringer offered as thanks.

A sucker. If there'd ever been a more appropriate gesture, he didn't recall it.

Rafe had spent every day until the new year in an alcohol-induced stupor, calling her at all hours, sending desperate text messages, even driving to her home in a stupid and embarrassing attempt to get her to change her mind.

"Mr. Sterling?" Hope's questioning voice cut through the morose memories.

He flipped the folder closed without reading any of the pages. He refused to be out of control over a woman ever again. But if he was expected to marry and produce an heir or two, he should at least want to go to bed with her.

"Perhaps of the three C's, compatibility and commitment are more important than chemistry?"

How much longer until he could dismiss her?

When he didn't answer, she filled the silence. "Can you tell me what it was about the first two candidates that didn't suit your needs? It will help me refine the search."

"Ms. Malloy..." He struggled to leash his raging impatience. "Show some fucking mercy, will you? Until ten minutes ago, I didn't know I needed a *candidate*."

She edged the third folder toward him.

With great reluctance but with a sudden urge to get through this, he thumbed it open. Another blonde. Another perfect smile. Another impeccable pedigree. "Since I didn't fill in your forms, I assume it was my mother who decided what college degrees and background were important?"

"Your sister rounded it out as far as activities you enjoy."

"Yet I don't see any of them who like to ride a

mountain bike."

"Not a huge demand in this part of Texas."

"Kayaking?"

"I'll add that to the next search."

He gave in to curiosity. "Was Celeste consulted?"

"I invited her to be part of process. She declined."

If Celeste had been involved, perhaps there would have been a redhead or a brunette. Even someone with pink toenails in peekaboo shoes.

For the second time, he resisted the impulse to hurl the files in the trash. Instead, he opened his top drawer and swept the offensive lot inside, then slammed it shut.

Hope uncrossed her legs and leaned toward him. Then, evidently thinking better of it, she sat back and recrossed them.

He swore her skin whispered like the promise of sin.

"Perhaps you should consider the options at a more convenient time," she suggested.

"I'll see you receive full payment." He stood.

"I've already received it."

His mother had written this woman a check for a hundred grand? "Thank you for your efforts."

"Mr. Sterling—"

He walked past her to the door and opened it.

She sighed but stood. After gathering her purse—a small pink thing shaped like a cat, complete with ears and whiskers—she joined him. Instead of leaving, as he'd ordered, she stood in front of him, chin tipped at a defiant angle.

Hope projected competence, but the heels and fanciful handbag gave her a feminine air. A sane man would think of her as a vendor or business associate, so he could slot her into the *off-limits* part of his conscience. She wasn't a potential date or wife. Or submissive.

He wanted her.

She isn't mine.

Fuck his conscience.

Before this ridiculous idea about finding him a woman to marry went any further, she needed to know the truth about him, the side he locked away and kept hidden unless he was at one of his favorite BDSM clubs, the side that Celeste should have informed his matchmaker about.

Bare inches separated him from Hope, and he halved that distance by leaning toward her. "Is there a place on your fourteen-page questionnaire to discuss sexual proclivities?"

"I'm not sure what you mean." Her knuckles whitened on her purse strap.

"Let me clarify." Rafe spoke softly into the thick air between them. "Kinks. Those nasty, scandalous things that people do in the privacy of their own homes. Things they don't talk about in public. Salacious acts that make them drop to their knees in church as they beg forgiveness. Would you consider that compatibility or chemistry?"

Tension tightened her shoulders. "Is there

something…" Her tone suggested she was trying for professionalism, but her voice cracked on a sharp inhalation.

After a few more shallow breaths, she ventured, "What do I need to know?"

"I'm into BDSM."

Her beautiful, pouty mouth parted a little.

An image scorched him—that of him slipping a spider gag between her lips, spreading her mouth and keeping it that way. He'd force her to communicate with her expression and her body, like she was now. "Your eyes are wide, Ms. Malloy. Are you shocked? Interested?" Her soul was reflected in the startling depths. "Curious, perhaps?"

It took her less than three seconds to close her mouth and regroup. "No. I'm wondering how I should phrase this for your candidates."

She'd lied. Instead of meeting his gaze, she stared at the potted plant near the window.

Rather than unleashing the beast that suddenly wanted to dominate her, he kept his tone even. "I'm sure you've had clients who like that sort of thing?"

Finally, after a breath, she looked at him. "I'll make some discreet inquiries of the candidates. What is it you're looking for?"

He ached to capture her chin and force her to look at him. "How much do you know about BDSM?"

She pulled back her shoulders, as if on more stable ground. "I've heard of it."

"No personal experience?"

"That's not relevant."

Damn her dishonest answer. Some? None? Would he be her first? Could he take her, mold her into what he wanted?

What the fuck was wrong with him? He'd already decided she was off-limits. "There are as many ways to practice BDSM as there are people in the lifestyle. No relationship is the same."

"Makes sense."

Mesmerized, he watched the wild flutter of her pulse in her throat. It was like oxygen to a dying man. He wanted more. "Some people prefer to confine their practices to the bedroom—at night, for example. Others, on occasion, indulge at a club or play party. A number of people practice it in varying degrees on a twenty-four-hour basis."

"Where do your…proclivities lie?"

Until now, he hadn't considered he might want a submissive wife. Over the years, he'd found it easier to go to the club. He was a Dom who would give a sub what she wanted, whether it was pain, roleplay, humiliation, a sensuous flogging, hours with torturous toys.

When he'd planned to marry Emma, he assumed she would work at a job that inspired her. Alternatively, she'd have been free to engage in social activities or charity endeavors like the wives of some of his associates. Giving up his clubs hadn't been a consideration. Nor had he allowed himself to think of calling his bride at five p.m. and telling her to meet him in the foyer of his loft, naked, with her thighs spread and cunt shaved.

Now, however, he couldn't banish the thought. And since his mother had already squandered a hundred grand, he figured he should be specific in his requests. More, he wanted Hope to know what she was getting into, even if she didn't yet realize he'd chosen her. "I want my wife to be submissive twenty-four hours a day."

"Can you clarify what you mean?" She clenched the handle of her kitty bag, seeming to pretend this was an ordinary conversation with a normal man.

Jeanine, the best executive assistant on the continent, entered the outer office. She'd been with Sterling Worldwide for almost thirty years, and with him for the past seven. With her polite smile and firm voice, she protected him against the world. "Morning, Mr. Sterling."

"Jeanine."

She angled her head toward Hope. "Everything all right, sir?"

"Unscheduled meeting with the Prestige Group."

"I see."

"My mother arranged it."

Jeanine scowled with understanding. Like a she-dragon, Jeanine would have protected him from his own mother. "Anything you need, Mr. Sterling?" She was asking if he wanted her to call security or to show the woman out. "Coffee?"

Her combination of savviness and loyalty made her indispensable.

"Just one cup, please. Ms. Malloy won't be staying."

He captured Hope's shoulders and pulled her into his office so he could close the door. He held on to her for a whole lot longer than was necessary but not as long as he wanted to. How would she react if he eased his first finger up the delicate column of her throat?

Would she surrender? Fight the inevitable?

Forcing himself to resist the driving impulse, he dropped his hands and curled them into fists at his sides.

"Proclivities," she prompted.

The word echoed in his head. "She'll wear a collar—my collar..." And because he could no longer resist, he traced an index finger across the hollow of her throat. Her pulse fluttered, and her breaths momentarily ceased. "My woman will know that she belongs to me and she will behave as such."

Hope's gaze remained locked on his. When she spoke, her voice wobbled. "And this...collar. She'll have to wear it all the time?"

"That's what twenty-four seven means." A devilish grin tugged at his lips. He kept his fingertip pressed to her warm skin. "It will be subtle, however. Nothing gaudy. Unless people knew, I doubt they'd think she was wearing anything other than a striking piece of jewelry. But her play collar, the one she wears in private with me or at a lifestyle event, may be different."

"Like at a BDSM club or something?" She

nodded, as if she were on ground she understood.

Not that he'd let her stay there long. "I enjoy showing off my sub. There's a certain restaurant in New Orleans, Vieille Rivière, that she will go to. And she'll join me when I visit people in similar social circles." *Including other Titans.* But there was a limit to how much he should tell her. "There are certain things I would want her to go along with. Bondage. Sensory deprivation."

"You mean like blindfolds and handcuffs?" There was no hesitation in her words, so he ascertained she'd made sense of what he'd said and decided that fell under the category of typical bedroom shenanigans.

"Among others, yes. I use blindfolds on occasion. I like gags so that my woman must beg with her eyes. Her tears are like dripping nectar from the gods."

Wide-eyed, uncertain, she sucked in a deep, disbelieving breath.

"Clamps," he added, skimming the column of her throat.

"I..."

"On her nipples, among other places. And I will want to her to wait for me at the end of a long day, on her knees, head tipped back, her beautiful mouth held open by a dental dam."

"You mean...she'd have to do this herself?"

"Prepare for my homecoming?" He imagined Hope parting her lips, sliding in the dam and positioning it, pictured her naked in front of the door, hungry for his touch. "Yes."

She retreated a step. "Mr. Sterling, I—"

"My wife will focus on me and my pleasure."

"That sounds rather old-fashioned."

"Does it? What you're not aware of is what I'm willing to do in return."

"In return?"

"I wouldn't expect a woman to give me everything she has to offer without me giving equal parts of myself. Her wants and desires will be my highest priority. I will give her the heavens if she wants them, the stars, the moon." He paused. "Then I'll take her to the depths of hell as she uncovers what sets her depraved soul free."

She shuddered.

"Can you find me all that in a *candidate*, Ms. Malloy?"

"You're rather particular."

"Indeed. I require a woman of impeccable breeding who presents her ass for my punishment when she displeases me."

The air conditioner kicked on. The whispering cool air did nothing to dissipate the heat between them.

He slid his hand around to the back of her neck, then feathered his fingers into her hair. "I want to kiss you, Ms. Malloy."

"Uhm…"

"Ask me to."

She scowled.

"I won't have you pretending that you're not

curious. When you're at home this evening, by yourself with a glass of wine, horny and considering masturbating—"

"That's not me." She shook her head so fast it was obviously a desperate lie.

"No? Ms. Malloy, the room is swimming with your pheromones. Deny it." She sagged a little against his hand, and he tightened his grip on her hair, as much to offer support as to imprison her. Then he continued as if she hadn't interrupted. "You'll remember this moment, fantasize about being mine."

"No…"

"Invite me to kiss you or tell me to release you. The power is yours. Yield to temptation or leave this room wondering if it's as good as you imagine it will be."

"Mr. Sterling, this can't be happening."

Despite her protest, she didn't try to escape. "I agree. This is the first time I've had three women"—four if he counted Celeste—"attempt to force me down the aisle." He paused. "And it's the first time I've had this kind of sexual longing for an adversary. Ask me to kiss you," he repeated instead of arguing. "Be sure to say please."

"Ah…"

He loosened his grip, and she leaned toward him, keeping herself hostage. Rafe didn't smile with triumph.

"Kiss me."

"There's nothing I'd enjoy more." That wasn't

the entire truth. There were a hundred things he'd like to do to her, but he made no move

Her internal standoff lasted longer than he thought it would. Excellent. She had a stubborn streak.

Hope glanced away and sighed. Then she looked at him with clear, confident eyes. "Please kiss me."

He could drown in her and be happy about it. He captured her chin to hold her steady. On her lips, he tasted the sweetness of her capitulation. "Open your mouth, sweet Hope."

She did, and he entered her mouth, slower than he would ordinarily, softer than he would if she were his submissive.

Hope responded with hesitation, and he continued, driving deeper, seeking more. Within seconds, she yielded.

She moaned and raised onto her tiptoes to lean into him. A few seconds beyond that, she wrapped her arms around him. Hope, his adversary, had now become his willing captive.

He released her chin and moved his hand to the middle of her back, then lower to the base of her spine.

Rafe drank in the scent of her femininity. His cock surged, not from ordinary arousal, but from soul-deep recognition. Her eagerness sought the Dom in him. It took all his restraint not to press his palm against her buttocks.

Earlier he'd said she'd be thinking of him as she masturbated. The truth was, he wasn't sure how he'd banish this memory of her — strength and suppleness in one heady package.

He plundered her mouth.

She offered more until she was panting and desperate, gripping him hard.

Instead of giving in to the driving need to rip off her clothes and fuck her, he distracted himself by tugging on her hair harder. As he'd requested, her eyes were open. *So goddamn trusting.* Did she have any idea how close he was to shredding the veneer of civilization that hung between them to claim her, mark her as his?

He ended the kiss while he still could. Her mouth was swollen, and he couldn't stop staring at her lips.

Hope took tiny breaths that didn't seem to steady her. She held on to him while she lowered her heels to the floor. Then, over a few heartbeats, she dropped her hands.

"Thank you, Rafe," he prompted.

"Are you serious? I'm supposed to thank you?" She continued to look at him and undoubtedly saw his resolve.

Would she give him what he demanded? "Unless you want me to spank —"

"Spank?" Her chin was at a full tilt.

"Spank." He repeated with emphasis. "Unless you want me to spank your pretty little ass so hard that you can't sit down after you leave here."

"That kind of behavior is unacceptable."

"Under normal circumstances," he agreed

without hesitation. "Unless you ask me for it." Part of him hoped she'd take him up on it. It would be a pleasure to prove she liked the feel of his hand on her bare skin. "I'll go first." He softened his tone, letting her glimpse his inner thoughts, a rare confession of his soul. "I enjoyed kissing you. Thank you."

"I..." She smoothed the skirt that he wanted to rip off her body.

"Look at me."

She followed his command. Then, with a soft and decidedly insubmissive tone, she said, "Thank you."

"Ms. Malloy, as I said, it was my pleasure."

Silence hung between them. Her inexperience thrilled him, and he wanted to give her another hundred firsts. Instead, he let her go. The real world—with its complex demands—was waiting. And if he wanted her at his feet, he had a lot of work to do.

"I'm not certain how much of what you said, and what we just did, is to get me to admit defeat, to quit..." She stiffened her spine.

"Maybe it started that way." His father's behavior had pissed Rafe off, and so had his mother's ambush, even Hope herself. He'd wanted to shake her as badly as he'd been shaken. As he'd spoken to her, his desires had churned to the surface. Until now—until *her*—he had been willing to confine his kink to a club. "It didn't end that way. That I promise you."

"I will ask the candidates about their openness to your suggestions."

Fuck. She wanted to retreat behind a facade of business, as if their kiss hadn't changed something. "Requirements. Not suggestions. Requirements. Be clear about that. If I'm to be saddled with a woman that I don't want until death do us part, there will be none of the hysteria that my family members seem to thrive on. My *wife* will know her place and her role, and she will meet my expectations. And to be clear, she *will* ask for my kiss. Like you did." He opened the door.

Jeanine was walking toward his office with a cup of coffee, and he waved her off.

Then, voice so soft that only Hope could hear, he finished. "You have a fourteen-page interview form. I will have something similar for the women you bring to me. It will cover things such as anal play, being shared with others, edging, exhibitionism. Shall I send it to you first?"

"Please do. It will save some time in your selection process." She started past him, and he snagged her elbow.

"And Ms. Malloy? She'll fucking address me as Sir." He was unaccountably furious at her rejection. At himself. "And if you come here ever again, so will you."

Her hand trembled where she grasped her purse strap. She flicked a glance at his hand before yanking her elbow free and continuing.

She paused at Jeanine's desk to say goodbye.

Why did that matter so much to him?

He should have snagged the cup of coffee and returned to his office to call his father, but Rafe continued to watch Hope. Each damnable step made her hips sway, and his still-hard cock throbbed in response.

At the door leading to the hallway, Hope paused, her hand on the knob. She glanced over her shoulder and met his gaze without blinking. He might have unsettled her, even shocked her. But he hadn't scared her.

Round one to the beautiful matchmaker.

CHAPTER TWO

Hell and a handbasket. The world shifted beneath Hope's feet. Who the fuck did he think he was? The Lord of Domination? And why had she responded with such abandon? As she strode down the marble hallway to the elevator, Hope forced herself to keep her chin high. It wasn't until after she'd pushed the call button and made sure she was alone that she allowed her shoulders to collapse against the wall, right beneath the scripted silver letters bearing Rafe's last name.

Celeste had warned that he was formidable and had coached Hope to be unflappable when dealing with him. Though she'd done a good job of presenting a cool exterior, nothing could have prepared her for meeting with the CFO of Sterling Worldwide.

He stood over six feet tall, was broad-shouldered and lean, showing he worked out as hard as he did everything else. As elegant as his suit had been, it hadn't concealed the force of his primal nature.

He'd studied her in a way no other man ever had. His questions had been pointed as he'd probed for her deepest secrets. Even though she had wanted to protect herself, she hadn't been able to look away from his threatening, turbulent deep-blue eyes.

The moment his mother and sister left the room, his danger had seared her. *"She'll wear a collar — my collar — and she will know she belongs to me."*

His voice had been cloaked in the most delicate silk, and his words had struck with a force that had left her speechless. They'd penetrated deep inside her brain, weaving an image until she pictured herself on her knees — waiting for his every command as he claimed what was his.

Any man speaking in such blunt, sexual terms would have triggered the same sort of feminine reaction from her. No. That was a lie. Every day, she spent time with rich, powerful men who had specific demands. Those words from anyone else would have left her cold. Rafe's image left her hungry.

Sex had always been unremarkable. It was required once a relationship progressed to a certain point, but it was a chore.

In Rafe's office, however, unfamiliar desire had

crawled through her. He'd been right about her pheromones. She'd never been aroused like that. When he'd caressed her throat, his prediction that she would ask for his kiss had become inevitable.

His mouth had demanded, and his tongue had plundered. Then he'd moved one hand to the small of her back. In that terrifying moment, she would have knelt for him, and part of her had unraveled at the idea that he might redden her ass. Even now she couldn't stop thinking about how his hand would feel on her naked buttocks. The wicked humiliation of it all…

When the kiss had ended, she'd been confused. Reality had crashed in on her. When had she become so wanton? Not knowing what else to do, she'd gathered her professional aura around her. The way he grabbed her elbow meant he sensed her withdrawal and had disliked it as much as she had.

She could have pulled away at any time. Why hadn't she?

The bell dinged, jarring her, and she pushed away from the wall. Her bag clutched in her hands, she rode the elevator to the lobby.

People strode past, some talking on phones, others staring at the screens, with most of them wearing earbuds, lost in a world of music, books, or podcasts. All were going through their day while her insides were in turmoil.

On the sidewalk outside, she paused.

Though it was ridiculous, she glanced up at the fifteenth floor and swept her gaze across the windows. Most were still dark. But at the end of the row, a man stood in one, unmoving, framed in glass and steel and power.

It couldn't be Rafe. He was far too busy running his conglomerate to look for her on the street.

No matter what her mind insisted, her heart had no doubt it was him. She'd had a connection with him that transcended common sense.

She shook her head and hurried to the parking lot where she'd left her car.

When she was inside with the doors locked, she exhaled. Her heart thundered as if she'd run down the pavement. And her skin was both hot and chilled. She allowed herself another thirty seconds to pull herself together before slipping her car into drive and navigating Houston's ever-thickening rush-hour traffic toward her own downtown suite of small offices.

In her purse, her phone vibrated half a moment before her upbeat marimba ringtone bounced through the passenger compartment, too loud and chipper for her current mood.

She glanced at the screen on her dash. Celeste Fallon. Curious, Hope connected the call. Her internship at Fallon and Associates during college garnered her a mentor and invaluable experience. The long, dedicated hours were rewarded with an invitation into Celeste's inner circle.

As usual, Celeste skipped a greeting. "He didn't like any of the women."

"No." Even though Hope had spent hours with

his mother and sister, searching through pictures and reading biographies of more than a hundred women, Rafe hadn't given any of them more than a cursory glance. "Is that a good guess? Wait—did you already talk to him?"

"I know Rafe."

"You could have saved me some time."

"Why on earth would I do that?"

Hope scowled. "You could have guided me in the right direction."

"Meaning what?"

Did Celeste know that he was into BDSM? "He has..." Hope stumbled around. How did she repeat what he'd said without revealing his secrets? "He's seeking a specific set of attributes in a wife."

"If you decide to look for a career in PR, see me first." Celeste's voice was droll. "You can't terminate your contract with him."

Hope's scowl deepened. As long as she refunded Rebecca's money, Prestige was under no obligation to the Sterlings.

"I know he's challenging—"

"That's not the word I'd choose."

"This is delicate, Hope." Celeste was direct to the point of bluntness, so her sudden vagueness was surprising.

"His tastes are unusual," Hope said.

"It's more than that. Finding Rafe a wife will open avenues that you can't imagine."

Instead of cruising through a yellow light, Hope stopped so she could concentrate on what Celeste was saying.

"There are others…"

Like Rafe? "Listen, Celeste…" She'd accepted Rafe's challenge. Pride alone wouldn't allow her to walk away. "I will find him a suitable wife."

"I knew I could count on you."

The car behind her blasted its horn. Without her noticing, the light had turned green. Before she could respond to Celeste, the call ended.

A few minutes later, Hope pulled into her spot in the parking garage. Although it was April, the humidity was oppressive, the sky a milky, churning gray. She slipped out of her blazer as she took the stairs to the third floor.

This morning, she was the first to arrive, and she unlocked the suite before walking into her office. After dropping her belongings on the credenza, she sank into the white utilitarian leather chair behind her glass-topped desk.

Her desk phone's light flicked on and off, indicating waiting messages. Since Skyler, her assistant, wasn't in yet, Hope listened to the first voicemail, from a potential client who preferred to talk rather than use email.

The second was from a woman she'd talked to last week at a business mixer, hoping to meet an older gentleman she'd seen listed on Prestige's website.

Rafe Sterling not withstanding, the week was off to a promising start.

A knock on her doorjamb made Hope look up.

Skyler stood there, carrying a tray that held two extra-large cups bearing the logo of their favorite shop. She also held up a small pastel-pink bag. If there was a God, there would be a chocolate cake doughnut inside. Without waiting for an invite, she sashayed in. "I come bearing gifts. A quad latte for the Matchmaking Maven."

Four shots of espresso? "Are you a mind reader?"

"You were still emailing me at midnight, and I know you had to get up before five to meet Mr. Sterling."

Greedy for the gift, Hope held out her hand.

"I want the details."

"Anything. Even my firstborn. Just hand it over."

Skyler held the cup just out of reach. "You have to promise not to leave anything out."

Except for the ones about the collar, the kiss, or how impossible it was to banish the image of waiting for him at the end of the day. "What's in the bag?"

"Exactly what you're hoping is in there. You just have to share the details in return."

"Anything you want to know," Hope lied. All was fair in love and doughnuts.

With a grin, Skyler handed over the latte, then shoved the bag toward Hope before dropping into a chair. "How did that colossal piece of McHottie sexiness take the news that he's getting married?"

"McHottie? You didn't just say that."

"His picture's in his file." Skyler flipped her long

blonde braid over her shoulder. To Skyler, hair was the ultimate accessory.

Hope took a sip before exhaling a deep, thankful sigh. The coffee was still hot, and Skyler had opted for whole milk instead of the fat-free version that Hope usually selected. It was heaven in a cup. "We don't refer to clients that way."

"Of course we don't." Skyler popped the lid off her cup and blew on the contents, sending foam skittering over the rim. "My question remains."

"He was less than enthusiastic." She'd expected that, however.

"He looked at the candidates, though. Right? And did you slide my folder in there?"

"You'd miss working with me too much."

"Yeah. Working is so much better than shopping and having spa days on an unlimited credit card."

Hope captured the corner of the small pink bag and dragged it toward her. If she ate the pastry, she would have to hit the gym before she went home. Suddenly that seemed like a reasonable choice.

"Who did he like the best?"

Hope broke off a chunk of the doughnut and popped it in her mouth. "No one."

"Are you kidding me? What man wouldn't want a former pageant winner?" Skyler took a drink. "Maybe he *is* waiting for me."

How had she managed her business without Skyler? Since she'd joined the team, business had doubled. She showed up with a good attitude, worked as long and as hard as Hope did, and she could be trusted with all their clients' secrets, which was why Hope added, "He has certain…requirements that we weren't aware of."

"Oh?" Skyler scooted back in her seat. "Do tell."

Until now, Hope thought she was unshockable. Their clients were from all parts of the globe, men who had the means to be as discriminating and unique as they wished. She'd had requests that a woman have a soft nature or that she wear heels at all times, even in the house. Other clients specified that any potential match had to be fluent in a specific language—French, Spanish, Arabic, Mandarin. Several had requested advanced degrees, including PhDs. A memorable octogenarian had been in search of a voluptuous twenty-something-year-old who was willing to read him bedtime stories. "He is into BDSM."

"He's into…" Skyler's coffee spilled over the side of her cup.

Praying her voice didn't waver, betraying her conflicted emotions, Hope continued. "He expects his wife to drape herself across his lap to have her ass spanked when she makes mistakes."

"That's hot. I'd fuck up all the time."

Hope raised her eyebrows.

"What? You wouldn't want Hottie McHottie to light up your butt?"

"No!" Hope guzzled the burning-hot latte to cover the fact that she was flustered at wanting just that. Then she leveled her gaze at her assistant. "You would?"

Skyler squirmed. "Oh, yes."

"And greeting him on your knees at the end of the day?"

"Yum. Bonus points if I get to be naked."

Hope's hand shook. "Are you serious?"

"Why not?" Skyler placed the lid on her cup. "Variety being the spice of life, right?"

Skyler's reaction was reassuring.

"Do you want me to ask the candidates if they're willing to be tied up and spanked by their future husband, or are you planning to call them?"

"Jesus." Hope shook away her thoughts and forced herself to focus on the problem at hand. Should she come right out and ask the women if they were amenable to a BDSM relationship? Or should she paint a vague picture? After all, *she* would have said *no way* until his compelling voice had wrapped around her and his touch had all but incinerated her.

Too bad she didn't have more time to craft a strategy. "He has a—I'm not sure what you'd call it—some sort of form for the potential women to fill in."

"Limits list."

"What?"

"It's a great way to talk about where each person is. The submissive can redline certain things—like humiliation, or an implement such as a paddle or a cane."

Hope shivered. "And you know about this, how?"

"Sorry to interrupt."

Tony Kingston, her new associate—and Prestige's lone male employee—stood in the doorway.

"Looks serious," he said. "Is this private?"

Most mornings, they all gathered in Hope's office or the conference room for an impromptu meeting to catch up and set the day's agenda. "Come in," Hope replied.

"You look as gorgeous as ever," Skyler said. "The purple tie is fabulous. Brave. Confident. Inviting without being too decadent."

"Uhm...thank you?"

"It was a compliment," Skyler assured him.

Tony did some modeling on the side. He stood a couple of inches over six feet tall, had well-defined biceps that came from lifting weights, and he offset his weakness for M&M's with grueling runs each night after work. His inherent fashion sense ensured he complemented his golden-brown good looks with the perfect attire.

When he'd first applied for a job, Hope had shied away from the idea of hiring a man, but Celeste had convinced her it was a good idea. Hope's mentor had been correct. With his wardrobe full of gray suits and bold-hued ties, he exuded class in an old-world way. His soothing tone invited intimacy, and his eyes promised trust. His quiet confidence appealed to men and women both. Since he'd come on board, Prestige had begun accepting female clients.

"All this coffee and sugar. Carbs. What's up?" He pulled back a chair, then sat in it with legs outstretched.

"We're just talking about the Sterling Worldwide heir and his kinky demands."

"God, Skyler!" Hope waved her hand. "Show some restraint."

"Sounds like my kind of conversation." Tony grinned.

"Not you too." The discussion spiked Hope's blood pressure

"Catch me up."

"He has a limits list," Skyler said.

Tony pressed his palms together. "He's twenty-four seven?"

Both of her employees looked at her, and Hope shifted. "Yes. Collars and..." She broke off another piece of doughnut to cover her discomfort. "He wants his wife to call him Sir."

"We're trying to figure out the best way to talk to the candidates," Skyler finished.

"It's delicate." He thought, then shrugged. "Our general nondisclosure should cover this."

Hope hesitated to even run this past the firm's lawyer.

"I suggest we talk to each candidate, see if she's at all interested in that type of relationship. If so, invite them to a mixer. He's adept at handling his own negotiations. We stay out of it as much as possible."

Hope nodded. "Skyler?"

"I think we should let them know as much as we can in advance."

"I disagree." Tony leaned forward. "As long as the woman is open to BDSM, it's up to Sterling to handle it."

Decision made, Hope nodded. "I agree with Tony. Skyler, after nine, start making the calls."

"To the women we've already presented? Or should we expand it to the next set of ten?"

"Let's start with the original five." Even though he'd professed not to like any of them.

Assignment understood, Skyler and Tony headed toward the door.

"Wait."

They stopped.

"See if we have anyone who likes kayaking or mountain biking."

"Mountain biking?" Skyler asked. "In Houston?"

"I hear Memorial Park has some trails. And we're not that far from Hill Country. There has to be someone who enjoys it, right?" Who also wanted to wear the collar of one of Houston's most eligible bachelors. And have his baby. She wasn't certain why those thoughts made her uncomfortable.

After Hope fled from his office, Rafe had crossed to the window and placed a palm on the wall as he looked down. He'd replayed their conversation, and he struggled to vanquish the thought of her as his submissive. He scened with women who were

51

experienced, but he was captivated by the idea of instructing her in the joys of surrender. He wanted her mouth to part from his caress of pain, gasp with the sting of pleasure.

Proving he already had power over her, she'd stopped on the sidewalk and glanced up. He stayed in place until she hurried off, as if frightened by what she saw.

She had reason to be.

When he crossed his office to return to his desk, he inhaled the scent of lilacs, and he wasn't certain whether or not he'd imagined it.

After shaking his head, he emailed her his limits list. Though she intended to use it to screen his candidates, he wondered which things she'd cross out and which she might be willing to try.

Those unanswered questions made his cock hard, so he shoved them away to concentrate on business. Getting his father reengaged with the business would settle the issue with Noah, take the marriage pressure off Rafe, and allow him to pursue the curvy little matchmaker.

Resolved, he'd called his father again. Annoyance flashed through Rafe when the call went straight to voicemail. He left a message before rolling the gnawing ache from his shoulder.

When the phone rang sometime later, he snatched it up, expecting his father.

Instead, it was Celeste.

"You met with Hope."

Like him, she rarely wasted precious moments

on pleasantries. "If that's what you would call it." He sat back.

"Don't blame her." And before he could say anything, she added, "Or me. We were tools for your mother's use."

As if Celeste would ever be a mere tool for anyone. "Which makes both you and Ms. Malloy complicit." He reached for the mug of coffee that Jeanine had brought a while ago. He'd ignored it until now. "Your input might have made their task a little less burdensome." He took a drink. The contents were tepid, but caffeine was caffeine and maybe it would help ward off the headache grinding at the back of his skull. "All beautiful. All...goddamn perfect." It was a glimpse of his ideal woman and make-believe life. No wonder he was pissed off.

"There's another matter..."

Celeste was a master of the expectant pause. In fact, she had studied theater along with psychology and business. A shrewder woman he'd never known.

While he waited for her to speak, he traced the logo on the cup. Instead of the Sterling crown, this one was emblazoned with the golden Titans logo, a laurel wreath cradling Athena's owl.

"You've had this thrust on you. So much responsibility. You're capable of it, no doubt."

"Get to the point, Celeste."

"I've just gotten off the phone with Gideon."

Judge Gideon Anderson was the chairperson of the Zeta Society, nicknamed the Titans by an enterprising young reporter sometime during the

1930s.

"Noah has been in contact with him, and the judge wanted to know if I'd spoken with Theodore. There's a steering committee meeting at the Parthenon on Saturday to finalize plans for the annual gathering. There's also some executive business that requires a quorum. Your father hasn't said he will be there. We can assume he won't."

"Christ." He stared at the owl representing wisdom. Was it a coincidence the paint was peeling from the edges?

For more than a hundred and fifty years, a Sterling had been seated at the board table.

"Noah offered to attend in his stead."

Tension gripped Rafe's shoulder, making pain from the bicycle crash jackknife through his body.

"Find a woman who will best suit your needs and take away any doubt or potential challenges to your role as the leader of Sterling Worldwide."

It was a warning, not a suggestion.

After Celeste rang off, Rafe pushed redial on his father's number.

"Ahoy, Rafe!"

In relief, he loosened his tie. "When are you coming home, Dad?"

"Not anytime soon. Lillibet wants to go on an around-the-world cruise for our honeymoon."

"Listen..." Rafe plowed a hand through his close-cropped hair. "A honeymoon happens after a wedding."

"I'm aware." Impatience clipped Theodore's

words.

"As far as I know, you already have a wife."

"Oh, for Christ's sake, Rafe. Don't burden me with your details."

"That you haven't taken care of. Bigamy is against the law. You'll need to file for a divorce if you're serious. Have you even spoken to a lawyer?"

"Lillibet wants this trip, and I'll damn well ensure she gets it."

"Whether or not you're still married to my mother?"

In the background, a female voice called out to his father, "Teddy! Teddy Bear!"

"She's always wanted to see Casablanca."

"Morocco?"

"So romantic."

"She does know it doesn't end well, right?" When his father didn't respond, Rafe prompted, "The movie. Bogart doesn't get the girl."

"I'm not sure she's interested in the details. We're leaving in May."

Next month?

"We've hired a crew for the *Lunar Sea*, and we're planning to be gone something like ninety days, maybe a hundred."

"Ted-dy!"

"Goddamn it, Dad. You need to think about the business."

"Ted-dy!"

"Coming, my love!" His father was laughing as he ended the call.

Rafe lowered his phone. Then, uncharacteristically, frustration overtook him, and he slammed it onto the desktop.

"Problem?"

He looked up to see Noah on the threshold.

This was turning into Rafe's lucky day. "What can I do for you?"

"Jeanine's not at her desk, so I took the liberty of seeing if you were in."

He wouldn't put it past Noah to have waited until Jeanine left. How long had he been there? How much had he overheard?

"I've been trying to reach Uncle Theodore."

"Have you?"

"There's a piece of property that might be become available in Hong Kong. High-density area. Looking at it for a boutique-type of operation."

"Send me the information."

Noah adjusted his tie. "It's not your particular expertise, is it?"

It wasn't. Rafe had spent a lot of his career at Sterling in the financial department. In addition to oversight and compliance, he'd been focused on expanding the company into new areas, muscling into parts of the hospitality industry that were ripe for disruption. But in his father's absence, he'd been sleeping less than usual as he juggled all the various arms of the conglomeration, adjusting to a steep learning curve while pretending his father was still in charge.

Aware of Noah waiting for him to snap, Rafe

countered with, "Is there a reason you're not confident in your own opinion?"

Noah blinked. "It's a lot of money."

"You have the authority as well as a budget. You're responsible for real estate acquisitions in Asia."

"I enjoy hearing Uncle Theodore's perspective."

Rafe also appreciated his father's guidance. Theodore might not want any part of day-to-day anymore, but it was his view of the industry that had shaped Sterling for the last generation. He might not like the responsibility, but he'd been damn good at it. "As I said, it's on you if it fails."

"You need to stop covering for Uncle Theodore." Uninvited, Noah took a seat and propped his ankle on top of his opposite knee. "I've been leaving him messages for a couple of weeks. And I stopped by the house on Friday. If he's not going to run Sterling Worldwide, he needs to be removed as CEO. The attorney I spoke to—"

"Close the door on your way out."

"Listen, Rafe, even you have to admit—"

"Close the door on your way out."

For long, tense moments, Noah remained where he was. But Rafe raised an eyebrow, refusing to yield.

Eventually, Noah stood. "Consider yourself warned."

When Rafe was alone in the reverberating silence, he sighed. Then he called his attorney.

With the few details that Rafe outlined,

Mercedes confirmed what Rafe already knew. As long as Theodore was absent, uncertainty abounded. Noah could file a lawsuit. Mercedes would challenge it, and perhaps a judge would throw it out. If not, Sterling Worldwide had a protracted, expensive mess in front of it. The press would feed from the carcass for years.

If Rafe were married, the succession would be clearer, making it much more difficult for Noah to prevail in court.

Rafe was trapped. Hopelessly fucking trapped.

Mouth set in a grim line, he ended the call, then pulled out the folders containing his bridal candidates. With determination, he flipped each one open in turn.

He glanced at the pictures and read the brief biographies that the women had written. And he reached his decision. None of the above. He wanted sexy Hope Malloy.

An hour later, Jeanine interrupted, saying that the Prestige Group was on the phone for him.

Heat flared in his blood, unexpected and unwelcome. To focus on his pursuit of Hope, he shoved away the desire that was so strong it disturbed him.

He pressed a button on his phone to accept the call on speaker so her voice could wrap around him. "Ms. Malloy." He kept his tone controlled.

"Mr. Sterling? This is Skyler Morrison at the Prestige Group. I'm Hope's assistant."

Disappointment crawled through him.

As if she hadn't crushed his fantasies, Skyler continued, "Hope asked me to call to let you know that we have a mixer scheduled for Thursday afternoon at four. We'll have a private room at the Ivy."

"I prefer to have it at the International." There was no reason for him to change the venue, except for the fact that he wanted this charade to happen at his club, where he was more in control.

Silence stretched for awkward moments before she said, "Everything is already arranged. The Ivy is an excellent choice. I think you'll find it suitable."

"I prefer the International Club." He'd enjoyed many fine meals at the Ivy, and she was right. The few private rooms made the upscale restaurant an adequate place for a business rendezvous.

Rafe told himself he preferred to do things on his terms. If he were honest, he'd admit it was more than that. He wanted to shake up Hope's plans and let her know he was in charge. And Thursday was too long to wait to see her. "Wednesday is better for my schedule. My contact is Barbara Thurston. I'll have her call you."

"Mr. Sterling—"

"Four o'clock?"

"We prefer to handle the arrangements ourselves."

"I'm sure you prefer to be in control. So do I." Hope might have avoided making this call, but that was the last battle she would win. "Let Ms. Malloy know I'm looking forward to it."

Skyler gave a frustrated sigh before conceding. "Wednesday at four. The International Club."

He grinned as he ended the call. *His round.*

CHAPTER THREE

"Is he a sadist?" Hannah demanded, distaste in her voice.

Oh, God. Is he?

Before they were able to call Rafe's potential mates the previous morning, he'd sent over his limits list. Most things Hope had some knowledge of, but there were a few things that had perplexed Skyler. Tony, however, had walked into the office, taken a seat, and proceeded to enlighten them. One shocked Hope. Another mortified her.

In the privacy of her home, she spent hours rereading each page he'd sent over, and each question had caused a reaction. Instead of simple yeses or nos, she'd imagined herself in the scenarios, secured to the bedposts, having orgasm after orgasm forced from her, having ice water drizzled on her stomach.

She'd been unable to sleep. When she was still restless at midnight, she'd gone for a run on the treadmill, hoping to unwind. It hadn't help much, and when she did drift off, she did so thinking of his damnable, demanding kiss.

"Hope?"

Hannah's sharp tone penetrated the fog clouding Hope's brain. "I'm here. Sorry." Hope blinked to refocus on her phone call. "I'm not sure about that." Did the fact that he wanted to spank his wife for any misbehavior make him a sadist? Or was it just part of the relationship? "Because these questions are subjective"—at least they seemed to be to her—"I think it's best if you ask him your specific questions when you meet him. We are hosting a mixer tomorrow evening."

"Look, Hope. I'm not *that* desperate for a man. There's no way I would ever marry a sadist."

Even if he's a gazillionaire?

"Can you find out for me? I don't want to waste my time."

"I understand. Let me get back to you with an answer." If she'd had any idea of the difficulties she would run into with Rafe as a client, Hope would have doubled her fee.

After ending the call, she left her office and strode into the main reception area. Since Skyler was on the phone, Hope went into the tiny kitchen. To her, as long as it held her favorite creamer, a couple of bottles of wine, and a stash of chocolate, it was the exact right size.

Since she'd eaten all the candy she bought for her personal use, she opened a bag of Tony's M&M's and helped herself.

She'd just finished savoring a yellow one when Skyler joined her. "That bad?"

"Hannah Morrison wants to know if our bachelor is a sadist."

Skyler dipped her hand into the treats too.

"Any luck with your calls?" Hope needed some good news.

"I talked to Adele. She said if I ever ask her something like that again, she'll end her association with us and blast us on social media."

The nondisclosure should prevent that, but she could always post an anonymous review and deny she'd done it. Hope exhaled. "If we survive this, every other client will be easy."

"Norah Minturn expressed interest in him...after asking about his net worth first."

Hope scooped up another half dozen candies. There was a reason Norah was one of the city's top financial managers.

"Ladies, ladies!" Tony edged his way between them and snatched away the bag. "A little respect, please. These are to be savored. One at a time. *One* at a time."

"We're going to need that back," Skyler said.

"Nothing's that bad," he insisted. "Unless the world is ending, this is my private stash, and grabby hands are not welcome."

"Hope has to ask McHottie if he's a sadist."

"A… *What?* Oh. Gotcha." Tony shoved the bag back at Hope. "Eat all you want." Without another word, he carried on toward his office and closed the door.

"Well, then." Skyler brushed her palms together. "I'll let you get it over with."

"You've been his contact person."

"About that…I've still got to firm up the next set of recommendations for you and confirm the arrangements with the International Club. Lots of work to do today. I'm very busy."

The main office phone rang. "Duty calls!" After a quick glance toward Tony's closed door, Skyler grabbed a handful of M&M's, then dashed toward her desk.

Hope returned to her office, then straightened a few things up. She watered the cactus on the windowsill, answered all her emails, even cleared out the receipts from her handbag. Then, out of busywork, she sighed.

Instead of picking up the phone, she stared at it. Mentally, she tried a few different approaches. They were all awkward — or worse, left her vulnerable and uncertain. She didn't want to know this much about him. But at the same time, she was hungry for the information.

What the hell was wrong with her? She needed

to find Rafe Sterling a wife. Instead, he'd upended her equilibrium.

Shaking her head at her cowardice, Hope snatched up her phone, searched out his contact information, then pressed the call button. She agonized through each ring and exhaled a relieved whoosh when she reached his voicemail. Damn it, even though his voice was recorded, the smokiness in his words sent little shivers of arousal skittering through her.

Since she had no business reacting to a client in that way, she cleared her throat before leaving what she prayed was a coherent message.

After the short reprieve, her anxiety spiked. Now she had to wait for him to call back.

Torturing her, he took most of the remaining workday. Tony and Skyler had already left the office, and Hope had been organizing her desk before heading to the gym.

In a small bit of retaliation, when the phone rang, she didn't answer until the last possible second, right before her ringtone trailed off. "Prestige Group."

"It's Rafe Sterling."

His voice sent tremors through her.

"What can I do for you?" he asked.

Her spine lost strength, and she sank deeper against the back of her seat. "As you know, we are setting up the mixer."

He waited without response.

She had no choice but to move forward. "I have

an…indelicate question for you."

"About…?"

What was the word he had used? "Your proclivities."

"That sounds interesting." Humor laced his words, as if he enjoyed making her uncomfortable. "Please, proceed."

Hope cleared her throat. *Fuck.* "Are you a sadist?"

He chuckled, low and sinister, titillating her. "From your tone earlier, I thought the topic would be much more delicate."

What did that mean? "So…" Her heart thumped in triple time.

"Can you be more specific?"

She squirmed. "I thought it would be a yes-or-no question."

"Maybe for some people it is. I find it a little more complex. Do I enjoy inflicting pain for the sheer joy of hurting someone?"

She wondered where he was. In his office? Looking out the window? Behind his desk?

"Is the woman in question a masochist? Does she enjoy it? Does receiving pain fulfill something deep inside her?"

"Fulfill something?"

"Masochists love to receive pain. It can be inextricably linked to their happiness. Or does she fear pain?" His tone took on a serrated edge. "Is it on her limits list? Does the idea scare her? Will she do anything to avoid it?"

"Your potential match says she won't date a sadist."

"The short answer is no. I'm not. Well, not in the strictest sense of the word."

Was everything complicated with him?

"However, I am more than happy to deliver the right amount to drive a woman wild. If she's a masochist, she will find that I'm willing to make her happy. Some people differ on their definition of sadism. What about delivering a spanking that the receiver thinks is too much but makes her come? Perhaps it's sadistic to duct tape a submissive to a chair and force her to watch a movie she hates. How about using vampire gloves to part her labia as I prepare to lash her clit?"

Her pussy throbbed. Uncomfortable, she shifted. He was answering a question, not speaking to her. He didn't want to do those wicked things to her, even if she was picturing him spreading her wide in front of him.

The door to the exterior hallway opened. Her attention jarred, she scowled and pushed back from her desk. Though it wasn't out of the question, guests didn't often stop in without an appointment. So, unless Tony or Skyler had forgotten something, there was no reason for anyone to be in the office.

Since Rafe was still talking, Hope covered the phone with her hand and called out, "Hello?" When there was no answer, her concern grew, and she left her office.

Hope froze when she entered the reception area.

Larger than life, intoxicating as well as overpowering, he stood near Skyler's desk.

Her momentary concern blossomed into relief, only to be replaced with a shocking surge of pleasure that mixed with a breathtaking sense of dread.

It might have been the end of the day, but his suit was impeccable. His silver tie was knotted high and tight, and his shirt was crisp and starched. He had the barest hint of an afternoon shadow, and he smelled of spice.

She had a feminine instinct to yield to him, but professionalism said she dared not. "Mr. Sterling." She ended the call, then held the phone in front of her to ward him off.

"I prefer not to answer questions about sadism in general terms." He didn't smile to dull the impact of his words. In fact, he sounded as if he were in a tough business negotiation rather than talking about sex. "I'd much rather discuss specific situations and ask my own questions in return. There might be some common ground, or something a sub might be willing to try."

She tightened her grip until she could no longer feel her fingers. "I'll convey what you've said to see if the potential match might want to have further conversation with you."

"And what about you, Hope?" He dropped his cell into an inner pocket of his suit coat. "You're not curious at all?"

"This isn't about me."

"You received my questionnaire." It was a

statement, not a question. He'd sent the email with a read-receipt request, so he knew the exact moment she'd opened it.

"I did."

"Did you learn anything about yourself?"

"Nothing that pertains to you," she lied. She had a number of questions, but for her sanity, she needed to keep him at an emotional distance. Returning to business where she understood the landscape better, she said, "As I mentioned in your office, we can set up private meetings with the candidates for you if there is mutual interest."

"Nothing at all?" His smile was lethal. "What sort of things were you curious about? What scared you?"

Hope kept her gaze riveted on his tie. "This is not an appropriate conversation." Even so, she couldn't find the words to ask him to leave. If she were honest with herself, she'd admit she didn't want him to go. In desperation, she said, "You're a client." Was she trying to convince herself or him?

"Are you familiar with a safe word?"

She forced herself to look up at his face. Then she wished she hadn't. His eyes were probing, giving her no place to hide.

"A safe word, Ms. Malloy?"

She exhaled. "I have done some reading. It stops a…well, whatever is going on."

As if he'd read her mind, he hooked a finger through the knot in his tie.

Her toes curled.

"What's your safe word?"

"You're my client," she repeated, voice catching.

"I'm not," he corrected. "My mother hired you."

Hope wanted to argue the technicality, but unaccountably, she didn't. She was a drowning woman ignoring a lifeline.

"Come here, Ms. Malloy."

She wasn't going to. Yet, just like the time she'd asked for his kiss, her treacherous body betrayed her, and she took a step closer, then a second.

"What would you like me to do with this tie?"

"Keep it around your neck."

"Is that the truth?" he pressed. His gaze enslaved hers. "Or should I punish you for not being truthful?"

She shivered, wanting that. "Mr. Sterling..."

"You're as safe as you want to be."

That was the problem. She wanted to be wild and abandoned. "We... I... Can't." She shook her head. It would be ridiculous to proceed. She tried again, with more force, "We can't." It would be *worse* than ridiculous. Rafe Sterling was starting to mean something to her. He filled her every waking moment, and not just because the Sterling account was the most challenging one she'd ever worked on. It was his damnable words about his proclivities.

"Give me a safe word. Something you wouldn't use in ordinary conversation, something easy to remember. Or tell me to leave."

A million emotions crashed through her. Fear and curiosity. Desire and doubt. Reality. It would be so much harder to find him the perfect match if she wanted him for herself. Not that she would, she rationalized.

He stood there, as patient as he always was because he knew her. Her capitulation was coming. They both knew it.

"A lot of submissives use the color red. Yellow to slow down."

"Eggplant." The word fell out, even as she was still telling herself she didn't need or want a safe word.

"Eggplant?" He laughed, breaking the tension, allowing her to see another side of him, one that wasn't as threatening or scary. As if he were an ordinary man. For some reason, that made him even more dangerous to her resolve. "Why eggplant?"

"I hate them."

"Okay, then." In an instant, his smile fled, and he was once again stern, leaving her reeling. "Tell me an instance when you might say that word."

Her rational brain screamed that she shouldn't engage in this conversation. But it had been years since she felt this alive. It was intoxicating. "When you ask me to do something that I don't want to."

"Not necessarily."

"No?"

"As long as it's something we've talked about and negotiated, you don't get to use a safe word."

"Like being duct taped to a chair and being forced to watch cartoons?"

"That might be included. Yes." He nodded, a

smile once again teasing his lips.

No doubt, she was falling for him. His softer side made him irresistible. "It sounds sadistic."

"It does, doesn't it? But if you have no objection to being tied or to watching television, and I put the two together, you don't get to safe word, unless there's something I don't know about. Or perhaps something will come up for you that you weren't expecting, an unpleasant memory, for example. In that case, we need to talk. Maybe we can make a change so that you're more comfortable with what I'm doing.

He crooked his finger, then pointed at a spot on the floor.

Hope hadn't considered that she might be a submissive. Like a few of her friends, she would own the fact that she'd had fantasies of being overpowered by a delicious hunk of manliness, including a particular actor bare-chested and wearing a kilt. But that she would have a physiological response to mere words and sexual demands? Getting a burst of pleasure and anticipation from being commanded by a man? Wanting him to dominate her? Worse, even though she wouldn't admit it to him, the way he'd threatened her with a spanking had intrigued her to the point that she couldn't banish it from her mind.

Without repeating himself, Rafe waited. Her heels were unnaturally loud on the wood floor as she closed the distance between them.

"Thank you," he said. "I can see your struggle.

Your frown. The thumping of your heart in your throat, the death grip you have on your phone. You're curious, and you are telling yourself you shouldn't be turned on. Perhaps you're thinking this may jeopardize our business arrangement, yet here you are. The first step in your submission is turning over your phone."

She tightened her hold.

"I'll put it on the desk." He extended his hand. "It will always be within reach. You can pick it up at any time. Call for help if you think you need it."

Even the suggestion that she might need help sent the room spinning.

With infinite patience, he waited. Would he really stand there all night? No doubt he would, if that was what she needed.

Shaking, she dropped the device into his palm.

"Very good."

His approval was a drug she couldn't get enough of.

He slid the device next to Skyler's empty candy dish. "Would you like to lock the door?"

She debated for a moment.

"BDSM is all about consent. Nothing will happen without your permission. Since this is our first time playing, you're free to use your safe word at any time. Anything on your hard limits list?"

"Canes scare me." She shivered. "And I'm not into sharing or being shared." That statement made her bring her chin up. "Nothing that will break my skin. Scars. Permanent marks."

"Understood," he acknowledged. "We'll discuss everything as we go."

His presence filled the room.

Hope moved past him to lock the door. Uncertain of what to do next, she allowed her shoulders to collapse against the wall as he turned to face her.

More than ten feet separated them, yet goose bumps danced across her skin as if he'd touched her.

"Take off your blazer, Hope." His words were soft, more inviting than commanding.

She nodded.

"I like the sound of your voice. I like to hear the catches, the breathlessness, the roughness, your hesitation, your fear."

Riveted, she looked at him.

"When I give you an order, I want to hear you say, *Yes, Rafe.* Or even better if you say, *Yes, Sir.*"

Calling him by the honorific would make this moment even more real. She pondered his request while he waited. Finally, softly, she said, "Yes, Rafe."

"That sounded sweeter than I could have imagined."

The tiny taste of his approval made her yearn for more.

"You're making me very, very happy."

She pushed away from the wall, then shrugged out of her jacket.

"Hang it up."

She was beginning the slide toward submission. He'd made simple, ordinary requests, and she'd obeyed.

"I didn't hear an answer," he prompted, and this time, his words were an intimidating purr.

"Yes, Rafe," she whispered desperately. "Anything you say." He'd demanded she talk to him. Her verbal acquiescence was part of the spell, a web that wrapped its inescapable silken strands around her. She hung the jacket on a nearby coatrack, then faced him, unsure.

He studied her, as if memorizing every detail.

A little unnerved, she covered her bare arms with her hands.

"Don't hide. I always want to see you. The parts you love, the parts you don't. I want your vulnerabilities as well as your strengths. All of you."

"You're asking a lot."

He was crossing an invisible line, one she'd drawn years ago to keep people — men — from getting too close. With a few words, he'd stated his intention of demolishing it. It made him more than scary. It made him dangerous.

"I haven't even begun." His words were a promise, buried beneath a warning. "Drop your arms."

Her safe word lodged in her throat. This was madness.

He hadn't asked her to do anything that made her physically uncomfortable, but the emotional implications terrified her.

Even though the silence stretched, he didn't repeat himself, waiting for her decision. Then, because it was inevitable, she lowered her arms.

He exhaled. In that moment, she realized how important this was for him as well. The knowledge fed her courage.

"Now unfasten the top button on your blouse."

It was too much to hope that he'd do it for her. Part of her wanted him to sweep her off her feet, do terrible things to her, and allow her to abdicate the responsibility. "Yes, Rafe." Her fingers shook a little as she complied.

"The second, please."

His gaze holding hers captive, she followed his order.

"Part the material."

She exposed her chest, revealing her cleavage and the lace outline of her bra.

"So obedient. Now come to me. I can't wait much longer."

With each step, her pulse accelerated. She wanted to please him, wanted this adventure, no matter where it led.

When she was in front of him, he asked, "On my list, what things intrigued you?"

Her insides rocked as if she were on a boat out in the middle of the ocean, away from any sight of land. "I think I might like to be restrained."

"Like with handcuffs, behind your back?"

"Or…"

"Nothing you could say would shock me."

"Yes. Or with a tie."

"Excellent. What else? Surely something

intrigued you?"

Hope took him at his word, that he couldn't be shocked. "Orgasm denial."

"One of my favorites." He grinned.

His expression faded so fast she wasn't sure if she'd imagined it. As he'd promised, he didn't appear surprised. Happy, maybe. But not shocked.

"Did you look it up?"

She recalled pictures of submissives who looked frustrated, one a bit dazed. She'd read accounts of how a Dominant had frustrated a sub for an entire week. The sub had said thoughts of sex dominated her days and that she'd climaxed in her sleep without touching herself. Hope wasn't sure whether that was fact or fiction. But she'd clicked through a half dozen similar stories. "Yes."

He waited for her to continue.

Hope wrung her hands, as if that would ward off his intensity. "The…" She cleared her throat. "The submissive gets close to coming and the Dom refuses to let her."

"It can be during a scene, or in general. Even as a punishment."

She wrinkled her nose. "I'm not into the whole idea of punishment."

"Even if you do something your Dom has forbidden?"

"Well…" Her tummy quivered. "Maybe. In that context."

He nodded. "Do you reach orgasm quickly?"

Shame and embarrassment flooded her. Was this

the way most Doms seduced their subs? By asking such personal questions? Destroying barriers in his path? Or was this something unique to him? "I...uhm..."

"Floundering won't save you."

"I don't date a lot."

"Do you masturbate?"

Heat flooded her body. Who the hell asked that kind of question? "Is this—"

"Necessary? Yes, it is. How many times a week do you masturbate?"

Her blood thickened, moving through her veins in sluggish little bursts. "It depends."

With a touch so gentle it unraveled her, he said, "If there's a question you don't want to answer or information you prefer to keep private, say so. But don't play games. If it's a question you can answer, do so."

He was forcing her to confront deeply personal thoughts. "I masturbate several times a week, sometimes more." Embarrassment danced through her, but she pressed on. "It helps me to sleep. Most nights I take a bath, and then sometimes I..." She tilted her chin back. "Play with myself."

"Not so difficult, right?"

Not once she'd shed her inhibitions.

"It becomes easier with practice. Honesty about your sexuality makes it easier for you to get your needs met." He released her wrist. "How do you do it? With a toy? With your fingers?"

"It becomes easier." She replayed his words for

encouragement. "It depends. Most nights I use my fingers. I have a dildo I like, and sometimes I use a vibrator."

"Are you naked? Or do you slip the toy inside your panties?"

"I'm...yes. Naked."

"And back to my original question. Do you come quickly when you masturbate?"

Sometimes in less than a minute. "Yes."

"And with a man?"

"I told you I don't date all that often." It was easier to protect herself if she didn't get too close. "To be honest, as you demand, I'm more self-conscious when I'm with a partner. Shy. Nervous. So sometimes I don't climax at all."

"And do you also play with your nipples, or just your pussy?"

Mortification gnawed at her. *He expects me to answer that?*

With infinite patience, he waited.

"Not my nipples."

"Show me."

Perplexed, she frowned.

"Take off your clothes, then lie on the desk and show me how you masturbate."

She stood there, agape. "Are you serious?"

Lazily, he lifted one eyebrow. "Was there anything in my tone to suggest otherwise?"

Oh. God. No. There wasn't.

Under his watchful gaze, she released another button. He didn't hurry her, and he didn't offer to help. Part of her wished he would—that way she wouldn't have to take responsibility for what was happening.

When she removed her shirt, he smoothed the material, then draped it over a nearby chair.

Her mind lurching from thought to thought, she reached behind her to unfasten her skirt. She worked the linen down her hips and thighs before letting it fall to the floor. Hope stood in front of him in bra, skimpy panties, and her heels.

"You're a spectacular woman, Ms. Malloy."

Even with his words of approval wrapping around her, it took tremendous effort to resist the urge to cover herself.

"Now give me your skirt."

She did, and once again, he hung it with care. Maybe it was ridiculous, but she drank assurance from that, as if his actions meant she could trust him.

"I'm waiting."

After unfastening her bra, she rolled her shoulders forward to lower the straps.

He nodded when she stood before him with her breasts bared and her nipples taut from the air-conditioning.

Her bra joined the rest of her clothing. Next, she wiggled out of her underwear. Most of the time, her dates had pulled her clothes off with haste, but Rafe seemed to savor every moment of her undressing.

"Do you shave all the time?"

She didn't need to ask whether he appreciated the small strip of hair or not. The approval gave his voice a roughened resonance. "Yes." She was glad she did. "I like it. Would you mind if I didn't?"

"Not at all. Whatever is comfortable for you. Women are exquisite, no matter their personal preference. Though I might request it of a sub just so she would be thinking of me during her grooming time."

She wondered what it would be like to have a man so involved in decisions she'd always considered private.

"And your shoes. They're sexy as hell, but I want you to be aware of how small you are compared to me."

At five feet seven without her heels, she didn't feel tiny next to many men. But once she was in front of him, in bare feet, several inches shorter and much more vulnerable, she was aware of his size and dominance.

Rafe eyed the desk again. "On second thought, do you have a conference room?"

"Down the hall, yes."

"Bigger than this?"

"Quite a bit. It seats eight."

"A better option, but I'll leave the choice up to you. You can hop up on here. I rather like the idea that you will remember this evening every time you walk into the office. A bigger table may be a little more comfortable."

She tipped her head to the side. "I'm not sure either will be comfortable."

"After sixty seconds, you won't even notice.

You'll be too busy begging me to allow you to come."

He wrecked her nerves.

"A sample of my wicked intentions?"

Suddenly it was all too real, and she wanted what he had to offer.

"Ask for it."

Her pulse stuttered, and her knees weakened. "I want... Yes."

"Come to me, sweet Hope." He pointed to a spot close to where he stood.

Knowing there was no going back, she hesitated for a moment. In a moment of madness, she looked at him. Panic seized her when she realized she was seeking reassurance from the man who had promised to redden her ass, arouse her, then deny her, punish her in her own workplace.

In his eyes, though, she read reassurance, a promise that she was safe. After a last nervous swallow, she did as he said. She took the three steps that brought her to him. The floor was cool against her skin, and she appreciated the stability when everything else swam with uncertainty.

"I appreciate your trust. I promise you, I will continue to earn it."

She nodded, the sincerity in his words compelling her to believe him.

"Spread your legs, Hope." As he spoke, he unknotted his tie, leaving the ends loose.

She did as he asked, and he held up his hand in front of her mouth. Though he didn't give her any instructions, she sucked on his finger.

"So sexy." He kept her gaze hostage as he extracted his finger, then trailed it down her cleavage, then lower still to outline her ribs, igniting a trail of damp heat over her skin.

Rafe skimmed the planes of her abdomen, then slid his hand between her thighs. She jerked as he brushed her clit. It had been so, so long since she'd had a man touch her this way. Until now, she hadn't realized how desperately she'd missed it.

"You're so delicate, Hope."

Because she didn't know what to expect, his touch was so much more intense than her own.

Several times, he slid back and forth, and she grabbed hold of his biceps for support. He pressed the small bundle of nerves, then backed off before teasing her again.

Her insides spiraled toward an orgasm. In a silent plea, she jerked her hips toward him.

Frustrating her, he stopped.

She sighed her disappointment. Her whole body was on fire and she needed him to extinguish the flames. She clamped her hand on his wrist, keeping his touch against her skin.

"No." His refusal was quick and sharp. "I appreciate how responsive you are. Imagine how much you will enjoy it when I do allow you to come."

"Maybe this orgasm denial wasn't such a good idea." His finger was so near her that she struggled against her reactions. "Can we renegotiate?"

"It doesn't work that way. You may safe word out if you want to stop the scene, but deciding you no longer like the rules of this game won't persuade me to change my mind. Understand?"

She sighed. "Yes, Rafe." Part of her was glad he'd refused. She didn't want him to change his mind. She wanted the experience.

"Conference room?" He tugged his hand away from hers. "Lead the way."

For protection, she reached for her shirt, but he stopped her with a sharp shake of his head.

He was pushing her past a lot of boundaries she hadn't realized she'd had. The moment she finished having sex with a man, she covered up in a robe or a towel. Once she'd taken the sheet with her when she'd fled to the bathroom after sex.

Barefooted, she walked down the hallway, aware of him right behind her.

She flipped on the conference room light. Before she was ready, he lifted her from the floor to sit on the edge of the table. Even though she wanted to present a picture of composure, she swung one leg back and forth, her body betraying the fact that she was outside her comfort zone.

He swept the audio-visual equipment onto a nearby chair. "Please put your hands behind you."

Despite his courteous words, it wasn't a request. She complied, and the position thrust her breasts forward a little. Her nipples were hard, and she was still aroused from the way he'd played with her in the reception area.

He returned to stand in front of her, arms folded, foreboding.

He thrilled her. He scared her.

"Legs farther apart."

She'd never been more exposed.

"I love seeing your pussy. I'd make you sit like this all the time if you were mine."

If you were mine. Mesmerized, she fixed her gaze on him. She wasn't his. This wasn't real. On some level, it was a mistake. *Remember that.* Sharing this with him was dangerous, yet she couldn't flee.

"Now scoot into the middle of the table and lie down."

Surprising herself, she wiggled back, cool polished wood beneath her bare buttocks.

He removed his jacket, folded it, then placed it underneath her head as a pillow. The scent of him, power and demand, clung to the material.

In his shirtsleeves, the cufflinks winking in the overhead light, he loomed broader, more intimidating.

"Show me how you masturbate."

Despite the knot of nerves in her stomach threatening to make her jump up and run for her clothes, she reached a hand between her legs. The first, barest brush against her clit made tension crash through her. His touch, his instructions, his dominance, had her dangling on the edge.

"Beautiful. Keep going."

She closed her eyes, trying to lose herself in the experience, but he interrupted, saying, "I want to see your expression."

Swallowing a sigh, she opened her eyes. Seeing him watching over her, arms folded like an aristocrat, heightened the naughtiness.

"Part your labia with your left hand."

She turned her head, then brought it back to center right away.

"At least you won't need to be spanked for that."

His sensual threat sent arousal through her.

"You asked whether I'm a sadist. I have to admit I can't banish the thought of slapping your cunt, making it red and swollen."

She would have said that was on her limits list, yet she suddenly wanted to experience the burn.

"Spank it for me."

Hope blinked him into focus. "What?"

"I was going to have you do it once. We'll make it three times since you hesitated." When she didn't react right away, "Shall we make it four?"

"No. No…" She shook her head.

"Five!"

She bit her lower lip as she eased her right hand away from her clit.

"Now six."

Hope squeezed her eyes shut in anticipation of the pain as she tapped her pussy once.

"That didn't count." Humor laced his voice. "Hold your labia apart."

"But that will hurt."

"That's rather the point, sweet Hope."

She did what he had said and gave herself

another soft spank.

"We may be here all night if I wait for you." He blazed her cunt with his hand, and she screamed, opening her eyes to glare at him.

Fuck.

"Rub it."

He stunned her by bending to lick her cunt, sucking on her clit, then pinching it until it was hard.

She screamed again, on the verge of an orgasm.

"You could come right now, couldn't you?"

Hope squirmed. "Yes." She could, and it loomed so close it hurt.

"Not yet."

Why the hell had she told him her deepest secret? It was sexy but frustrating beyond words.

"Put both of your hands on your legs and count backward from ninety-nine to one."

It didn't help.

"Out loud."

Her voice and uneven breaths filled the room. When she reached fifty-seven, the air conditioner clicked on and her overheated skin began to cool, but the need to climax hadn't diminished.

Unconsciously she squeezed her legs together, hoping to ease the discomfort.

"Legs apart."

Did he see everything? She gritted her teeth as she spread her thighs.

"Your cunt isn't even swollen. I must not have hit you very hard."

"It didn't feel that way to me."

"You were at forty-six, and I didn't give you permission to stop counting."

"Yes, Rafe."

"I may make a recording of you saying that. It's intoxicating."

"Forty-five."

His soft laugh wrapped her in intimacy.

When she reached ten, he used two fingers to spread her labia. She arched her back, aroused all over again.

"Clamps would work, but since I don't have any, we'll do this for now."

"This is fine."

"I'm sorry?"

His voice was a whiplash.

"This is fine, Rafe."

"I guessed that would be your response."

His approval sent shivers through her. The power of his tone shocked her, and her continued craving for his approval made her reel.

"Now, sweet Hope, spank your pussy six times without stopping. Make them real, make them count, or we will begin again." He spread his fingers wider, making her whimper. "If you choose not to, I will take over. I can make you a promise that you won't like it if I do."

She believed him.

Summoning courage, her insides in turmoil, she delivered six stinging slaps to her pussy. Then she dropped her hand to her side as tears burned her eyes.

He remained in place, keeping her pussy on display, and air caressed her damp skin. The pain receded right away, but her clit pulsed with demand.

"How close are you to orgasm?"

"Very," she confessed. The mention of it made her tummy tighten.

He stroked between her legs, making her tremble. Then he delved inside her pussy. She thrashed, wanting to escape, wanting more.

"Rafe..." She lifted her head from the soft pillow he'd created. "Sir!"

He pulled away.

She collapsed again and would have rolled onto her side to escape if he hadn't placed a hand on her chest to trap her in place.

"Is this sadism?" he asked, voice soft and inviting. "I'm causing you distress and it's arousing me. Deliberate infliction of pain, and it's the best drug on the planet."

She finally understood the complexity of his question. Her pussy had blazed when he spanked her, but he had left behind a cascade of demand.

"I want you to place your heels flat on the table so that you can lift your pelvis up."

"We're not finished?"

"On the contrary, Hope. We've barely started."

He'd already shattered her boundaries.

Her whole body shuddered as she lifted her buttocks and braced herself. With a firm grip, he took hold of each ankle and repositioned her feet so that they were uncomfortably far apart. Humiliation lanced her as she was exposed, her pussy all but in his face.

"Your skin is red. My favorite color. I love how swollen your flesh is. Please play with your nipples."

She shook her head to clear it.

"I won't ask twice."

That terrible tone was back, reverberating with thunder.

The wood beneath her was uncomfortable, but playing with herself while he watched was even worse.

Legs wide in a commanding stance, he stood off to the side of her, removing his cufflinks and turning back his shirtsleeves. She'd never considered a man's forearms to be sexy before, but his were.

He dropped the gold studs near her head. The design—an owl, framed in leaves—caught her eye for a moment. The bird's emerald eyes flared. "Stay in position and continue to stimulate your breasts and nipples."

His raised eyebrows indicated he was waiting for her affirmative response. Since her mouth was dry, her words were barely audible. "Yes, Rafe." With him watching, her nipples were more responsive than ever, and her pussy dampened again.

"The scent of you is filling the room."

She was too turned on to care.

He moistened his thumb and pressed it against her clit. It was still swollen from her spanks and from his brutal slap. In seconds, she was on the verge of an orgasm. Instead of continuing to toy with her, he slid two fingers deep inside her.

Her body weakened, and she dropped her rear to the table.

"Back into position. Concentrate on staying there."

This time he didn't help her, and she struggled to lift herself as she continued to pinch, then release her nipples. The orgasm he wouldn't permit took on a need of its own. In desperation, she moved her hips.

"I'll make you wait even longer if you don't heed my wishes."

Damn him.

He slid in and out, finger-fucking her, obliterating all thought.

"Hope," he snapped.

She was undone, unable to think or act.

He pulled out his fingers, and she whimpered.

"Do as you're told."

"You *are* a sadist."

"You're enjoying it," he countered. "By your definition that would make you at least a little bit masochistic."

"No! I hate this. I want to come."

"Breathe through it. The worst part will pass."

Dear heavens above, why had she ever mentioned orgasm denial?

Rafe gave her a few seconds longer to recover before gripping her ankles. He held them in place, offering some leverage. "Now back into position."

Since she couldn't escape and—thank God—he wasn't touching her most sensual places, she exhaled a shuddering breath and somehow found the emotional and physical strength to force her hips off the table again.

"You've got the most gorgeous pussy." He reinserted his finger and crooked it to find her G-spot.

Her legs quivered. "Rafe!"

"You can endure this."

"No. No, no, no, no. No...no, I can't." Sweat slickened her body.

He moved away, and her overheated body chilled. The moment she recovered, he flattened her clit with his thumb and pushed a finger inside her. Then he took her arousal and used it as lube to press against her anus.

That was something she'd always worked up to with men, but with him it was logical. He seemed to have no sexual hang-ups, and because of that, she didn't protest.

He worked his finger back and forth until it was seated in her ass.

Then with his other hand, he tormented her already abused pussy. A million sensations zinged through her. No man had ever brought her to this state.

"Tug on your nipples. I want them stretched out."

She did, whimpering from the pain and tossing her head back and forth, desperate to escape the torture, and trying to hold the orgasm at bay.

When the edges unraveled, her vision blurring, he blazed her pussy with a slap that shattered the silence. She screamed as she came.

Hope wasn't aware of him moving, but her buttocks collapsed against the table. Her ass burned and her pussy ached, and he swallowed her cries with a burning kiss that turned her inside out.

He trapped her hands, crushing her breasts against him. Rafe consumed her.

She wasn't sure how long she lost sight of reality, but when she was able to breathe, he was cradling the side of her face with one of his hands.

He was smiling when he said, "You came without permission."

She scowled. "Someone didn't give me a choice, Sir."

"It doesn't mean the lapse won't be punished."

"Oh my God." She struggled up onto her elbows. "You can't be serious."

"I am. Lapses mean correction, and you're going to get a well-deserved spanking." His statement was blunt, but there was tenderness in his eyes.

The disconnect between that and what they'd done perplexed her. "Is it always like this?"

"Like what?" He helped her to sit up, and he picked up his jacket, smoothed the wrinkles, then draped it around her shoulders.

"I don't know..." She gathered the lapels and drew them together, partially to warm up, partially to hide from the vulnerabilities he'd exposed.

"You're gruff but thoughtful."

"Maybe not in all relationships, but for me? Yes. I like this part of the BDSM dynamic. The aftercare. I want you to enjoy it as well. And there can be a hell of an emotional component to any scene, even a short one, resulting in a hormonal rush and crash."

Too well, she understood what he was speaking about.

"It's crucial the Dominant be there for the submissive as long as needed. When we play, I will ensure I take care of your needs."

"That was the most intense orgasm I've ever had." It had been the difference between a rainstorm and a hurricane.

"Pleasing you is my greatest reward."

"You say that as if you mean it."

"I do. Now, for your spanking, would you like it at your house or mine?"

The hot desire that lashed her told her it would be a terrible mistake to spend more time with him. "Mr. Sterling—"

"After what we've shared?" His words were light, but a reprimand lay beneath.

She wrapped herself even tighter. "Rafe." Using his first name created greater intimacy, as he no doubt wanted. "We shouldn't go any further."

"That's fine. If you mean it, please use your safe word."

CHAPTER FOUR

Damn him.

Spending more time together would be disastrous for her emotional state, yet her safe word lodged in her throat.

Rafe didn't move away from her. His stance — feet rooted to the floor, arms folded — spoke of resolve, making it clear that he would wait as long as necessary for her to be honest with both of them.

After endless moments, she whispered, "No."

"Let me take you to dinner. Then we can decide which house to go to." He offered his hand.

After a short hesitation, she took it. He helped her from the table, and she stood in front of him, no longer client to vendor, but submissive to Dominant.

"I've spent plenty of time thinking of you since yesterday morning." His voice was rough with gravel. "You're everything I imagined."

And he was more than she'd dared to dream about.

Since the table was smudged from her feet, buttocks, and the shattering orgasm, she said, "I need to clean it."

"You could leave it for the morning." His grin was cheeky, a contrast to how serious he was a few moments before. "The reminder will be a nice start for your day."

With her luck, Tony or Skyler would arrive first and they'd know what she'd done in the office. There would be dozens of questions that she didn't want to answer. "No, thanks." On unsteady, bare feet, she pulled out a soft cloth and furniture polish from a storage cabinet.

He plucked his jacket from her shoulders and draped it across the back of a chair.

No way was she cleaning the room nude with him standing there. She froze. "I'll meet you in the reception area." Where her belongings were scattered on the floor.

"I prefer to watch."

An hour prior, she would have bet money that she would not be naked in front of one of her clients. More, she would have scoffed at the idea that she'd allow him to drive her to a soul-splintering orgasm.

Hope's heart slammed, and she exhaled. With

quiet power, Rafe had exerted his will, and she'd yielded, not because he overwhelmed her, but because her own scandalous behavior had been unusual and thrilling.

She picked up his cufflinks. Though they were a pair, the designs were mismatched. One was engraved with an odd-shaped Z. The other, the owl with gemstones for eyes, she'd seen when he took them off. The same symbols were probably on his ring. She traced the lightning-like Z pattern. "This is unusual. Do they have special meaning to you?"

"It represents the Zeta Society."

"The..." Hope blinked. She'd heard of it, in shadowy terms. A few years ago, she'd come across an article in her favorite online magazine. Most of the quoted sources had been anonymous, and she'd learned that the organization had been formed in the nineteenth century, and they had thousands of members worldwide.

The initiation fee was reported to be five figures, with burdensome dues. Despite that, the wait list to join was years long. The society supposedly owned an estate on the banks of the Mississippi River in Louisiana. The reporter had asked for an invitation to the yearly meeting, dubbed the Oak Valley Gathering. Their denial hadn't deterred him. Instead of entering through the gate, he'd snuck over a fence. Before being apprehended by security, he'd gotten as far as spying on the bonfire that was the ceremonial opening of the event.

Rafe was studying her.

"You're a Titan?" The moniker had been bestowed almost a century prior by an intrepid reporter who saw a group of prominent society members gathered in New Orleans. In his newspaper coverage, he called the men Titans, and the name had stuck.

Rafe remained silent for a few more moments. "One of my ancestors, John Sterling, was a founding member."

The information was a lot to take in, and she wouldn't have met him, except for... "Celeste." Her mentor's words echoed... *There are others.* At the time, Hope had assumed that meant BDSM adherents. Had Celeste been referring to the Titans? "Is Celeste also a member?"

"I've already said too much."

"I see." That was a lie. She didn't understand at all. "So, your wife... Do I need to know about this for finding you a bride?"

"No. Any woman I marry will be made aware of the Zeta Society when it's appropriate."

Hope stroked the lines of one of the laurel wreaths.

"The owl represents wisdom."

"It looks like Athena's owl. From mythology."

"I'm sure it is. The founders were familiar with Greek traditions from their time at university."

"How long have you been a member?"

"Since I turned eighteen. It's tradition. Not every Sterling joins. But the vast majority do."

"Including women?"

"We started admitting them at least half a century ago."

"Very progressive." She offered him the cufflink. "This is all very cloak-and-dagger."

"Secret, yes. Nefarious? Not at all. We exist so that people from all over the world have a place to gather and have discussions away from the glaring eye of the media as we talk about ways to make the world a better place."

"Are you going to make me sign some sort of blood oath so I don't go to the press?"

"You're a smart woman, Hope. I trust you."

They both knew she'd be out of the matchmaking business with no prospects if she didn't maintain her clients' confidentiality.

He rolled down his shirtsleeves, then extended a wrist toward her.

It was a simple unspoken request, but she fought an internal struggle. It seemed natural to do this for him, yet it spoke of emotional intimacy. With a soft sigh, she threaded the metal through the slit in the material.

"Thank you."

The huskiness in his words sent a ripple down her spine. Without being asked or instructed, she seated the second link in place as well.

"Perfect." He adjusted the cuffs. "Now my jacket?"

When she hesitated, he captured a lock of her hair and tucked it behind her ear. How could she refuse him?

Hope held his expensive jacket while he shrugged into it.

"It smells like you," he observed.

"Sorry."

"Don't be. I may never clean it again. Your scent — it's lilacs, isn't it?"

She nodded as he turned to face her. The approval in his eyes made her curl her toes into the cool flooring.

"I'll make dinner reservations."

"I haven't agreed to go with you." She wasn't sure which one of them she was reminding.

"I'd enjoy the honor of your company." He dropped a kiss on her forehead.

Charming or otherwise, he was impossible to resist.

"Is seafood okay?" He suggested the Bluewater Bistro, one of Houston's ten best restaurants. "They have one of the best wine and champagne selections in the city."

Her remaining resistance drained away. He'd had her at wine. She suspected he would have moved on to dessert if she'd still protested. With that kind of epicurean temptation, she didn't stand a chance. "Sounds wonderful."

When she didn't move, he added, "Hurry."

He stood near the door, a Titan who helped rule the world, as she shined the table. When she finished, he placed all the electronic equipment back where it belonged.

Her pussy was still damp, her ass a bit tender.

He'd read her well. She was going to go to dinner with him and allow him to spank her ass for coming without permission. Then, like Cinderella, at midnight, she'd return to her regular life.

After she'd put away the cleaning materials, she led the way to the reception area. He went into the bathroom to wash his hands. Since he'd left the door open, she watched him refasten his tie and straighten the knot.

He flicked his glance to the side, and in the mirror, their gazes met.

Desire arced through her. It was as if he was reminding her of what they'd done and what he intended later in that night.

By the time he had finished up and joined her, she was dressed.

She excused herself to shut down her computer and turn off the office lights. In the distance, he made reservations, the deep tones of his voice reverberating through her.

After grabbing her bag from her bottom desk drawer, she made a call of her own, to her next-door neighbor. "I know this is a lot to ask. I need you to feed the Colonel."

"Girlfriend, you can't pay me enough to take care of that hell-spawn."

Hope sighed. The last time Caroline had looked after the Colonel, the cat had escaped. By the time the hissing, shrieking feline had been corralled, Caroline had an armful of scratches, a bite mark, and emotional wounds. "I wouldn't ask if I didn't have to."

"I still have PTSD."

"There's a bottle of your favorite wine in the refrigerator."

Caroline was silent for a moment. "Is it leftover from the other night?"

"No. This is a new one that I've been saving." Silence echoed over the line, but Caroline hadn't hung up. Waiting for the deal to be sweetened? "There's a cheesecake in the freezer. It's topped with chocolate." Hope had ordered it for Skyler's upcoming birthday. With luck there was time to replace it.

"I'll need a Starbucks gift card too. Chocolate goes with coffee."

"Done." She didn't even ask how much. "Thank you. Seven o'clock, sharp." Or all the building's residents would know that the Colonel had missed her can of tuna.

"You owe me!"

"Anything," she swore, ending the call before Caroline could change her mind.

"The Colonel?" Rafe inquired when she met him at the door.

"My mom's cat. Well, mine now. I inherited her."

"The Colonel is a she?"

If he wanted to go to her house, he needed to know her deepest secret. "She's a Somali. Long-haired, a tail like a fox. My mother took her in when the woman who owned her deployed to

Afghanistan. When the woman returned, she made a hundred excuses about why she couldn't take the cat back. The truth was, the Colonel is a tyrant."

He grinned.

"You laugh now, but you haven't met her. Her original name was Samantha, but because she's so bossy and wants everything her way, my mom nicknamed her the Colonel." Which had been much better than Tyrant. "It stuck."

"So how did you end up with her?"

"No one else would take her, and I didn't have the heart to take her to the pound. I doubt she would have found a new home."

"Did something happen to your mother?"

Emotion clawed through her. "Yes." She reached for the doorknob. "Shall we?"

He curled his hand over hers. "I'm sorry for your loss."

"She was involved in a one-car accident after she'd worked a double shift at the hospital. The investigators said it appeared she fell asleep at the wheel." As horrible as it was, that news hadn't surprised her. Once Hope had left home, her mother hated the loneliness. She'd taken extra shifts all the time, even the overnight ones. In her remaining free time, she had volunteered at a veterans' charity. "It was almost two years ago." A knot of pain lodged in her throat. "I keep waiting for it to get easier."

"If you want to talk about it, I'm an excellent listener."

After swallowing, she was in control again.

"Thank you." She left it at that. Watching her mother's pain had taught Hope to avoid dependence on a man. Keeping her fractured soul buried was still the best way to accomplish that. "Shall we?"

He let her go, and she turned the knob, then locked the door behind them when they were in the hallway.

"I'm happy to drive us," he said when they reached the elevator.

Being in an enclosed space with him? No escape? Breathing him in? "I thought we'd take separate cars."

"It will be easier if we're in one. Then we can make plans for whose house we will go to."

Once again, she reminded him, "I haven't said yes."

"And you haven't said no."

The elevator doors slid open, and he ushered her inside.

"So tell me, Ms. Malloy —" He turned to her, backed her into the corner, then pinned her arms above her head, her purse dangling from her fingers. She gasped as he dragged her skirt hem up her thighs and burrowed his fingers beneath her panties to find her damp pussy. He stroked her clit, hard, just this side of brutal. "Am I a sadist?"

She gasped, and Rafe smiled in sweet victory.

Maybe he wasn't a sadist in the strictest sense of the word. Until now, he would have denied that he was. Yet nothing ignited him like the soft sounds of her gasps and her sweet little whimpers. Her cries were the icing on top. "Could you come for me right now?" He pinched her clit.

"God, Rafe…" Her words were a whimper. Her golden-hazel eyes were wide as she looked to him for guidance and permission. "Yes. Yes. I could."

Her pretty little pleas would echo in his ears for the rest of the night. He slid his finger inside her cunt.

"I…" Like the best kind of horny and helpless sub, she ground her pelvis against his hand.

He found her G-spot, pressed it, played with her clit even harder, waited for her breaths to turn to gasps. Then he pulled away his hand.

She sagged forward, and he caught her. "You can't mean to leave me like this."

"Yes. I can." He removed his hand from beneath her skirt, helped her to stand, then smoothed back her hair as the elevator swooshed to a stop.

"You *are* a sadist." She strode ahead of him across the lobby. He let her, enjoying the crisp click of her high-heeled shoes on the marble and the sight of her stiff spine as she took steps as long as her tight-fitting skirt allowed.

At the glass door, she paused.

"I've changed my mind about orgasm denial."

"Pity. I enjoy what it does to you. All that tension. Frustration. Even the anger." He reached around her to grab hold of the oversize handle. "My car is parked at the curb."

She shivered.

He schooled his features, so he didn't grin. Houston's ever-present spring humidity draped them like a wet woolen sweater. "Looks like rain." And he wouldn't mind if she got drenched.

Not responding, she strode through the exit.

Using his remote control, he unlocked his SUV, then opened the passenger door. He offered his hand to assist her, but she didn't accept. Instead, she slid in and clutched her bag in front of her as if it were a lifeline.

"Perhaps you'd like to hike up your skirt and masturbate without coming while I drive to the restaurant?"

Her mouth formed an adorable O.

"No?" he asked. "You'd prefer not to? Then I suggest you be grateful for the orgasms I give you rather than express your displeasure when I withhold them." He closed her inside the vehicle.

When he slid behind the wheel, she was still looking straight ahead.

Since it was so late in the evening, the drive to the seafood restaurant on Westheimer took less than fifteen minutes.

The valet took the car, and Myrna, the owner herself, greeted them. When she learned that it was Hope's first visit to the Bluewater Bistro, Myrna signaled for an employee to bring over a rose, then guided them to a quiet corner at the back of the dining room. Rather than a table, they'd been given a booth, so he could slide in close to his still-pouting matchmaker.

Hope set down the flower, the petals a shocking splash of red against the white tablecloth. Rafe had a sudden idea of what to do with the stem.

Myrna extended a high-end tablet toward Rafe. "May I get you a drink? Or would you like a minute to settle in?"

He glanced at Hope. "Any preference? Wine? Champagne?"

"Champagne?" Her eyes widened. "Do you mean it?"

"They have it by the glass."

"In that case, yes."

He swiped his finger across the screen a couple of times, not stopping until he reached the sparkling wine section. After scanning the list, he offered a recommendation.

She smiled. "Sounds wonderful."

"Two glasses," he told Myrna.

"My pleasure." She conveyed the order to the server whom she introduced.

"They know you here," Hope mentioned when they were alone, a basket of yeasty rolls on the table between them. "Is it a favorite place to bring dates?"

"Fishing for information, Ms. Malloy?" The thought pleased him.

"I thought it might be something I could tell the candidates about you."

He shook off his sudden annoyance. Was she trying to prick his ego? "I come here because the food is superlative, and it's not at one of my hotels so

I can relax more, away from business. Besides, if I took out a lot of women, my mother wouldn't have needed to hire you."

The server returned with the wine, then left again when Rafe said they needed a few minutes of privacy.

"To a fruitful partnership." He raised his glass.

She clinked hers against his rim, then took a delicate sip. "Oh wow." Then she went quiet for a moment. "Oh, my God. Yum."

"Glad you approve." She didn't hide her pleasure, and he savored her reactions. "How's your pussy?"

"What?" Over the top of her flute, she cast him a glare that would have castrated a lesser man. "You can't talk like that in public."

Rafe was intent on doing far more than that. "I'll give you that orgasm now if you want."

"What?" She checked to see if anyone had heard his outrageous suggestion. Her drink sloshed as she slid the glass onto the table.

"You said you didn't want orgasm denial anymore."

"I didn't say I wanted public ones!"

He picked up the breadbasket and offered it to her. "Roll?"

"You're impossible, Mr. Sterling."

"So I've been told."

With the focus of a gemologist cutting a diamond, she selected the roll with the crispiest crust. He watched her butter it, then take a bite. She closed her eyes and made a sound of satisfaction. Sharing this made him realize how empty dining alone every night was.

While waiting to order, she turned their discussion toward the women she'd been interviewing for him. His patience snapped. He didn't want to think about the perfect Miss Texas runner-up or a blonde doctor or anyone else. "Mind if we save that conversation for business hours?"

She inhaled. "Then what do you want to talk about?"

"You."

"Why? You're the client. One of Houston's most eligible bachelors."

"Who is having dinner with a seductive woman who I want to submit to me." When the thought had first formed, he'd meant for the remainder of this evening. But the idea of stretching it for a longer period interested him. There were a million things she might enjoy, and he didn't want another Dom to be her instructor. "Let's start with your name. Does it have any significance?"

She pressed her lips together and stared into her glass.

The fact she'd avoided the question surprised him. "Was that too personal?"

"Not many people ask." A few seconds later, she dragged the wine toward her and kept hold of the stem. "My dad was in the army."

"Was?"

Rather than give him a direct answer, she

responded with, "I was born while he was deployed, and...my mother couldn't get hold of him to let him know she was in labor. Of course, she was nervous, but she refused to think anything but positive thoughts." She gave a half smile that was heavy with grief and touched with bravery. "He didn't make it home alive. He never met me."

Rafe reached across the table to curl his hand over hers. He expected her to pull away, but she didn't. "It couldn't have been easy, growing up without your father."

"My mom..." Hope paused, as if searching for the right words to convey her emotions. "She did her best, but..."

He continued to hold her. In his peripheral vision, he saw the waiter heading in their direction. Then, noticing their body language, he instead walked toward another table. "Go on."

"She didn't recover...spent a lot of her time lost in the past. She worked as a nurse at an army hospital, taking care of soldiers, as if she could maintain some sort of connection with him." Hope blinked. *Trying to clear the memories?* "Sorry. You didn't need to hear all that."

"She didn't remarry?"

"No. She believed that she and my dad were soulmates."

"And you? Do you believe in fate that way?"

"I'm pragmatic. The idea of someone being all-consuming terrifies me."

The server returned, and she tugged her hand

away and picked at her roll. After consulting Hope about her preferences, Rafe ordered an appetizer.

Before he could ask another question, she leaned forward. "What was it like to grow up in luxury as the heir of a multibillion-dollar conglomeration?"

"Not as exciting or as comfortable as you might think. Loaded with expectation. I went to nursery school at age three, then boarding school." How did he describe an upbringing that was silent, at times frigid? "When I was home for summers and holidays, I spent a lot of time with my grandfather, instead of with my parents. He believed in hard work, so he hired me as the general errand boy at the Sterling Downtown the moment I turned ten. On my thirteenth birthday, I became a bellboy. I was allowed to keep tips, but my paychecks went to pay for my education. My senior year of high school, I worked as an assistant concierge. And then in college, when others slept late or went on vacation, I worked as a manager for several different properties. I did an intern year in Asia."

"What was his rationale?"

"He didn't want me to be self-centered like my dad."

She winced and pushed away her plate, and he realized she hadn't taken a single bite.

"My great-great-great..." He frowned. "Maybe one or two more—I forget how many—grandfather emigrated from Norway in search of a better life. He understood the value of hard work, and each generation has tried to instill that in the next. My dad, you may or may not know, was not the family heir."

"No?" She pulled the glass toward herself again, then sat back and crossed her legs.

The feminine picture she presented made him forget the past and think about the immediate future.

"You were saying?"

Rafe prided himself on his ability to focus, yet Hope distracted him. "My uncle—my dad's brother—was killed in a car accident. Since the terms of the family trust are clear—a woman can't inherit, and a male must be married to become the heir—my father married my mother."

"And if you're to succeed…"

"My cousin, Noah, is married." To a woman who was as much of a social climber as he was. "They have a couple of kids." That they had packed off to boarding school. Rafe suspected neither of them wanted the responsibility of being parents. "He'd like my father to step down from the CEO position. And since Noah's married with children, he thinks he deserves to fill the role. He would begin to sell off most of our brands."

"Would that be bad?"

He'd considered that question. "My great-grandfather was forced to do that around the time of the Great Depression in order to forestall bankruptcy. As the extended family grew stronger, they loaned him the money to get out of debt and buy back the properties. That was in the 1940s and early 50s. He swore it wouldn't happen again. It wasn't until thirty years ago that my grandfather was able to repurchase the Le Noble in New York." One of the chain's crown jewels, a five-diamond property near Grand Central Station.

"I had high tea there once."

"Remarkable, isn't it? And that is what Sterling is about. The experience. Exceeding expectations at every turn. Would a new owner understand and value that?" He scowled. "The brand is well respected worldwide," he said when they were alone again. "And it is profitable. With some changes, returns could be even greater. For example, we're considering adding a luxury cruise line with several small exclusive ships and a couple of medium-sized ones. We won't be competing with value carriers, but instead we'll be creating a new market. I'm also developing an idea to create high-end housing opportunities, villas and mansions that families can stay in for weeks or months if they desire. Imagine that you could have a house in Tuscany with a wine cellar at your disposal. Or a villa in Monte Carlo. Perhaps a chateau in the Swiss alps. No need to worry about the taxes or maintenance or housekeeping."

"Or cooking?"

"Or cooking," he confirmed.

"If I must..." She laughed. "Is this where I say, 'take my money'?"

He enjoyed her expressions. Whether she was happy or upset, excited or teasing, the emotion filtered across her face. "So if we sell, would we get as much as it's worth? How many corporations have the kind of money necessary? There are a limited number of hoteliers with the capital and resources to buy us out. Would the Sterling name be discontinued? I believe the future is bright, both in economy travel and the luxury markets. To me, this is more than a business. It's my family's legacy. I'm in no hurry to tear it down."

"Which is why your grandfather spent so much time with you. He wanted to instill that in you."

Noah had enjoyed a pampered childhood with lazy days and trips. After college, he'd traveled the world—staying at various Sterling properties. His version of learning the business had included ordering twenty-four-hour room service and judging the food quality and wait times. He'd even compiled a spreadsheet to show where there was room for improvement. Not that Rafe objected to that. In fact, that kind of reporting was appreciated. But Noah had done it all on company money, and he'd traveled to exotic destinations and made outrageous demands. To make matters worse, he was—by all accounts—a lousy tipper.

The server brought crab cakes, and Hope moved her rose to one side to make room for the platter. She pricked her index finger on a thorn, reigniting his hunger for her, something he'd never had trouble controlling before.

She sucked on her finger. "That hurts."

"Not as much as what I'm thinking about doing to you."

Her eyes widened.

"I want the thorns on your pussy." He transferred one of the appetizers onto her plate, then scooped the second onto his. "The question is, are you going to do it beneath the table? Or wait until we get home?"

Hope dropped her hand and curled it into a fist in her lap. "Are you serious?"

"I am."

"You want me to…" She trailed off. "I'm not sure I understand."

"Hike up your skirt, then scrape the thorns up your inner thigh."

"Mr. Sterling, *you* are a sadist."

With her, yes. He couldn't hide his grin at her delicate outrage. "Of the worst kind, it turns out."

Her gaze flickered to the rose, then back at her plate. Though she didn't respond, she was clearly thinking about his suggestion.

"How did you like the way I spanked your pussy? Did it hurt as much as you imagined it would?"

"Yes, but…"

"But?" he prompted.

"The sensations were… What I mean is… The orgasms were…"

Her struggle was as real as it was delicious. "The pain added to the heightened sensations?"

"Yes."

"Then do it."

Until she discreetly wiggled around to lift the

hem of her skirt, he wasn't sure she'd do as he'd requested.

His cock surged as her knee brushed his. He made sure the tablecloth guaranteed her privacy while she lowered the rose to the seat.

Her hands trembled, and her breaths crashed into each other. "Maybe it's the champagne." She sounded deliciously bemused.

"It's the curiosity. The risk." There were so many more things he'd ask of her when they visited Vieille Rivière, his favorite private restaurant in New Orleans. "The reward you're hoping for later. It might hurt. Tomorrow morning perhaps you'll notice a small scratch that will remind you of this evening. If nothing else, it's an experience you won't get with anyone else. You're hungry for that, aren't you, sweet Hope? The opportunity to live, to explore?"

"Yes," she murmured. "But it will hurt."

"Especially when you press the thorn against your clit."

Her skin went scarlet, then drained of color.

"Then you'll be so aroused you'll wonder how you'll make it to my house without an orgasm. You may even consider giving into the temptation of excusing yourself to the ladies' room, but since you'll be on a video with me while you're in there, you won't have the opportunity."

"You can't mean that!"

"Which part? Forbidding you to masturbate? Or the part where you'll be on the phone with me?"

"Either." She scowled. The lines trenched between her eyebrows would scare a lesser man.

"For clarity, I meant both."

The server joined them. "Everything okay, Mr. Sterling?"

"Fine. Thank you, Stephen."

"Let me know if there's anything else you need." With that, the man left them alone again.

"Meet my gaze," Rafe instructed Hope. "I want to see each of your reactions."

She had to scoot around a little.

"I'm waiting."

Hope drew her lower lip between her teeth as she pressed the stem against her skin.

"How is that?"

She whimpered. Slowly, she moved her hand higher. Breathless, she stopped and looked at him.

"Make sure you have a thorn pointed toward your pussy." Her almost imperceptible movements and tiny sighs told him she would, indeed, enjoy his vampire gloves—dozens of tiny spiked nubs burrowing into her at the same time.

She turned the stem a little. "I'm nervous."

"Good."

"Good?" Her eyebrows were drawn together in shock and question.

"Fear is powerful, isn't it? Your insides are trembling. Fight or flight has been triggered. Everything inside you is rebelling at my request. Everything you've learned is warning you not to do it. Yet you know—or at least suspect—that the high you will experience will make any fleeting pain worth it."

From the way she frowned at him, she didn't want him to be right.

"What's going on inside you? Has your heart rate increased? Palms a little damp? Hot shivers? Cold? Are you trembling?"

"Yes. All that."

"And to think, you could just be having dinner alone. Or worse, with some man who bored you, talking about current events, discussing your day at work." He took a sip of his drink, appreciating the dryness and notes of vanilla. "There's some risk, for sure. You could be caught. Myrna might see you and kick us out of here, perhaps ban us from all her restaurants. You might be so turned on that you have a difficult time containing your reaction. Maybe our server will suspect what you're doing and pretend not to notice. At any rate, you're tempted." Would she do it? Ms. Malloy was a perfect lady, and wondering if she would color outside the lines was a tantalizing prospect. If she did, her acquiescence would fuel his masturbatory fantasies for days, maybe weeks.

She took her sweet time deciding, and that made her surrender that much sweeter.

Hope moved her hand a little and bit down hard on her lip as she forced the thorn against her cunt. Rafe could have exploded in that instant. It wasn't just her shocked, rapturous expression. It was more. Her obedience. Her thirst to receive what he offered.

"Sweet God, Hope." Beneath the tablecloth, he moved his hand on top of hers and pressed, digging the thorn in harder, imagining it snagging her silken panties.

"Rafe…"

He held it against her another few seconds, until she inched back. Then he released his grip.

With her shoulders shaking, she dragged in a few shallow breaths. "That's… It didn't hurt like I thought it would. Maybe because of my underwear? But…" She placed the rose back on the table. A single petal fell from it. "The idea of what we did, I mean, in public." She crossed her legs. "It was hot. And you're right about what was going on in my brain. The…"

"Mindfuck?"

"Yes." She reached for her glass and her hand trembled as she lifted it. "Addictive."

He had a million more experiences for her, including a few they could start on tonight.

CHAPTER FIVE

"After you." Rafe opened the door to his condominium. Hope hesitated for a fraction of a second. Everything else that had happened until now, she could excuse. Rafe and his overwhelming presence had swept her up in the moment. But coming home with him, after he'd said he planned to spank her?

"Hope?"

As always, patience radiated through his voice. If she told him that she'd changed her mind, he'd take her home and leave her there.

Which meant the problem wasn't the powerful and seductive Rafe Sterling. It was her. Clients had asked her out before. Until today, she'd turned them down. But with Rafe, the more scandalous his behavior, the deeper she was drawn into his web.

Trembling, she stepped across the threshold into the inviting, expansive white-marble entryway.

He followed, closed the door, then turned the lock. A shiver feathered down her spine, one that had nothing to do with the air-conditioning and everything to do with the lethal heat that blazed in his eyes when he turned her to face him.

"I'm glad you're here."

"I'm —" Not knowing what to say, she broke off.

"Show me your thigh."

So much for thinking he might give her some time to get settled.

He held out a hand for her purse. He placed it on a bench that might have been an old church pew.

When he regarded her with one raised eyebrow, she lifted her skirt. She was shocked when she didn't see any abrasion from the thorn. Even though the scratch was imaginary, she could have shown him the exact path it had carved. Her clit throbbed still, from the phantom pain.

"You'll have to do it harder next time."

She wanted to. What did that say about her? Hope dropped the hem of her skirt and the material fluttered back into place.

"May I take your blazer?"

His switch from a sexual Dominant to courteous host tipped her world off-balance.

She shrugged out of her jacket, and he hung it in

a coat closet near the door.

"Let me show you around so you're comfortable."

That wasn't a word she would have chosen to describe being in his place.

"Your house is a surprise," she said as they passed a black baby-grand piano.

"Is it?"

"I thought you might live in River Oaks or Tanglewood." Or another of Houston's pricey gated communities, even the Woodlands where he could have a sprawling estate. Instead, they'd ridden the elevator to the ninth-floor penthouse of a modern-looking condominium in Uptown. When they'd driven onto the property, they passed tennis courts, several swimming pools, and a running track. Though he'd left his car in the parking garage, there were numerous spaces outside, and there was a wooden portico covered with vines to create an inviting shaded gateway to the entrance of each of the complex's three buildings.

"I didn't see the point in getting a house since I don't spend a lot of time at home. A condo requires much less maintenance. And I like the amenities."

"Like the concierge?"

"It's handy. It's also close to bike trails. I can reach them without having to drive anywhere."

The space was contemporary, with floor-to-ceiling windows. A balcony off the main living area had a seating area with oversize chairs, end tables, umbrellas, and, of course, a bicycle.

His fireplace mantel had no personal touches. The room was filled with decorator-inspired vases and art. Even his furniture was stark—black leather with no welcoming pillows.

On the other hand, the kitchen was a chef's delight, with a pot filler over the six-burner stovetop. The vent was streamlined and gleamed.

"I'd offer you champagne, but that will have to wait until after your spanking."

The way he spoke to her, as if it was inevitable, sent rockets of desire straight to her pussy. "Uhm. Okay. Why?"

"You need to be in full charge of your responses, and I need to be aware of you and your reactions to what we are doing. But I can offer you a club soda or mineral water."

Since her mouth was dry and she wanted to occupy her hands, she said, "Mineral water would be nice."

He took down a glass with a thick stem, filled it halfway, then squeezed some fresh lime into it. "Shall we go outside?"

She nodded as she accepted the drink. "The view is spectacular," she said once they were on the patio. From here, there was a perfect vantage of the empty tennis courts and a young couple splashing each other in the swimming pool. Beyond, buildings glistened in the fading sunlight.

"Invites you to go and explore the city, doesn't it?"

She turned and rested her back against the

railing. "Is this complex owned by Sterling Worldwide?"

"No. We don't do a lot of that kind of development, but it is something I'm interested in. It's a departure from our core strength, so I would want to proceed with caution."

"Cautious isn't a word I associate with you."

"Why not?" He frowned, puzzled, but not challenging, inviting her response.

"You seem...ambitious."

"The two aren't incompatible. I like to win. So while I move forward, I do so on situations that require very little risk."

"Which is another reason to use a matchmaker."

"Clever way to convince me not to ask for the return of my mother's money."

She tried to grin, but the reminder that she needed to find him a wife with whom he would share this view every day bothered her enough that she distracted herself by taking a sip of her mineral water.

"There's more to see," he told her.

The dining room table was oblong, glass topped, with seating for ten. "Do you entertain a lot?"

"No. The designer my mother hired suggested I needed something this size to fill the space, and I didn't have the heart to turn it into the exercise room that I wanted."

As part of the dining room, he had a fabulous bar area. Stemware of various sizes and shapes lined up on two rows of glass shelves. As if this were one of his hotels, several more mirror-lined shelves held gorgeous bottles of liquor, all premium brands. The patio could be accessed through a set of French doors. "You should consider hosting parties. This place was made for it."

He shuddered, and she laughed. The shared experience softened her tension and demolished barriers. If she wasn't careful, she might start to like him.

Rafe showed her the study, complete with a built-in desk and a wall of bookshelves, another fireplace, and a television. This room had a couple of comfortable-looking chairs, lamps, and a settee. Because of a smattering of magazines — back issues of *Houstonia, Texas Monthly, Sterling Getaways* — along with the TV remote control on the coffee table, she guessed this was where he spent a lot of his free time. As with the rest of the home, this room had no personal effects.

"There's a private elevator over there." He pointed to a door that looked as if it might be a pantry.

"A private elevator for your condo?"

He shrugged. "It's helpful for moving furniture."

"Which you do a lot?"

"Or as a timeout place for naughty subs."

"Whew. Good thing I don't know any of those."

"Yeah." His quick grin transformed him into a more approachable man. "Good thing. Would you like to see the upstairs?"

She paused, knowing what that meant. His private space. His bedroom. Her spanking. Dread and anticipation unfurled. "Ye—ees." The word broke into two syllables as she stumbled over it. She was trying to sound sophisticated or at least submissive, yet she was as unnerved as a virgin.

"You delight me." At the bottom of the marble staircase, he paused. "I'd like you to get undressed."

As always, he shocked her. "Here?"

"It will change your mindset."

"And make me cold."

"Not for long. Your ass will be hot soon enough."

Unable to maintain her composure while his expectation overwhelmed her, she lowered her gaze. He took the glass from her and set it down. Her voice cracking, she asked, "Are you staying dressed?"

"At least for the moment."

"Is that part of your approach to BDSM?"

"It can be."

His shockingly clear eyes radiated power. A lot of executives wore comfortable clothing, but she thought his tailored suits were sexy and classy. Once again, her gaze traveled to his tie as she had a sudden fantasy about being restrained.

"Besides, I like looking at your body. It's easier not to give in to the temptation to fuck you if I'm dressed."

"I wondered about that."

"We haven't discussed it. I want you to understand that BDSM and sex are often separate things. One doesn't have to lead to the other."

"If…" Had she lost what little remained of her mind? Hope cleared her throat, then tried again. "I'm open to it."

"Me too."

The growl threaded through his words heated her. Maybe he was right that she didn't need to worry about getting cold. She removed her shoes and left them near the bottom stair.

He rolled the glass between his palms as he watched her. She discarded her blouse, then her bra. Beneath his gaze, her nipples hardened.

"You could do this for me every day, and I would appreciate it."

Rafe made it easy to be brave. She unzipped her skirt, then worked it over hips that had always been too wide. It whooshed to the tile floor. Then she stripped off her panties.

"You can either bring your clothes upstairs or put them over the back of the couch."

She opted for the couch, though the old her would have clutched them in front of her body to use as a shield.

"Precede me, please."

Obeying with this request was more difficult than some of the others, even the one to drag the rose up her bare thigh. Her body's flaws would be exposed to him.

Affecting bravery, she pulled back her shoulders and began to walk up the stairs. She had reached the landing before his footsteps echoed behind her. He was following, but at his own languid pace.

"Take a left turn at the top," he instructed.

The second story was as spectacular as the first. He had a guest room with a large window that was covered with a blind. It had its own private bathroom.

His home office was as tidy as the rest of the house. One wall was covered with renderings of various Sterling hotels, some in winter settings with snow covering the nearby mountain peaks, another with an open-air lobby with the warm waters of the South Pacific beckoning. There were others in Asia, the Le Noble in New York City, the Maison Sterling in New Orleans, and the Sterling Parkland in Washington, DC, complete with a view of the White House or Lafayette Park. A coffee-table book of the company's history lay atop his credenza.

Pictures and portraits lined the walls, and there was a framed family tree.

Earlier she'd suggested that it must have been exciting and wonderful to be the wealthy heir apparent of the Sterling empire. Obviously, it was also a burden. Though he was a young man, he had a weariness about him that spoke of grave responsibility. "This is part museum."

"That's on purpose. It reminds me of what I'm working toward."

"As if you'd forget?"

He showed her the bonus room with a television and more unused couches. A full-body workout machine stood near the window. "It has interesting possibilities for securing you in place while I do nasty things to you."

She glanced over her shoulder. He wasn't smiling, and a diabolical gleam spiked through his eyes.

"The tour is over. I'm impatient for a taste of you."

He invited her to precede him into the oversize master bedroom. There were windows on two sides, meaning it would be a sundrenched space during the day. And he had a small table and chairs.

"I'd start every morning off right here, I think." It would be a perfect nook for journaling or planning her day.

"You're welcome to see how it works for you." He placed her almost-untouched water glass on the nightstand.

Another temptation. She wondered if this was how she would end up in hell, by eating one forbidden fruit at a time.

"Come here." His tone was sharper than it had been earlier, skittering her pulse into a frenzy. He pointed to a spot in front of him.

She crossed the cool floor to stand where he indicated. Then, unsure how to act, she shifted her weight.

"Please help me off with my jacket."

She walked behind him and thought that performing the act might be awkward, but instead it was easy, part of the dominance he was using to define their roles.

"It goes in the closet." He pointed. "On the valet."

She'd seen that type of wooden structure in magazine ads and on designer television shows, and until now she hadn't been sure what it was called. It had a shelf for his personal effects, a drawer for storage, and a couple of hooks, perhaps for a tie and a belt.

On the side wall, he had a vault. And there was a wooden panel that might have resembled a wardrobe, except for the fact it was built into the wall. The large luxurious walk-in closet smelled of leather and pulsed with masculine power. His organization was meticulous. His suits and shirts were arranged by color. Next came casual wear, khaki pants and polo shirts. Sports shirts and shorts were folded on shelves. She supposed it made him more efficient, but part of her yearned to mess up his life, even a little bit.

"Stalling won't save you," he called out.

Hope gripped the material tighter, so she didn't drop it. "Coming!" She draped the jacket over the back of the valet on the piece of wood curved to resemble a hanger, then smoothed the wrinkles from the fabric. There was no reason to be scared of what would come next. *Who am I kidding?*

When she returned to him, his smile of appreciation was the encouragement she needed.

"Undo my tie."

"I'm not sure where to begin."

"You'll figure it out. The more you struggle, the

more I'll enjoy it."

She stretched to reach the knot, and getting so close to him caused her tender nipples to brush against his shirt. He filled her vision, swamped her senses. If this kind of arousal was constant in BDSM, she wasn't sure she could bear it.

Hope worked the knot free.

"Take it all the way off."

"Should I put it away?"

"No. Offer it to me, then turn around and place your hands behind you." He held her gaze. "Tell me you understand."

This was her first experience with bondage, and her pulse fluttered. "Yes, Rafe." The words were magic, making her want to obey.

Hope pulled his tie free. A primitive instinct compelled her to fold it in half, then in quarters, before extending it toward him.

"You're a natural."

She turned, expectation spiking in her blood, and laced her fingers at the small of her back, waiting.

With perfunctory movements, he wound the silk around her wrists. "How's that?"

It wasn't tight enough to cut off her circulation, but there was no give in the fabric, making her aware of his power.

"I want you to use your colors if you're frightened too much." He feathered the words against her ear.

"You're planning to scare me?"

"Oh, yes. The exact amount." His breath was warm on her skin, and tiny goose bumps dotted her arms. "Some fear is good for you, sweet Hope. It will keep you in line."

And if it doesn't? A sense of preservation kept her from challenging him aloud.

He swept her from her feet to carry her to the bed. He laid her on her back, her hands still fastened, imprisoned beneath her.

Her mouth dried as he crossed to the closet. He returned less than a minute later, carrying two things, a thin paddle and leather-thonged implement she recognized as a flogger.

"This one is for beginners."

If that was true, she didn't want to see the advanced version. The fear he had mentioned chilled her.

"The falls are wide, so it's going to be a thuddy sensation." He picked up the handle. He held the flogger above her chest, the angled tips skimming her skin. Watching her reaction, he danced the leather over her breasts, the light touch awakening her nerve endings. Her nipples became even tighter, and she drew her shoulder blades toward each other, trying to arch.

He moved lower, across her ribs, down her torso. Without being told, she spread her legs for him.

"Sweet, sweet Hope." Avoiding her cunt, he gave her legs and inner thighs leather caresses.

"Please." She wanted the whole experience.

He moved his wrist, then flicked the strands between her legs.

This was more than a touch; it was quick bursts of flat pain. She understood what he'd meant by thuddy, and she loved it. "This... Yes."

"Say my name."

"Please, Rafe." Then for the first time, because it was natural, she added, "Sir."

"I'd put a ribbon around the moon for you." When he flicked his hand, sending the flogger flying against her cunt in a brutal kiss, she screamed his name.

"Did you come?"

"I..."

He pulled the implement away. *"Did you come?"* His carefully enunciated demand made her shiver.

"You know I did. But it's not my fault."

"Does that mean you're blaming me for your misbehavior?"

Ever since he pressed the thorn against her, she'd been on a knife's edge. The fact that he'd denied her a climax several times had made her more orgasmic than ever before. Sensing danger, she answered, "No. Sir. I meant that I've been so turned on by your skilled"—*evil*—"ways this entire evening." She opened her eyes, unaware that she'd closed them.

"Celeste mentioned you should go into PR. I concur."

He returned to his closet. Something tinkled, like metal playing on wood. His cufflinks? Then silence echoed around her. Her trepidation built, as he no doubt intended.

When he exited, his shirtsleeves were rolled up. He'd never been sexier.

"I will be with you in less than sixty seconds."

She nodded. The man was masterful. In leaving her tied in the middle of his bed, naked, flogged, her pussy sizzling, she was hyperaware of her submission to him.

Though she strained her hearing, she couldn't quite make out what he was doing.

In less time than he'd promised, he carried a wooden chair into the room.

"This will suit our needs." It was serviceable and sturdy, like something out of an old-fashioned classroom. "In fact, I may leave it in here permanently." He placed it near one of the windows. "Please come to me."

Since her hands were tied, his request challenged her. She wriggled toward the edge of the mattress.

Watching her with avid interest, he said, "Now I want you on your knees, then turn around."

"I suspect I'm not the first one you've given this direction to."

"You'd be wrong."

Startled, she stared at him.

"You're the first submissive I've had in this bed."

Since she wasn't sure how to respond, she accepted his help to her knees. "You like watching me struggle."

"It's as exciting as fuck. I'm considering ordering you to grind your pelvis against the mattress and watching you get yourself off. Shouldn't take much since your cunt is already hot from my lash."

An illicit thrill raced through her. What the hell was it about him that turned her into a sex fiend, horny for each new experience?

"In fact—"

"No. No, no, no, no, no. No."

"No?" In his maddening way, he raised one of his eyebrows. "No is not a safe word."

She knew that.

"Oh, yes. I want to watch you fuck my bedding."

She was humiliated. Worse, she was aroused.

"Back into the middle of the bed." He held on to her while she faced away from him. Then he checked her bonds and tightened them again before lowering her facedown onto the mattress. "Now do the nasty to my bedding," he said.

Thankful her heated face was buried in the covers, so he couldn't see her, she awkwardly rotated her hips.

"Again, with more enthusiasm."

"*God.*" She made the same stilted move.

"Get out of your head. Pretend I'm not here, if that's easier."

How could she? His scent lingered everywhere, and his words rumbled in her head.

"I mean it, Hope. Stop thinking. Do, rather than worry."

Having her hands tied behind her back restricted her movements and shifted her body weight. But that meant she could use the leverage to stimulate her breasts.

"Stalling any longer will make your upcoming spanking even worse."

Concentrating on following his orders, she shifted her upper body back and forth.

"Better. I love watching your ass shimmy."

She scowled, relieved he couldn't see her face.

In a few minutes, she grew tired and frustrated. When he relented, she exhaled. A spanking had to be better than this.

But he wasn't done with her. He rolled her onto one side, then folded a pillow in half before placing it between her legs and under her lower torso. The position forced her ass into the air, and it placed her pussy against the pillow.

"Now hump it."

The Egyptian cotton rubbing against her cunt turned her on. She stopped trying to create friction against her nipples and instead focused on thrusting against the pillow.

"That's it."

Once she shut out thoughts of how obscene she must look with her buttocks clenching and wiggling, she appreciated his murmurs of approval. He had been right when he'd suggested that she'd easily be aroused because her cunt had been tormented by orgasms, the rose, and his flogger.

A climax loomed out of reach. And no doubt he

intended to punish her for coming when his lash had struck her. She moaned.

"I love hearing your sounds. Somewhere between pleasure and desperation. Grind it harder."

I can't. She did. The increased sensation was a lick of pleasure. "Rafe…"

"You're not ready yet."

"I am!" Now that he'd refused her, she was frantic.

"Wait."

She slowed her movements a little, trying to back away from the pleasure.

"I didn't tell you to stop fucking it."

"But…"

He unleashed his flogger on her ass, driving her.

Crying out from the exhilaration, Hope adjusted her position as much as possible beneath his lash and without the use of her hands so that her labia was parted farther, putting more of her body in contact with the pillowcase. "Rafe. Rafe." She ground her back teeth together, trying to distract herself.

He continued, lighting up her buttocks and upper thighs. It was too much and at the same time not enough.

"I love seeing you helpless like this. Needy. Hungry. Your greedy little cunt."

His words dragged her back to his sensual reality, and her ability to hold on much longer was unraveling. "Sir!"

"Perfect."

She exhaled in gratitude, but instead of him

granting her relief, he tossed aside the flogger, then turned her onto her back. "What?" she demanded as breath whooshed from her lungs.

He dragged the pillow from beneath her and threw it to the far side of the mattress before spreading her legs and kneeling between her thighs.

She studied his strong face, and this time there was no smile of approval, nothing beyond intense focus. "Are we going to have sex?"

"Oh, yes." Instead of unbuckling his belt, he leisurely plucked at her semierect nipples, teasing them until they were engorged and standing straight up.

Her arousal returned in force, and she lifted her hips in invitation.

He released his grip and instead placed his palms on either side of her hips.

"I thought we were going to have sex." She scowled at the confounding man.

"Your spanking is first."

Frustration gnawed at her. "So you're not going to let me come?"

"You'll get to come as often as you like when I'm fucking you." His eyes darkened. "But for now? No. I'm staying here until you're no longer on the edge."

His games were infuriating, yet they left her vibrant and alive.

He proved to be a patient man. Rafe remained where he was, preventing her from drawing her legs together to try to sneak some relief. The whole time he kept his gaze trained on her, showing interest in nothing other than her actions.

When her skin had cooled, and she'd regained control over her breathing, he instructed, "Stay in that exact position."

He waited for her to nod before he left the bed. "When you're ready, turn yourself over, then make your way to the edge of the mattress, feetfirst."

Her earlier task should have meant she'd no longer be embarrassed in front of him. *Wrong.* Having him loom over her with folded arms while she inched toward him, trying to avoid rubbing her pussy so she didn't come, made her very aware of her femininity.

Hope had expected him to stand there while she maneuvered off the bed, but he was there to steady her, his grip sure. "Thank you."

"I'll always be here for you, Hope."

For a glorious second, she allowed herself to bask in his words before reality crashed back into her. He wasn't hers, and she wasn't his.

She shrugged out of his grip, then turned to face him. She wished he wasn't so handsome and that his web wasn't so thick.

"You've earned that spanking."

"*Earned?* Like it's some kind of honor?"

"In the most wonderful way."

"Mmm-hmm."

"How was the flogging?"

She recalled the pain that had excited her, then receded right away. "I liked it."

"Perhaps you'll enjoy the paddle as well."

It was on the bed, behind her, but it loomed as a threat. "Not convinced."

"It's a different kind of pain. Depending how I use it, of course. It will be a flat, dull pain. I won't let you bruise—"

"Are there bruises from the flogger?" She turned her head, as if she could see her rear.

"No. I'm not saying it's impossible, but I didn't use a lot of force. Were you hoping for some?"

Scandalized, she opened her eyes wide. "No." But the idea swirled in her mind.

"You're an ineffective liar." He grinned.

"Can we get the spanking over with?" The longer they waited, the worse her nerves were becoming.

"You don't get to set the pace, sweet Hope. That's known as topping from the bottom. I promise to honor your safe word. But there can be no misunderstanding. I'm in charge."

"Yes, Rafe." She said it so quickly that her lack of sincerity had to be obvious.

"Because you're attempting to manipulate me, we'll also play with the butterfly."

CHAPTER SIX

"Butterfly?" Now what had she gotten herself into?

"It's a purple vibrator. You'll find it on the bottom shelf of the wall unit in the closet." He removed the tie from around her wrists. "Don't stall."

With a sigh, she returned to his closet and hung the tie from the valet. The wood panel she'd noticed earlier stood open, displaying an array of BDSM paraphernalia. Her mouth dropped open. Now she understood why he'd sent her to fetch the butterfly. It was so that she'd see his dozens of torture devices, floggers in different lengths and sizes, one made from chain that terrified her. He had an assortment of paddles and canes, along with cuffs, numerous skeins of rope, blindfolds, a gag made from a ball, and others near it that were from metal and appeared to be made to hold a mouth open.

"Also four of those long fabric strips," he called out. "With metal clips on the end."

She suspected he intended to use them to restrain her.

"And two sets of cuffs!"

Earlier, she could have pulled out of his tie, but these would keep her secure. It unnerved her as much as it excited her.

She picked up the silicone vibrator from the bottom shelf. It had two straps attached, and it appeared innocent enough. A little voice whispered that it was anything but.

Carrying the items he'd ordered, she walked back into the bedroom. He'd stripped down the bedspread and top sheet.

"Thank you." He dropped a gentle kiss on her forehead.

The contrast of his caring and unrelenting nature both occupying the same space at the same time unbalanced her.

He took the strips from her, then said, "Please put it on."

While he attached the restraints to the bedframe, she pulled the butterfly into place. The silicone was firm and cool.

"That looks sexy on you."

She wrinkled her nose.

"I'd like you in the middle of the bed. On your back."

To keep the thing in place, she moved gingerly and pressed it against her body. "Oh!"

"Imagine once I turn it on."

Hope had to fight to stave off an orgasm just getting into place.

He fastened the cuffs around her wrists and ankles, then positioned her spread-eagle and helpless. "Everything okay?"

Except for the terrible awareness of her exposure.

"Let me clarify—no problems with circulation, with the cuffs being too tight?"

"No." Her voice was too soft even for her to hear. "I mean, I'm okay. I'd prefer a spanking to more orgasm denial."

He sat on the bed next to her. "I acknowledge what you've said." He captured a lock of hair and played with it.

"But you won't change your mind, will you? Because you're the Lord of Domination and you're in charge."

"Lord of Domination?"

Oh, God, she hadn't said that out loud.

His smile was both swift and triumphant. "I like that. You can use it in place of my name in your phone so that whenever we talk you'll be reminded of this moment when you were helpless and terrified."

Hope sighed, loving and hating this dynamic. It

was anything but boring, unlike how her sex life had been until this point.

"Shall we begin?"

He waited with seeming bountiful patience for her consent.

"Yes, Rafe."

With a nod, he stood, adjusted his shirtsleeves above his elbows, then went into the closet.

Was he gone for an inordinate amount of time or did it just feel like it because she was left alone, helpless, aware of her nudity and her journey into submission, a bit anxious about what to expect?

When he returned, he was carrying a rectangular fob about an inch thick. "Is that what I think it is?"

"A remote control, yes. The power to make you whimper and beg and cry."

His grin was terrifying.

Instead of returning to sit next to her as she had guessed he might, Rafe slid the chair across the floor until it was positioned at the foot of the bed.

Then he stood, adjusted the elastic straps a little higher up her legs, used two fingers to part her labia, then snuggled the butterfly into her pussy. His touch, impersonal and precise, made her wiggle. She ached for him to get her off. Instead, he readjusted the black strap on her left thigh once more, making it even tighter, before taking a seat.

He watched her as she fought to relax. It took a couple of minutes for her to release the tension in her muscles, sink into the mattress, then find patience and peace, feelings that were unfamiliar to her. Only then did Rafe flip on the device.

A soft sensation flickered across her clit, grabbing her attention. Before she could do anything other than take a shallow breath, he turned off the switch.

"How was that?"

She'd been afraid the vibration would be something she'd struggle to tolerate, but it hadn't been bad. Much less intense than she'd feared. She lifted her head a little to see him. "Fine."

"Are you ready?" His grin promised there was something to be wary of.

"Yes." The word didn't come out as strong as it would have been even thirty seconds before.

Rafe slid his forefinger across the switch.

A faint hum filled the room, and the butterfly fluttered against her clit, this time with more force. She sucked in a gasp. "God almighty." Her toes curled. For the first time, she tugged against her bondage, trying to escape even as she sought more. "Rafe!"

"This is hotter than watching you trying to get yourself off on the pillow."

She tried to picture herself, no secrets from his sharp gaze, her pussy spread and held wide.

He notched the switch higher.

She screamed. Earlier this evening, she was sure it wouldn't have seemed so extreme, but since he'd kept her teetering on the edge for so long, this was difficult to bear. Hope dug her heels into the mattress, trying to use it as leverage to lift herself, but his bonds were too secure.

A million electrical zaps arced through her pussy. "I... I..." In under a minute, she needed to come.

Her body went rigid, and she closed her eyes...only to have the room go silent, the vibrator turn off. She exhaled a deep, shuddering breath, the type she had after a long run or during interval training on the elliptical at the gym.

"Discovering how easy you are to arouse is gratifying."

Rafe gave her no time to answer or recover. He turned the vibrator to high, making her cry out. She tried to roll to one side to escape, and because she couldn't, she tightened her buttocks in a vain attempt to ignore the powerful toy.

He continued to run the vibrator hard while she wailed his name.

She couldn't move or touch herself.

Rafe sat there, master of all, keeping her panting and desperate.

Her safe word offered an escape, but Hope didn't want to grab it. No one had ever demanded so much of her. It — Rafe — would destroy her.

Her pussy was stretched by the relentless toy when he allowed her to rest.

Even though it was turned off, little shocks pulsed through her. It took a full minute for her to drag her pulse back under control.

She wasn't aware of him moving, but he stroked her hair back from her face. Hope blinked. Approval radiated from his eyes. And for that drug, she'd endure anything.

"One more denial. Can you do it?"

Hope wanted to respond with *"Do your worst."* But the truth was, she wasn't that brave. As he'd said, he was much better at this game than she was, and she'd be smart not to test him. "Yes, Rafe."

He pressed his thumb to her lips, then stroked one of her eyebrows.

When he sat on the chair, she braced herself, tightening her muscles. But… The vibrator barely fluttered, just an exquisite kiss against her genitals.

She sighed with pleasure. After the vibrator's rigorous shuddering, she appreciated the gentleness. No longer needing to fight, she surrendered. "So nice…"

After a few minutes, the flicker from the silicone, combined with a low-grade hum, unnerved her. Unlike the previous two times, this wasn't an avalanche of arousal. It was a small wave that started in the distance, then grew, crested, then crashed against the shore. "Rafe! Damn it!" Because it came from the furthest recesses of her body and had taken so much time to build, this was stealthier, so much stealthier than the earlier ones had been. She was helpless. Why the hell had she wanted him to do his worst? "I can't…" *Fuck.* With the way her limbs were restrained, there was no way for her to dislodge the annoyance or get enough pressure to achieve completion.

He stood and walked around the bed to stand

beside her.

"I'm…" She couldn't form a coherent sentence.

"Almost there," he agreed. He squeezed each of her nipples in turn, making her yelp.

He pulled the shimmering device from her for a second and she breathed out a heartfelt "Thank you."

"Don't thank me yet." He increased the speed and pressed it into her, hard.

She sobbed, unsatisfied and drained.

"I imagined you to be fierce" — he turned off the remote and tossed it onto the nightstand — "but I had no idea how incredible you'd be."

He kissed her, mouth-fucking her. She responded in kind, taking and giving, tasting.

When he ended the kiss, his eyes were heavy. "I want a thousand more nights like this."

So do I. Life had taught her not to wish for the impossible, but she was.

He left her long enough to unclip her bonds. Though he didn't remove her cuffs, he rubbed her skin. Then, fortunately, he lowered the elastic straps from her hips.

"If you threw that thing away, I'd do a happy dance."

Rafe helped her up, and she wrapped her arms around her upturned knees, recovering. Reverberations rocked her body, and she needed an orgasm.

Rafe picked up the paddle before moving the chair to where it had been. He placed the spanking implement on the nearby table, within easy reach.

"Come here, Hope." He pointed to his lap.

"You're still going to spank me?" After all that?

"I am, indeed."

Rafe appreciated the seductive, sleepy haze in Hope's golden eyes. It reminded him of the first rays of dawn before the sun fully emerged.

He extended his hand in her direction and she climbed from the bed and took tiny, hesitating steps. At first, she kept her legs wider than normal, as if hoping not to arouse herself. But for the last couple, she pressed her legs together. She was in such distress that his dick hardened to granite.

She stood in front of him, her head tipped back.

"Tell me why you're being spanked."

"For coming without permission."

"And?"

She curled her hands at her sides. "Because you're the Lord of Domination and you said so."

He grinned. "Yes. That's correct." And he wanted to show her the beautiful, sensual side of BDSM. "Over my lap, please."

"I..."

He offered his hand again. She slipped her small palm against his; then he helped her to get situated, ensuring her fingertips could touch the floor. The truth was, he would keep her safe, always. "Relax your head. If you keep it tense, you may get a crick in your neck." When she didn't follow his instruction fast enough, he pressed his hand between her shoulder blades, easing her into position.

Before she could arrange herself, he lifted one knee to unbalance her. As she tried to press her palms against the floor, he placed one of his legs behind her knees, trapping her with her full ass on total display, her buttocks where he wanted them.

He'd promised her no bruises, so he took his time caressing her skin, then rubbing it vigorously.

"Uhmp."

Because of her undignified position, it would be difficult for her to speak, and her moans suited him fine. He continued to rub until her flesh turned a satisfying pink.

"This..." She squealed. "Not...spanking."

"It's part of it." He could do this all night. Rafe gave her a few gentle swats, making sure there was plenty of blood flow to the area he intended to paddle.

"That's all?" Despite his admonition, she turned her head to look at him. "I thought it would hurt."

"That wasn't the spanking." He chuckled at her innocence. "It was a small warm-up."

"Oh." She allowed her body to go limp.

"I'm going to give a few with my hand."

"Yum." Her gasp thrilled him.

After placing a hand on the far side of her waist, he spanked each of her buttocks.

She sighed and settled into him more. *Damn. Her trust...* He rubbed the affected spots. "The next will be a little harder. Breathe through it and accept. Struggle will make any pain more problematic. But it will dissipate if you sink into it." He stroked between her legs. As hot and swollen as her pussy was, it wouldn't take much to turn her on.

He gave her two more fast swats.

"Oh, Rafe. I have to… You have to let me…"

"No." He delivered the last two that he intended to give her with his hand. "How are you doing so far?"

"It's so…amazing."

Her surrender humbled him. "My sweet, sweet Hope." He wondered if she'd say the same thing when he switched to the paddle? He stroked her for a few seconds until she tightened her buttocks and began to buck. Before she could come, he pulled his hand away. "Rafe!"

"We're almost there," he promised, picking up the paddle. "This will hurt more than the hand spanks." He pressed the wood against the fleshiest part of her ass. "Remember my advice?"

"Breathe. Accept it."

"Close enough." He pulled back the paddle, then swung it, hitting the place he'd intended.

She lifted her head, her hair spilling around her like a curtain.

"Breathe," he prompted.

As if starved for oxygen, she gulped for air.

"And again."

She did.

"Better?" He pushed his hand against the heated spot.

She nodded, and the clip fell from her hair to

clatter against the hardwood floor.

The pink of her skin was the stuff of fantasies. He'd dream of it forever. "Ready?"

"Yes."

He aimed for a spot right above the other. Afterward, he stroked away the pain.

"Oh, God."

She didn't have to tell him the problem. He smelled her pheromones. She liked this. This sexy woman was born for him.

The third strike of the paddle was the searing brand of his possession.

"Rafe!"

This time, he didn't touch the mark, didn't try to take away her pain. Instead, he savored the sight and her whimpers. *Mine.* Hope was his, whether she acknowledged it or not.

After the fourth, she understood what to do and found the rhythm he set. Instead of tightening her muscles, she kept them loose. "Beautiful," he told her.

He paddled her again, much harder this time. The shameless sub tried to grind her cunt against his thigh. "Hussy." Christ almighty. He couldn't enjoy her more.

"Please, please, please."

"Say it."

"Sir!"

She turned the honorific into a plaintive wail. It took extraordinary resolve not to lift her, hold her against him and give her the orgasm she so prettily begged for. "Last one." He aimed for her sit spot, so she wouldn't forget it for a long time.

Even though he warned her, she didn't clench. "Ask for it," he encouraged.

"I want you to paddle me, please."

Like he'd promised earlier, she was begging for it. Pride filled him, and he let the paddle fly.

She cried out as she pushed herself from the floor.

He kept her legs pinned, but this time he rubbed away the pain and pressed a hand against her pussy to distract her. "You did well. Not that I expected anything different."

Hope was shaking as he helped her up. He kept her close where he wanted her, maneuvering her body so that she sat on his lap. He pulled her against him, locks of her hair draping across his chest. Her body was chilled, and he stroked her arm to chase away the goose bumps while she took a few short breaths.

They remained as they were for long minutes. Eventually, she placed a palm on his shoulder to push away from him.

"How was your first spanking?" He brushed back her hair to see her expression.

"It was…" She opened her mouth, but no words emerged.

He understood her conundrum. He wasn't sure what it meant to him to spank her, either. Her reactions had softened a part of him that he hadn't realized he'd walled off. What they'd shared had been physical, but emotional as well. Pain. Pleasure. Tying them together, knotting a bond that he might not want to undo. Her screams, cries, gasps had been real in a way nothing else had ever been for him.

"This sounds ridiculous..." She paused. "I liked it. The pain went away fast, and then I was hotter than I'd ever been." She pressed her palms together. "I'm not sure how much more I want or could take. I'm ready to lose my mind. The need to orgasm... It's...more than uncomfortable. I can't think about anything else."

"Sweet Hope, if you were mine, I might keep you like that. Send you to work each morning with your clit throbbing and an order not to touch yourself. Forbid you to wear underwear, perhaps. Call you several times a day and instruct you to masturbate without getting yourself off."

"That's terrifying."

"Good." He stood and carried her to the bed, where he placed her on the edge. "Undress me."

"Finally." She reached for his belt.

Her hands trembled. From their play? Or from anticipation? Her fingers slipped off the buckle once before she managed to release it. Then she pulled the leather free of its loops. "Roll it up and leave it on the nightstand. In case I need to thrash you later."

She gasped. "You wouldn't!" Her mouth said one thing, but her eyes gleamed.

What had he unleashed?

Hope unfastened the button at the top of his trousers. Before she could lower his zipper, he said,

"Shoes and socks."

Her movements fluid, she accepted his hand, slid from the bed and onto her knees. Why in the name of fuck had he resisted the idea of being involved with a woman who was into the lifestyle?

He lifted each foot, and she untied his shoes and removed each of them before taking off his socks. "While you're there, you can remove my slacks."

"Yes, Rafe."

Every time she said that phrase, her words were more natural, music and eroticism lacing through them.

Hope pulled down his zipper, the rasp an audible promise of her submission. She released her grip and his pants fell to the floor, leaving him in his tight-fitting black boxer briefs.

Rafe stepped out of the trousers, and she scooped the garment from the floor. "Would you like me to put this on the valet?"

For a moment, he was taunted by the idea of tying her to the wooden structure, perhaps making her hold on to the shelf, or the part meant for his suit coat. His valet as bondage equipment. Delicious. "Thank you." Hands on her shoulders, he assisted her up.

She paused at the closet door to look back at him. Her eyes sparkled, and her ass bore a few fine lines from his paddle. He couldn't wait to dig in his fingers and reignite her pain.

As if reading his mind, she hurried.

When she returned, he said, "You may finish

what you started."

Hope unbuttoned his shirt, then removed it, noticing the bandage on his shoulder from the biking accident over the weekend. He'd been so into her that he'd forgotten about it.

After clearing her throat, she asked, "Your underwear?" She clutched his shirt in front of her, not that the action would save her. "Are you going to take them off?"

"You are. Being on your knees will make it easier."

"I might have guessed you would say that."

"Then next time, feel free to make that an assumption." He grinned, more determined than ever that there would be a next time.

She knelt, her face inches from his crotch. After almost no hesitation, she placed her hands inside the waistband, then worked the material over his penis. "Oh!"

"Oh?"

"Your...uhm..."

"Cock? Dick?" He couldn't hide his grin.

"Wow."

He was hard and had been most of the time since he'd walked into her office and seen the look of shock on her face. Having her respond to him, then marking her conference room table, had made his erection painful. Now that he was free of the constraints of a somewhat civilized society, he desired her with need that bordered on savage. "On the bed or I will fuck you on the floor."

She scrambled, but it wasn't fast enough for him.

Rafe grabbed her upper arms, pulled her up, then turned her away from him and bent her over the bed, forcing her breasts into the mattress. "I'm out of patience."

"Good."

Her face was buried in the sheet, and the word was muffled, but he'd take bets he hadn't misheard her. "On your toes. Push your ass toward me."

"Yes!"

So she didn't get away, he dug the fingers of his left hand into the flesh near her hipbone. With the other hand, he dragged open the drawer in his nightstand and fished out a condom.

He pressed his knees against her thighs while he sheathed himself, then he reached between her legs to squeeze her cunt. She cried out, coming all over him. "That was hot." He spread her buttocks, then used his grip to lift her higher so that he could slide his dick into her. "Put your arms over your head. Stretch them as far as you can."

"Fuck, Rafe…"

Even though she was wet for him, the angle and his size made her pussy tight, the entry difficult.

He had to control himself and slow down.

"I want…"

He did, too. Rafe slipped in and out, short, easy movements until she accommodated his length. When he was seated, he stopped.

"Do me! Fuck me, Rafe. Do it. Please!"

"I love it when you use manners. So sexy." He

leaned over, fed the words into her ear, and she bucked beneath him. Once he was in control of his emotions, he began to move inside her, this time pulling almost all the way out before easing back in.

"Oh, God." She formed her hands into fists.

He stroked her clit, forcing her to writhe. The fact that he had so much power over her went to his head faster than the finest bourbon.

She climaxed, her internal muscles clenching around him. He tightened his jaw to stave off his ejaculation.

When it was over, her body went limp on the bed.

He bent his knees to move inside her. He dug one hand into her hair, then worked his free arm between the mattress and her so that he could hold her in place.

After a few moments while she recovered her energy, she moved with him. When he was sure she was turned on again, he jerked his hips harder. Her body bounced with her responses, and she murmured his name.

"That's it." When he was unable to wait any longer, he came inside her. "God*damn*." For him, this was about more than sex. She filled a place that he hadn't known was empty.

He loosened his grip on her hair, and she laid her head down but didn't try to move away from him.

As the final shudders went down his spine, he stroked the sides of her breasts. She made some tiny, unintelligible sounds.

When he was aware of time and place again, he knew her legs had to be tired. The whole time, she'd been on her tiptoes. He had more appreciation for her than any other woman he'd been with. Everything he'd offered, she'd accepted, with unadulterated desire.

He pulled out, then helped her onto the bed. Saying nothing, she curled on her side. Rafe left the room long enough to dispose of the condom before joining her. She didn't seem to be asleep, nor was she awake.

After grabbing the bedding, he crawled onto the bed beside her, curled his body around hers in some sort of caveman-like protection, then covered them both.

In his arms, Hope dozed, and when she woke enough to shimmy her sweet ass against his cock, she got his interest.

Following his orders, she grabbed a condom and rolled it onto his hard cock. Then she rode him. Rafe grabbed her ass, digging his hands into the places where he'd spanked her. Her breathless whimpers were all he could hope for.

They found a rhythm, and her lips parted a little as her eyelids slid closed.

"I want to watch your reactions."

Obediently, she kept her gaze on him. The golden color of her irises darkened, and she struggled with his order as her pussy constricted on his cock. "Come for me, Hope."

She lifted her hips, meeting each of his thrusts, moving with him in a timeless, primal beat.

This time, her orgasm came in a series of tiny gasps that fed his response. With her, sex was more than a driving hunger. It was a fevered connection.

When he was certain she was satiated, Rafe took his pleasure. When they were both dizzy, breathless, he rolled to his side. Savoring the moment, he tucked her next to him.

She sighed and blinked, fighting off sleep.

He left her long enough to dampen a washcloth with warm water. When he returned, she mumbled a protest about being disturbed. "Shh," he soothed as he bathed her.

"That feels good."

He kissed her forehead, cherishing her. She smiled, and he tucked the blankets around her. Once she was asleep, he took a quick shower, thinking of her, realizing how different his interaction was with her than with submissives at his clubs. He always took care of the women he scened with, but she meant more to him than any other woman had.

Naked, warm from the shower, he climbed into bed with her. He smoothed her hair and snuggled her close. How was she going to react when she realized he didn't intend to let her go?

CHAPTER SEVEN

Hope froze as awareness and horror crept over her. It wasn't dawn, and she was naked in Rafe Sterling's bed. Thank God he wasn't in the room with her.

She let out a long sigh. What in the name of everything sacred had she been thinking? The man and his sexiness had made her forget she had a brain. She was stupid, crazy attracted to him. He was right about the pheromones, but she couldn't allow it to happen again.

She jumped from the bed and hurried to the bathroom. Every muscle burned, and her pussy ached. She had to be a mess.

She stood near a mirror and contorted herself so

she could look at her ass in the mirror. There wasn't a mark on her body. How was that even possible? There was no doubt she'd been used last night, spanked, tied up, fucked hard. He'd made her beg to come, ask for punishment. What was worse was that she'd wanted to.

They'd had sex, several times. Once in the middle of the night, even. She'd half woken, shivering from the air-conditioning. Seeking warmth, she'd scooted across the bed toward him. He'd captured her, and his dick had been hard.

Although she wasn't sure how he'd managed it while still mostly asleep, he'd grabbed a condom, put it on, then taken her from behind, holding her waist tight while he slid in and out of her. After she'd had a delicious orgasm, she'd drifted off, satiated.

She pulled her hair on top of her head before remembering that her clip had hit the floor in his bedroom.

Time to get out of there. She'd been hired to find him a wife. The sooner she did that, the better for her emotional state — before she fell for him.

The scent of coffee wafted through the air, encouraging her to get the day started and face Rafe with her decision to end this now.

Unable to brazen her way through the morning after, she hurried into his closet to find a robe. The arms were far too long, and she had to roll up the sleeves so they didn't cover her hands. She wrapped the belt around her waist twice before tying a knot so secure it was at least as good as the ones he'd used on her.

Their scene replaying in her mind, she hurried to the bedroom to drop to her hands and knees to search beneath the bed for her hair clip.

"I see you're up."

She bumped her head on the bedrail before looking over her shoulder to see him standing in the doorway, two cups of coffee in hand.

Damn him.

Dressed in tailored slacks, polished shoes, and a crisp shirt, he took her breath. Even though he had no tie on, his cufflinks were in place. He might have been casual, but his look still spoke of power.

"Looking for something?"

She pushed off the floor and sat back on her calves. "My hair clip."

"On the nightstand. I found it last night."

If she hadn't been so intent on escape, she might have found it. "Thank you." She hurried to her feet; then she grabbed the clip and secured the metal in place, hoping the act might stabilize her ping-ponging emotional state.

"I brought you some coffee."

It shouldn't have surprised her, but Rafe waited for her to come to him.

Once she was a few feet from him, she inhaled his masculine scent, unmistakable resolve combined with the spice from his shower.

"You were everything I could imagine."

There was nothing she could say in response. The evening had revealed parts of herself that she'd been unaware of. "Thank you for the coffee." She accepted the cup and took a drink, not because she wanted it but because she was desperate to escape the scrutiny. The brew was strong and rich, inviting her to linger, something she dared not do. "I'll get dressed and call for a ride."

"No." He shook his head. "I'll drive you home and take you to work."

"That won't be necessary."

His eyes turned dark, the cold twilight after the sun had set.

"I will see to you, Hope."

"Mr. —"

"Don't." Rafe held up a hand. "Don't pretend that it didn't happen, that you're unaffected, that you didn't scream my name, beg, then ask for more."

Coffee nearly spilled over the rim before she steadied her hand.

"It happened. I liked it, and so did you."

"You're a *client*." She wondered which one of them she was trying to convince.

"And don't you damn well dare pretend it doesn't matter." He closed the distance between them. With aching tenderness, he tucked a stray lock of hair behind her ear. "We're two consenting adults who had an amazing scene. Admit it."

She exhaled. "It doesn't change anything."

"Your clothes are downstairs," he told her. "When would you like to leave?"

Her victory had been too easy to trust it. "Ten minutes?" That was long enough for her to finish the coffee, clean up, and dress.

He nodded. He picked up his coffee cup, pivoted, and headed toward the doorway.

Damn it, she didn't want him to go.

As if sensing her indecision, he stopped, then turned back to her.

With three steps, he was in front of her. He placed his cup on the nightstand. She remained rooted where she was, and she slumped in relief when he cradled her shoulders.

She was up on her toes again, and he claimed her mouth with ruthless intent, a potent reminder of what she'd offered last night and a glimpse of what part of her hoped he still might demand in the future.

When Rafe released her, she was shaken, her mouth bruised from his passion.

With that, he left. If she'd thought she could steady her emotions, she'd been wrong. She sank onto the edge of the bed and wrapped her arms around her knees to recover from the storm that was Rafe. It wasn't until minutes later that she was steady enough to join him downstairs.

Fortunately, he was nowhere in sight.

He'd folded her clothing and stacked it in a neat pile on the bench near her purse. After snatching up her belongings, she dashed into the powder room.

She was pulled together and ready to face him when she emerged from the bathroom, dressed, shoulders squared, wearing mascara and some hot-pink confidence-faking lipstick. She'd tucked last night's panties into her purse. It was the first time she'd ever gone without underwear, and she feared Rafe would realize it.

Showing there was no end to his surprises, he was standing in front of the stove when she found him. He'd set two plates on the countertop and poured them each a glass of orange juice.

"Morning," he called out when he noticed her. "Mushrooms, onions, green peppers okay in your omelet?"

The sweet scent of toast filled the air, and oil sizzled in a pan. "I don't eat breakfast."

"You need the energy after last night."

So much for forgetting the events had happened. In a horrible betrayal, her stomach grumbled. "Yes."

"Do you mind grabbing some napkins from the pantry?"

She'd been hoping to escape, not get drawn into an intimate kitchen scene that made him more human and less the Dominant who'd introduced her to a dozen deviant delights. "Do you do this every morning?"

"Cook?" He turned toward her wearing an apron with *Some Like It Hot* embroidered on the front. "Yeah. I would eat croissants and doughnuts if I didn't cook."

"And the problem with that is what?" She found the napkins and carried them to the countertop.

He ladled beaten eggs into the pan then tossed in a handful of veggies. "Cheese?"

"The more the better."

"A girl after my heart."

Since he was facing the stove, she couldn't read his expression. She hopped up onto a barstool, then shifted because her bottom was a little sore.

"There's more coffee in the carafe."

"I've had enough. Thanks."

This time, he did look at her. "I'd like another one. With cream."

She wished she'd called for a ride. Each moment that ticked by deepened their ties. "You're closer." Where had she found the courage to say that?

"You're being difficult." He reached for a wooden spoon and waved it in her direction.

Reading the threat, she climbed off the stool as she asked, "How much cream?" Hope closed her mouth to prevent the reflexive Sir from slipping out. Side-eyeing the spoon, she refilled his cup, then removed a carton of heavy cream from the refrigerator. No wonder her coffee had tasted so good. At home, she poured in liberal doses of sugar-free vanilla imitation creamer. This was a definite upgrade.

"That wasn't so difficult, was it?" he asked when she placed the cup onto the counter beside him.

Before he could ask for anything else, she fled for the safety of her stool.

A few minutes later, he plated their food, then joined her.

The food was exceptional, and he made small talk while they ate, charming her, regaling her with stories of the Sterling company's history. "We were the first to have running water in guest rooms."

She recalled historical hotel images featuring water basins and pitchers. "I guess I'd never considered that there was a time that didn't exist."

"And televisions."

"What?" Hope gave a mock shudder. "No TV? Say it isn't so!"

"We started in New York City in 1947. As you might have imagined, it was an upgrade that many people appreciated. That became a strong selling point for families traveling with children. We were also the first to install air conditioners in public areas, after my great-grandfather stayed in the Maison Sterling in New Orleans, during what might have been a heat wave. In the late 1920s."

It made sense that the hotel had been in the South. "I had no idea air-conditioning had been around that long."

"It took years to have them in all rooms, as you might imagine, and it wasn't until the late fifties that we launched an effort to bring it to every hotel in our portfolio. Many of the amenities in today's travel industry were innovations pioneered by my family. Central reservations, telephones, hotels at airports. My grandfather, Barron, the one I worked for, traveled coast-to-coast, visiting our hotels. He'd sit in the lobbies, pretending to be a guest, and he'd talk to people about the things that would make their stay better. We've continued that tradition. Our executives are required to travel two weeks out of the year as if they were a regular consumer, sometimes under a false name if they're known in the industry. No comped rooms. No upgrades. One of the weeks must be in hotels they haven't stayed in before. They interact with the associates in valet, baggage handling, concierge, restaurants. And they report back to the head of their division. I'm thinking of expanding the program, down to regional managers."

As much as Hope tried to keep an emotional barrier between herself and Rafe, she couldn't. He was animated, charming. The constant glimpses of the complex man bothered her, making it impossible for her to think of him as nothing but a hard-ass Dom or uncaring tycoon. He was still speaking, so she shook her head to focus on him.

"He ran the company for over half a century, and he didn't take a day off—not even Christmas— until he ended up in the hospital on his deathbed. Even then, he asked for reports to be brought in. Less than an hour before he passed, he summoned his family members and gave them specific instructions about how he wanted the company run. There were no warm goodbyes. Instead, he was trying to convey his vision to those of us who would carry on."

Rafe's story was a bleak reminder that he might lose everything if he didn't find a wife, soon. "I'll...er...do the dishes." She wadded her napkin and tossed it on a plate.

"No need. My housekeeper, Sienna, will be here later."

"Housekeeper?" She couldn't keep the note of

wistfulness out of her voice. That sounded like pure luxury. Still, she rinsed the dishes, then stacked them in the sink before putting away the unused food.

"We make a good team."

She didn't want to make a good team with a man who belonged to another woman.

"Five minutes?" he asked.

"I'll be ready." In fact, she was anxious to leave now. While he climbed the stairs to the second story, she crossed the room to look out the window. Because it was still dark, her reflection bounced back at her—untidy hair with tendrils curling against her neck, arms folded with her hands on her shoulders.

Hope didn't recognize herself. Her eyes had lost some innocence. She was now a woman who knew something about BDSM, and more, had learned about herself, what she liked, what she wanted. Regular sex—the kind that had bored her—would no longer be okay. She craved the excitement, the unknown, the bite of pain, the strain of being on her knees, waiting.

Rafe was ready in less than five minutes, and she met him at the bottom of the stairs. She stood in front of him. The cut of his suit coat was exquisite, tailored to fit his broad shoulders but also emphasize his lean waist. His shirt was crisp and white, and his dark gray tie had silver swirls, something of a cross between a paisley and the yin-yang symbol.

The emeralds in his ring winked in the overhead light, a stark reminder that he belonged to an exclusive and secret group of people who wanted to run more than their own companies.

She was a matchmaker, the daughter of a nurse and a soldier, from humble beginnings. She might spend time with Houston's rich and somewhat famous, but she was an outsider, someone who provided them with a much-valued service.

"Shall we?"

Outside, he helped her into his car, and again, the seat cradled her as if designed for her. He programmed in the address she provided before easing into traffic. While they drove through the quiet streets, his cell phone rang, and Celeste's name showed up on the car's display screen.

"Do you mind if I take it?"

Curious, she responded, "Not at all."

Surprising her, he answered on the car's audio system. "Morning, Celeste. Say good morning to Hope Malloy."

There was no pause before Celeste responded, "Well, hello, Hope."

Hope shot him a wilting glance. There had been no reason to acknowledge her presence.

"I'm driving Hope home."

"Very good."

Was it too much to wish that the seat would swallow her? Rafe seemed oblivious to Hope's discomfort.

Always one to focus on business, Celeste continued. "Are you free to talk?"

"Yes."

Hope expected him to switch to a headset, but

he didn't.

"Noah telephoned me last night."

"Did he?"

Hope pulled out her cell phone and pretended to be interested in reading her email. The truth was, she didn't see a word on the screen.

"Yes, along with other directors on the steering committee."

Hope slid a glance toward him. Was Celeste talking about the Titans? Hope shook her head. That the secret society was real, with a steering committee and intrigue, took her aback. And that he hadn't made the call confidential was even more startling.

"And the purpose of his call?"

"To suggest your father be removed from his position."

Rafe's fingers tightened on the steering wheel.

"He's recommending himself as the replacement. On the grounds that Theodore isn't performing his required duties. He missed a phone conference call yesterday. With no apologies or acknowledgment that he'd received an invitation. Judge Anderson had us hold while he attempted to reach your dad."

Judge Anderson? The one who was in the news all the time?

When Rafe didn't respond, Celeste continued. "You could offer to take his place at the next in-person."

"Isn't that this week?"

"Saturday. I can't tell you how the others will

react," Celeste warned. "You might be asked to leave. But I'll speak on your behalf."

"If I can't ensure that Dad will attend, I'll be there." With a promise to be in touch and a brief goodbye, he ended the call. "I apologize for the interruption." He depressed a button on the steering wheel to disconnect the line. In the ambient streetlight, Hope saw tension grooved next to his eyes. "If I can't talk some sense into my dad, I'll go see him this morning."

"Okay." She mentally began a mad scramble. "I'll need to reschedule the mixer."

"I'll be back in plenty of time."

"How can you do that on such short notice?"

"The company has a plane. The executives fly commercial when possible, but sometimes urgency prevails."

Of course he had a plane.

"You could go with me."

"What?" She turned to look at him. "No. I can't. I have a job. People to talk to." Including women who might want to be his wife. But the invitation excited her. To jet off to the coast on a whim? Traveling on a private charter? How divine would that be?

"Another time, then."

There wouldn't be another time. "Since you have personal business to take care of, there's no need to see me to the office." The sooner she extracted herself from this situation, the better.

He didn't respond. She wasn't sure that meant

he agreed or that he'd set his course and refused to deviate.

When he pulled up in front of her high-rise apartment building in Midtown, she found out. He came around to open her door, assisted her from the passenger compartment, then followed her up the path.

With her hand on the metal plate to push through the glass door, she paused. "Rafe—"

"Was there anything I've said that suggested I was open for negotiation?"

There wasn't.

"Unless you'd like to have an argument right here in public—which I'm happy to indulge—and make us both late for work, I suggest you save the energy." With that, he placed his palm about six inches higher than hers and shoved the door open. "After you."

She couldn't win this battle so she sighed her frustration and entered the building.

"I need to make sure we don't let the Colonel out," she said when they stood in front of the door of her tenth-floor apartment. She turned the knob and bent to extend her hand across the entryway.

Foiled, the Colonel screeched, shredding Hope's remaining nerves. She scooted the feline back several feet, and Rafe followed her inside. Without needing to be told, he closed and locked the door behind him.

The Colonel turned toward Rafe and hissed.

"Sorry." To avoid a catastrophe, Hope scooped up her pet. "I warned you about her. She doesn't like anyone."

"We'll be fine."

"You're brave. She also bites and scratches."

"All that?" He turned his gaze toward the animal. "She doesn't sound all that different from her owner."

Hope winced. "Am I that bad?"

"All I'm saying is I'm not intimidated. She can do her worst."

"We'll see." All normal human beings were at least wary of the Colonel. Some were scared. All had good reason.

He reached to pet the cat. The Colonel pulled her paw back and struck. "She is feisty."

Hope stroked the cat's head to calm her down. "I tried to warn you."

"I'm enchanted already."

"You're giving me reason to question your sanity." She put down the Colonel, who dashed to the far corner of the room to climb to the top of her enormous carpeted jungle gym. Somalis were known to be curious and energetic, so Hope was on a constant quest to keep the animal entertained and physically worn out. The Colonel glared at them from the top perch. She dug her claws into the edge, and she appeared ready to pounce and attack. "At least we know where she is. You sure you want to wait for me?"

"I've told you, Hope..." He caught her shoulders and drew her close. "I'm not intimidated. Not by you or the creature that shares your home."

He was going to kiss her. He leaned toward her, and she steeled herself. More than ever, she had to keep her emotions walled off to him.

But instead of kissing her, he released her and stroked her cheekbone. "How long do you need?"

Confounded man. He knew how to play her. Now that he'd refused the affection, she wanted it. Damn her. And her freaking topsy-turvy reactions.

Annoyed, she said, "As long as it takes."

"Sweet, sweet Hope. I'll still spank the attitude out you if you need it."

She didn't. "No." Worse, she did. Somehow, she managed to avoid the confession. "There's a coffeemaker in the kitchen." He couldn't hear the warble in her voice, right? "Make yourself comfortable." Hope hurried to the bedroom and closed the door. Then her conscience prevailed, forcing her to issue a warning. Yanking open the door, she called out, "Stay on your guard around the Colonel."

"Again—"

She slammed the door. And he laughed.

Frustration, with herself as much as with him, still poured through her as she stripped off her clothes and took a hot shower, expecting him to walk in on her. She reminded herself to be grateful when he didn't. Unwanted disappointment tasted bitter.

After she shut off the water and wrapped a towel around her, the sounds of his rich baritone reached her. Then, more than a minute of silence was followed by a singsong crooning.

Freezing in place as she was slipping into a pair of panties, she tilted her head to listen.

"We might as well be friends, Samantha."

He was talking to her cat? And he'd remembered her real name from last night? Hope shook her head. The man was certifiable.

The Colonel hissed. Hope grinned. Some things were consistent.

Even though he was waiting for her, she didn't hurry through her morning routine. She'd told him he didn't need to drive her.

When she exited the bedroom, wearing a long-sleeved shirt, a skirt, heels, and a blazer — her form of armor against the rigors of the day, including Rafe's marriage mixer — he was holding a framed picture.

"Your father?" he asked.

"Right before his last deployment." She nodded. "It was the last one my mother had of him."

"It must be hard." He slid the photo back onto the shelf.

"I don't know anything else." At times, school had been difficult — father-daughter dances, when her class had made Father's Day gifts.

"This was his also?"

He pointed to a triangular-shaped shadowbox that displayed an American flag.

"Yes. He was buried with full military honors. This one draped his casket." Why she displayed it, she didn't know. When she'd cleaned out her mother's apartment, Hope had taken her father's smiling picture and the flag and displayed them on her shelves, in the exact same position her mother had. It hadn't occurred to Hope to do anything else, not even pack them away in the trunk that she used as a coffee table.

She'd brought that too, from her Mom's. It was a time machine of sorts, filled with the memorabilia that Cynthia had carried with her everywhere she went. The box contained her husband's effects, photos, love letters, a wind-up watch, ribbons, mementos, his army-issued dog tags.

Each year on the anniversary of his death, Cynthia would open a bottle of wine and the trunk. She'd hold each item, one at a time, and the tracks of a thousand tears would stain her cheeks.

"Sorry to bring up something so painful."

Hope tried for a brave smile. On some level, her mother's ghosts had become her own. Hope, too, had her own grief ritual, commemorating her mother's birthday. "Let me get the Colonel her breakfast. Then I'll be ready to go."

"I'll do it."

She frowned. How could he be so damn likable?

"She'll have to like me after that, right?"

"About that..." The cat still glared from her perch. "It didn't work for my neighbor."

"Where's her food?"

When he made his mind up about something, he followed through.

"Hope?"

"On the bottom shelf of the pantry."

Instead of waiting for her, he led the way into

the kitchen.

She followed but stayed in the doorway where she could keep an eye on the cat. The moment he opened a can, the Colonel lifted her head. Rafe pulled off the lid, and the Colonel meowed.

"So far so good?" He made himself comfortable, opening a drawer to find a spoon. "Does she get the whole thing?"

"Yes."

"No dry food?"

"I told you she was bossy. I tried her on dry a few times. She goes on a hunger strike."

He grinned. "I like a female who knows what she likes." He crossed to the cat dish, picked it up, carried it to the sink, then washed and dried it.

"Now she's going to expect that too."

"Samantha!" He scooped the food into the glass bowl. "Breakfast!"

The Colonel leaped from her perch and skulked into the kitchen.

He carried the dish to the placemat with a happy face on it. The Colonel flicked her big, bushy tail, then sat and waited until he moved back to the other side of the kitchen. "Not ready to be friends? I'm a patient man."

Without being asked, he replenished the Colonel's water.

Impressed, Hope said, "I'll let you know when I need a babysitter for her."

"Bring her over anytime."

She pushed away from the wall. "Bring her

over? To your place? Where she'll tear up your very expensive furniture and dance across your piano keys?" She shuddered. "Knock over all your designer-exclusive pieces?"

"It will keep her entertained. Right, Samantha?" He bent to scratch behind the feline's ear. He received a fast, unpleasant swat for his efforts.

"I'm not sure if you're patient or persistent."

"Different sides of the same coin."

"Did she break the skin?"

"No." He didn't bother checking. "Any other chores before we leave for work?"

"My office is out of your way."

"You've got two choices, Hope. You can leave here over my shoulder or on your own two feet."

She gaped at him. "What?" From the firm set of his jaw, she didn't dare ask whether or not he was serious. "I'll walk."

To his credit, he didn't gloat. "Is there a procedure so the Colonel doesn't escape?"

"No. I dash out right after I feed her, while she's occupied." Hope appreciated that he'd thought of the cat. "At other times, I have to get her a catnip treat or there will be a wrestling act at the door."

"She does have you trained."

"I know who is in charge."

"That will come in handy. Shall we?" He opened the door and waited while she locked it.

At the end of the hallway, he rang for the elevator, then placed his hand in the small of her back with a possession that she liked and was disturbingly comfortable.

Traffic had thickened, and his phone rang several times, keeping their conversation brief. She was grateful for the reprieve and emotional distance. She needed it before walking into the office to make more calls to find him a wife.

At the curb in front of her building, he stopped in a no-parking zone.

"Thank you for the ride." She reached for the handle.

"Wait."

"It's —"

"Not necessary. I know. Save yourself the argument." He checked the mirrors, then exited the car to round the hood before opening her door and offering her a gallant hand out.

"Do you always get your way, Mr. Sterling?"

"I do my best. Sometimes I come up short. Not often." He shrugged. "Not when it matters."

Before she had a chance to answer, he dug a hand into her hair, sending her clip skittering across the sidewalk. "Much better," he said, eyes gleaming with sexual intent.

She wrapped her hand around his wrist. They couldn't. Not here on the street where anyone could see them. Yet she didn't use the word that would stop him.

Appearing unconcerned by the commuters heading into work, he placed his free hand on her rear. As if he knew precisely where he'd spanked her, he squeezed her right buttock, sending a fresh flare of recognition through her. He backed off right away, moving his palm to the place between her shoulder blades. She was helpless to look away from his face, unable to find her voice, trapped by his grip.

"Open your mouth."

Even though her brain urged self-protection, her body's response to him was automatic.

He claimed her tongue, plundered inside, made her remember his dominance. She responded, giving him what he wanted and what she craved.

Rafe left her on edge, pulsing with awareness. "No orgasms, Hope."

"What?" Her mouth was bruised, her mind swimming in endorphins and confusion.

"You heard me."

"I did. I just don't believe you made that request."

"It wasn't a request."

In response to his command, arousal clawed at her. Since they didn't have a relationship, there was no way he'd ever know. But the fact that he'd thought of it and set off fireworks inside her pussy — he had to know that.

He let her go, then crouched to pick up her clip. Instead of returning it, he slid the metal into the breast pocket of his suit. "Do you mind?"

Did he want to keep it as a trophy? "It's fine." She had others in her desk drawer.

"Leave your hair loose? I want to imagine you like this all day."

Sighing, Hope scooped back wayward strands.

"Will you?"

Why was she agreeing? That wouldn't help her put distance between them. Then again, maybe it was because she didn't want to refuse him anything. "Yes."

He walked her to the big glass door and opened it for her.

"Have a safe flight."

"See you this afternoon."

With a quick smile, she entered the building.

She paused near the large reception desk and looked back. He stood on the sidewalk, watching her. In the last few seconds, he'd put on a pair of sunglasses that made it impossible for her to read his expression. He did, indeed, always get his way.

Not that it mattered. In a week, perhaps as soon as a few days, he would no longer be part of her life.

She clutched the straps of her purse so tight that her knuckles whitened. If only she could convince herself that forgetting him was a good thing.

CHAPTER EIGHT

The sight of Skyler's desk made Hope freeze in horror. Memories of the previous night assailed her. It had been a mistake to get physical with Rafe at her workplace. She should have confined her explorations to his home. Or the restaurant. An image of the rose's thorn returned, making her flush and squeeze her legs together.

The front office door slammed open and Skyler rushed in. "Oh my God!"

Hope's pulse slowed as she turned back to face her assistant. "What?"

"Nice try." Skyler grinned. "I saw you canoodling on the sidewalk. My boss. The cool and calm and in charge Ms. Hope Malloy, president and

CEO of the Prestige Group, was all but doing the nasty outside the building." She fanned herself. "I didn't get a good look at the guy, what with those sunglasses and his back being to me. But damn. He's hot. Dish."

"We have work to do."

"Are you serious?" Skyler's mouth fell open in disappointment. "You're keeping it a secret?"

That was the plan. Except… Hope exhaled.

"I brought doughnuts." Skyler lifted a white bag from the depths of her purse.

"Can't tempt me today, Satan."

"Which means you already ate. I know you don't make breakfast for yourself. Which means that hot guy made you breakfast?"

"Would you stop?" Despite herself, Hope grinned. It had been a rare treat.

"Seriously?" Skyler walked in and dumped her purse on the desk, with no idea that one of their clients had considered bending Hope over the surface a little more than twelve hours before.

After plonking herself into her chair, Skyler extracted both pastries and placed them on top of the bag.

"That's sorcery."

"You're not hungry, remember?" She studied both before picking up the vanilla-glazed cake doughnut.

Which meant she'd left Hope her favorite — the chocolate one.

Looking at Hope, Skyler took a bite and made

soft noises that sounded orgasmic.

Hope's fingers twitched. She knew what the confection tasted like, how sweet and puffy and mouth-watering it was. A need for a sugar rush crashed through her, threatening her resolve.

She reached for it, and Skyler, the most horrible, worst assistant ever, yanked it away. "Uh-uh. Talk first. This doughnut is truth serum."

The battle was real. Sugar in exchange for a confession. Hope's resolve waned, and Hope sank into her chair.

Skyler broke off part of the chocolate pastry and edged it toward Hope.

"You're coldhearted."

"Persuasive." Skyler nodded. "I prefer to think of it as persuasive."

"Cunning," Hope corrected.

"Whatever works." She took another bite. "Go ahead. It's going to be better than you remember. They're still warm, but they won't be for long."

Bested by an assault on her sweet tooth, Hope sighed and took a bite. Warm and gooey, the icing exploded in her mouth. "God."

"I told you. You should always trust me. Now… Back to your admirer. From what I could see, he wanted to devour you."

Hope stared at Skyler above the doughnut poised in front of her mouth for the next bite she was sure to need. "You couldn't have seen all that."

"Au contraire. I was facing him as I was walking down the street. There were like a million people heading to work—"

"Or ten."

"Whatever." Skyler shrugged. "You were his entire universe."

"That's an exaggeration."

"Nope. Not at all. He stood there watching you forever. Quit keeping me in suspense. I need a name."

Stalling, stalling, she popped the doughnut in her mouth and chewed. When she couldn't stall anymore, she braced for the inevitable. "Rafe Sterling."

"Our client?" Skyler dropped her pastry. "*That* Rafe Sterling?"

As if there could be two even in a city the size of Houston.

"Shit. Shit."

Hope nodded. "One and the same."

"Oh, shit."

That was about right. "Yeah." Hope took another bite. "I'm going to need the other half."

"You are going to need a full dozen. I should have gotten you a latte, too. I'll get Tony to stop on his way in." Skyler shoved both doughnuts across the desk. She typed a text message into her phone, then said, "Okay. Tell me everything."

"Uhm." There were things Hope would not reveal to another human being. "No."

"No? Crap on a cracker, it has to be bad."

Hope chose her words carefully. "If you'll recall, I had to be the one to call him to find out if he was a sadist."

"Right." Skyler glared. "Come on, Hope."

"He wanted to discuss it in person. Over dinner. That's how it started."

Skyler waved her hand, brandishing the doughnut. "So how did it end? Somehow you went from dinner to a public groping the next morning?"

Hope slunk down in her seat.

"Sorry." Skyler didn't sound the least bit contrite. When Hope failed to respond, Skyler widened her eyes. Her voice filled with wonder and awe, she asked, "What happened in between? Is he a sadist?"

"Let's say I..." How much to reveal that would satisfy her assistant but not give away secrets? "I learned a few things about what that might encompass."

"Such as?"

"There seem to be a whole host of behaviors that could be considered sadistic by some and pleasurable by others."

"Did he—"

"I'm not answering anything else about what happened after I left the office and when I returned."

Skyler was silent for a moment. Then she tried a different approach. "What did the Colonel think of him?"

"She tolerated him."

"Ha! Which meant he was at your apartment."

"I told you—"

"River Oaks? He lives in River Oaks, right?"

"Uptown. And that's the end of what I'm saying." Hope forced an edge of finality into her tone. "Back to business."

Skyler nodded. "What does this mean for our contract with Mrs. Sterling?"

After everything Hope had learned about his family's dynamics, she understood why Rafe's mother had hired them. Time was of the essence. This morning's call from Celeste had reinforced that. "Nothing has changed. To my knowledge, we haven't been fired. Which means the mixer is still on."

"After that kiss? You're kidding me, right? Right? You spent the night with him, and you still want us to find him a wife?"

More than ever. Before she became any more attached. Last night, this morning, had been a huge tactical error. Not just because he was a client, but because she'd promised herself she would never become besotted with a man the way her mother had. Love had destroyed her mother, and if she wasn't careful, Hope would fall into the same trap. Rafe had elicited responses she hadn't known she was capable of. He'd taken her to the edge of orgasm and dangled her over the precipice. Then he'd cared for her, tucked her in, taken care of her cat, seen her to work. It would be too easy to fall in love with him. And far too dangerous.

"Earth to Hope. Come in please?"

She shook her head, aware that Skyler had spoken a couple of times. "Sorry. What?"

"I asked if you're kidding me. Shouldn't we tell Mrs. Sterling that we are not able to fulfill this contract?"

"He needs a wife." To convince herself, Hope brushed her hands together to dislodge invisible crumbs. "I'll call Hannah and give her some information to see if she'd like to be included on the invitation list. If you'll confirm today's details with the International Club, we'll be fine."

"Are you sure that you're sure?" Concern telegraphed across Skyler's voice. "Like, extra sure, sure?"

"I'm okay." Resolved, Hope stood, then snatched up the rest of the doughnut.

"Hey, boss?"

Hope paused at the entrance to her office.

"You sure you're okay? Because I wouldn't be."

"Yeah." The lie left Hope's mouth dry.

"She's a beauty, isn't she?"

Turning, Rafe leashed his impatience. His father hadn't agreed to see him, but Rafe had flown in regardless. He hadn't found his father at the oceanfront condominium he'd rented in St. Pete Beach, and in desperation, Rafe had asked Celeste to track his father's cell phone. At first, she'd refused to help. That wasn't a service that the Fallon Group offered. But she had numerous employees with dozens of contacts. And because the Theodore situation also affected the Zeta Society, she'd been persuaded.

After discovering Theodore's location, she'd hazarded a guess that he was on his boat, registered as the *Lunar Sea*. His dad's car was in the marina's parking lot, and Rafe picked the lock on the gate leading to his dad's boat. Rafe had boarded the yacht and roused his father and Lillibet from bed.

Pacing with impatience, Rafe had returned to the deck. Though the boat was comfortable, he couldn't imagine it cruising the Atlantic. A few minutes later, Theodore, in bare feet and a robe, had joined Rafe.

"The boat," Theodore prompted. "She's a beauty. Can I offer you a cup of coffee? Bloody Mary? Bellini? Mimosa?"

"I won't be staying."

Lillibet joined them. Her blonde hair was fluffed around her face, her eyelashes were in place, and her lips were painted bright red. She wore silver platform sandals and a pair of sunglasses that covered more than her bikini did. In her left hand, she had a filled champagne flute, and her ring finger was strategically placed so that the engagement diamond winked in the sun. Rafe wondered how she managed the weight of the rock and the filled glass.

With a great show, she leaned forward, made a cutesy sound, and kissed Theodore on the cheek, leaving behind traces of her lipstick. "Don't be long, Teddy Bear. I already miss you." As she moved off, she gave Rafe a little wave that was part hello, part goodbye. "I'll be in the hot tub, lover, waiting for you."

One hand on his waist, Theodore watched her go. He stayed where he was, riveted, besotted, as she climbed the stairs, her sleek muscles contracting with each step.

Rafe was a cynic. But even he recognized that Theodore didn't look at his wife the same way. Had he ever? Maybe he was in love. And so what if he was? Everyone around them was dealing with the repercussions of his behavior. "When are you going to stop this, Dad? You're needed at home."

"Well, even if you don't want coffee, I do. Having an uninvited guest wasn't how I planned to start the day. Make yourself comfortable while you're here."

Theodore disappeared inside the cabin, leaving Rafe to exhale his irritation. He glanced at his cell phone to see if Hope had returned his last text message, the one where he'd reminded her not to touch herself. Words couldn't convey how much he wanted her to disobey him.

There was nothing.

Frustrated but undeterred, he decided to change his approach.

He sent an email with instructions to Jeanine, then repocketed his device.

When Theodore returned, he was carrying a mug of coffee, but even from several feet away, the scent of whiskey wafted toward Rafe. "Is that necessary?"

"This one's for you," Theodore said, extending

the mug.

"I don't drink in the morning."

"Well, then, don't mind if I do." With a shrug, Theodore took a long drink. "I hated running Sterling Worldwide. Didn't plan on getting married."

"We all have to do things we'd rather not."

"Your mother is a good woman. Bit of a stick up her ass, but she did her best."

"Don't fucking go there," Rafe warned, a growl in his voice. His mother was a good woman. And she cared a lot more about Sterling Worldwide than the man who owned the company. Rafe would be damned if he'd listen to anyone say anything bad about her. No matter who they were.

"Duty. Responsibility. Think of what others will say. Go to work. Increase the wealth. Take the right vacations. Go to work. Increase the wealth." Theodore gazed out over the gorgeous blue water. "Even the fucking Zeta Society. Take your place. Do the right thing." When he looked back at Rafe, he did so with clear, lucid eyes. "I abdicated."

Rafe pulled off his sunglasses. "Dad. Listen to me—"

"Call it retirement if you must."

"You're too young."

"What's the sense in having all this"—he extended his hand and swept it wide, encompassing the world, not just the marina—"if you don't enjoy it?"

"Future generations are counting on you."

"I did my part. Added to the damn coffers like I

was supposed to. Produced the requisite heirs." He took a drink of the coffee he'd said was for Rafe. "Now, my boy, it's up to you. I quit. Firing myself. If you want my advice? Let that little prick have it."

Rafe scowled. "Noah?"

"He's got ambition and a wife who popped out the squalling brats." He shuddered. "Thank God Lillibet doesn't want kids. Best thing about her."

Rafe ignored that in favor of staying focused. "I talked to Celeste. Noah has indicated he wants your seat on the Zeta's steering committee."

"Better him than us."

"Judge Anderson has been trying to reach you. You missed a telephone conference call."

"I was busy."

"There's a planning meeting Saturday." For more than a hundred and fifty years, a Sterling had attended every session.

"Let Noah go. He's a schemer, Rafe. I said ambition, but hunger or thirst is a better word. He wants power. You're goddamn rich, boy-o. Let him have the headaches. The trust is inviolate. You'll get a piece of anything he makes. I'd watch him, though. He's got plenty offshore in Switzerland. Panama, even. You have enough money to live the life you want. The one you deserve. If you don't want to get married, don't. Have girlfriends for as long as you can keep getting it up. Sleep in. See the world. Enjoy your time on the planet."

Fury colored Rafe's world. Nothing excused his father's adultery. "The company legacy means nothing to you? The struggle? The sweat? Our obligations? Grandfather—your dad—made it clear that we have a duty to do good in the world."

"Haven't lost a minute worrying about it." He clapped Rafe on the shoulder. "Be sure you listen well. I'd hate to have you make an unnecessary trip. I'm not coming back, boy-o. Not now that I'm out."

Previous generations had sacrificed for Theodore to squander the riches? "If that's the case, Mom will want a divorce."

Theodore shrugged. "I'm sure she will. Make it easier for me to marry Lillibet, at any rate."

"You'll lose half of your money, assets, homes." Years down the line, Lillibet might get the rest.

"Rebecca is a fine woman. Good, solid stock. Devoted to you kids and growing my career. She deserved better than I gave her."

Rafe tried one last time. "Mom is willing to pretend none of this happened."

"Why the hell would I want that?"

The edges of Rafe's temper frayed. "Your actions are destroying our family."

"An unfortunate byproduct of my happiness."

Selfish fucking bastard. "You would only have to work part-time. We could sort out something. I'll take over more responsibility. You can take long vacations as we plan your exit strategy. Maybe over the next year, two at the most." Give Rafe time to convince Hope to marry him.

"I'll be in… Where was it Lillibet wants to go? Monaco?"

195

"Morocco?"

"Oh, yes. Casablanca. I think I told you I've hired a captain. He starts next week. I'll be able to start taking this baby out of her slip."

Jesus. Rafe exhaled. *Fuck.*

"Look, son. No. I'm giving you a gift. From my insight." He tapped his temple, as if showing off his brain's prowess. "Getting up, going to work—there's more to life." His eyes, so much like Rafe's own, were clearer than Rafe had ever seen them. Rebecca's suppositions weren't correct. Theodore Sterling was in control of his faculties. "Take my advice, son. Get out while you can. Talk to the lawyers. It's not worth it. None of it. Do what you want with your life. Have you ever thought about what that might be?"

"I have." More than ever, Rafe knew. Sterling Worldwide was his. His responsibility. His fucking good fortune.

"I'm glad we've had this chat." Theodore released his hand, a physical representation of his emotional resolve. "I'm living *my* life. Not the one everyone else wanted. I sacrificed thirty fucking *years*," he reiterated. "That's more than a life sentence."

"I need six months," Rafe pressed. "It's not that long. Give us some time to set up a transition. Avoid a crisis."

"I'll be in Morocco by then. Just like Bogey and Bacall."

Was Theodore even listening? "It was Humphry Bogart and Ingrid Bergman."

"You're sure? It wasn't Lauren Bacall? The two were legend together."

"Bergman. I warned you it has an unhappy ending. They don't end up together."

"Teddy Bear!" Lillibet leaned over the rail, her nipples all but peeking out from the hot-pink bikini top. She waved her empty champagne glass and her diamond blinked in the sun.

"Coming, darling!"

"This is the life you want?"

"My plumbing is working again for the first time in years."

"Dad." Rafe shoved his sunglasses back into place. This trip had been as useless as it was frustrating. "There are certain things you'll need to handle before you leave."

"If I'm available. Don't have much time for business."

"At least answer your phone when I call."

"It's rarely convenient."

"Bye-bye, Rafe." Lillibet gave her annoying wave once again.

"I'll show myself out."

"You don't mind?" his dad threw over his shoulder as he headed for the stairs.

For a moment, Rafe studied Lillibet. His father had met her at his club. She'd been the front desk hostess, in charge of greeting members, taking them to tables in the dining room, ringing their massage therapist, or wishing them a good workout. Beyond that, Rafe knew nothing about her.

With a squeal, dripping wet from the hot tub, she ran to greet Theodore.

Rafe left the *Lunar Sea* without looking back. That was what he needed to do. Move forward. Focus on the future. His father's choices showed Rafe how selfish he'd been in some of his. His refusal to get over Emma and find a suitable woman to marry was now causing succession problems in the business and adding undue stress to his mother and sister's lives. Funny how easy it was to see his father's flaw and how difficult to recognize the one inside himself.

In the car that would take Rafe back to the regional airport, he phoned Mercedes to set up a legal meeting for the moment he returned.

Then, once on board the plane, he called Celeste on her direct line.

"I can say with some confidence that Dad's not coming to the Saturday meeting."

"You'll attend in his stead?"

"I'll be there. What do you know about Lillibet?"

"In what way?" Celeste's voice sharpened.

"Who is she? I know how they met, but I don't know her background."

"I'll find out." Without wasting any more time, she hung up.

The plane was taxiing when he called the office to let Jeanine know about his return time and his afternoon plans. "Did Ms. Malloy receive her gift?"

"I checked a few minutes ago. It was out for delivery."

"Very well."

He sat back as the pilot took off. The earth beneath Rafe grew smaller in the window, and the altitude gave him perspective. He hadn't planned to be CEO for years, maybe decades. But now that the company was going to be his, he had a future to secure.

After the attendant had brought him a cup of coffee, he sent a message to Hope.

New Orleans this weekend? We can leave Friday afternoon. There's a particular restaurant I want to introduce you to.

Several times, he checked his phone to be sure he hadn't missed a message. It took over an hour for her to respond.

Everything's set for this afternoon's mixer.

Since they'd met, he might have won a couple of rounds, but this one definitely went to her.

He'd spent his adult life avoiding relationship drama. And now...? Now, he realized life was more intriguing than ever. He lived for another hit of her.

Indeed, she'd won the latest skirmish. He, however, intended to be the ultimate victor.

Rafe reached for his phone one more time to make reservations for dinner Friday night at Vieille Rivière in Louisiana. He was nothing if not persistent.

CHAPTER NINE

Hope's knees wobbled as the express elevator she rode with Skyler and Tony whooshed to a stop on the sixty-first floor of 1 International Plaza, a stunning five-sided tower that housed some of Houston's premier companies. Though the Prestige Group had hosted mixers at many of the Bayou City's most outstanding venues, they'd never used this facility.

The doors parted to reveal a large lobby area with gleaming marble floors and floor-to-ceiling windows. A woman wearing a black skirt suit and a warm smile stood a few feet away. "Welcome to the International Club, Ms. Malloy."

When the trio exited, the woman extended her hand. "I'm Barbara Thurston. Mr. Sterling requested I take very good care of you."

With her purse, Skyler nudged Hope's ribs. Hope glared at her assistant. That morning, Rafe had sent a bouquet of red roses, with thorns. Not wanting to look at the arrangement all day, Hope had placed the vase in the conference room, in the middle of the table, which bore a smudge that she'd missed cleaning. She hadn't been able to hide the flowers, but she'd kept the texts private. It had taken resolve she didn't know she possessed to stop herself from responding.

Last night, Rafe had sent her the names of two submissives he'd scened with in the past and recommended she call them as references. Despite her resolve to avoid him, she'd closed her office door and made the first call to Sara. Sara had said she'd adored playing with Rafe. He had been considerate and fulfilled her desires. Knowing he'd been involved with the sweet-sounding submissive had spiked envy in Hope. But as far as references went, Sara's words were reassuring. Hope had called the next sub too and received a similar glowing recommendation.

Part of her had hoped she'd learn something bad that would give her a solid reason to bolt.

Skyler cleared her throat, bringing Hope back to the present. She'd been lost in thought while Barbara had been speaking. "Sorry?"

"I was asking if this is your first visit to the

International Plaza."

"It is."

"We're delighted to have you here. Our observation deck is renowned for its city views." Several pieces of modern art adorned the wide-open area, similar in theme to ones on the street, tying the inside of the building with the exterior and providing a visual bridge to the nearby arts complex.

Hope tossed a glance over her shoulder at Skyler and Tony. Skyler's mouth was parted, and Tony adjusted his yellow tie.

"If you'll come with me, I'll get you settled in."

Refusing to be anything but confident in her decision to retain the account even though that meant she had to face him again, Hope followed the concierge to the Bayou Vista room at the end of a long hallway. The area was enclosed by frosted glass etched with the Houston skyline.

When she stepped inside the intimate space, her breath was taken away once more. She was drawn toward the windows, even though she was trying to focus on the room's setup.

"It's a common reaction," Barbara assured her. "Take your time."

Over the past few years, Hope had been rocked by some incredible views, including a revolving rooftop restaurant atop a downtown hotel. But this was fifteen floors higher than that, soaring over all the nearby buildings, offering a stunning skyscape, as far away as the ship channel. Closer in was the aquarium with its famous Ferris wheel. Buffalo

Bayou with its paths and parks and green space that meandered through the city, provided an inviting space in the concrete jungle.

Tony joined her, adjusting his tie. "I wonder what it costs for a corporate membership."

More than the Prestige Group could afford, no doubt.

"I'm happy to send across some information," Barbara said. "The fact that Mr. Sterling invited you here will have some sway with the membership committee, I'm sure."

Since she didn't want to say it wouldn't be necessary, Hope smiled. Access to this facility would be amazing, but amazing came with a price tag.

Tony glanced toward Skyler. "You can see that glass-bottomed pool that goes off the edge of that apartment building." He pointed to a building in the distance.

That feature was remarkable, and a video of a woman appearing to walk off the front of the apartment complex, with the street forty stories below, had gone viral. While Hope considered herself adventurous, she would never swim where she could see cars and people below her.

"Come have a look," Tony invited.

"Oh, hell no," Skyler replied, her features blanching.

Hope turned. "Are you afraid of heights?"

"No. Uh, I'm fine. Good. Just making sure everything is okay. You know, the food and beverages." Skyler glanced at Barbara.

The woman joined her, which left Hope no choice but to follow.

A champagne fountain sat in the center of the room, flowing with amber bubbly. A bottle stood off to the side, bearing a label so expensive that she would only purchase it for a major celebration.

He'd also provided chocolate-covered strawberries, a cheese tray, and an assortment of fresh veggies.

There were a few high bar tables scattered around the room, covered with white tablecloths. Each had a centerpiece consisting of a flickering candle and a sprig of bluebonnets — the Texas state flower — in a small vase. Jazz music, played low, provided a sophisticated background without being so loud that it would disturb intimate conversation.

A staff of two stood in place, ready to serve.

"If there's anything you require to make your event more successful, please let me know." Barbara offered a business card with her personal cell phone number on it. "I'll be here until your event wraps up. And of course, the staff can handle anything you need."

"Thank you." Hope slipped the card into her kitty purse, then stowed it beneath a table. Skyler placed her handbag alongside Hope's.

"I could get used to this kind of mixer," Tony said. "Think about the type of clientele we'd attract. People would be dying for an invitation to come here."

Hope stood. "Don't even."

"Tell me we can have some of the champagne," Skyler implored.

"A taste test would be appropriate, I think." Tony nodded. "Make sure it's palatable."

"I'm sure it's fine," Hope responded.

"Yeah. Fine." Skyler smoothed her skirt.

Hope didn't have any rules against drinking at Prestige events. In fact, it might be more awkward if they didn't occasionally have one in hand. She just made sure they caught a ride home if they imbibed, and to ensure everyone was on their best behavior, employees were not permitted anything more than two glasses per evening.

"I'll be the official taste tester. I'm all about being a team player, as you know." Tony picked up a flute and filled it.

"Selfless," Skyler said.

Hope and Skyler stood next to each other, watching as he took a sip.

"You were right. It's fine." He sighed, as if suffering. "I suppose it will work since we have nothing else." He stuck the glass back under the waterfall.

"Want one?" Skyler asked Hope.

"No." She needed every advantage she could gather where Rafe was concerned, which meant she had to keep her mind clear, even if that meant forgoing a glass of one of the best sparkling wines on the planet.

Skyler took her first sip and her eyes rolled back. She bent her knees in a mock swoon. "Oh, there so is a God."

"It's that good?" Hope asked.

"Better than that. Orgasmic, even."

"You make that face when you orgasm?" Tony asked.

"Do *not* answer him!" Hope snapped.

Skyler made a circle over her head, indicating she had a halo.

"Business. We're here for work," Hope reminded them. They'd talked to seventeen candidates and ended up with four who might consider a BDSM relationship with the right millionaire.

Tony was on his second champagne when the first potential date arrived. Destiny Faulks owned a graphic design firm. She was petite, energetic, and had a brush of purple streaked through her blonde hair. Skyler went to say hello while Tony met Charlotte Lewiston, who played with the symphony. He led her to the center table where he offered her a glass of champagne.

Minutes later, Hope welcomed their third guest, Norah Minturn. Though young, the woman worked for a hedge fund management group and had already started to earn a reputation as being savvy and bold. She was from old money but left her trust fund untouched, preferring to make her own mark on the world.

Even though she was deep in conversation, Hope knew the moment Rafe opened the door. Oxygen rushed from the room. Her heart rate turned thready and words died in her throat.

She was caught in his unseen tractor beam. Unable to stop herself, she turned toward him. Their gazes locked, and he tipped his head to acknowledge her. Heat flooded her, as well as her instinct to succumb to his dominance. Realizing she was ignoring Norah, Hope shook herself. She made eye contact with Skyler, signaling she needed assistance. Then she turned back to Norah with a polite and practiced smile. "If you'll excuse me for a moment?"

"That's Rafe Sterling."

His gaze was a livewire, and Hope shivered at the force of his attention. She hid her annoyance at Norah's non-question. "Do you know him?"

"No." She stared at him, unblinkingly. "But I want to."

After unclenching her back teeth, Hope smiled. "You'll get a chance."

"When you said you had a successful businessman for me to meet, I had no idea you meant *him*." Hunger and interest laced her tone. "He stands to inherit a billion dollars." Norah took a breath before cupping her hand near her mouth to keep the conversation private. "He wants to tie me up and order me around?"

For a reason she didn't dare name, Hope's smile faded. "As I mentioned, that would entail a personal discussion between you and Mr. Sterling."

Skyler finally arrived with Destiny to include Norah in their discussion.

As if he were royalty, Rafe had remained where

he was, just inside the door, waiting for Hope to come to him. As if he were royalty, she went.

The air around him sizzled, supercharged.

She hesitated. In this business setting, it would be inappropriate to hug him, and a handshake would be ludicrous.

Seeming to enjoy her struggle, he waited her out, studying her, not making any move to extract her from the conundrum.

In the end, she opted not to touch him. It was much safer that way.

In a voice loud enough for others to hear, she said, "Excellent choice of venues, Mr. Sterling." Did her words sound as forced to him as they did to her?

He continued to hold her gaze. "The view is second to none."

With a broken inhalation, aware of Skyler watching them, Hope continued. "Everything is perfect. All the details. The room…" She was babbling. Damn it. Damn him and the smile toying with the corners of his lips.

"You received my flowers?"

"Thank you. But you need to stop."

"Why?"

"Why?" She blinked. "Do I need to list the reasons?"

"You don't like flowers?"

"That's not the point."

"So you did enjoy them?"

"Mr. Sterling, please. Let me introduce you to your candidates."

"Is this how it's going to be?" That telltale warning tic in his jaw was back. "Foisting me off on others?"

"I'm here to do a job. You're here to save your empire." *She* had to remind herself of that. Hope flicked a glance toward her assistant. By prior arrangement, she hurried over. "This is Skyler Morrison, the heartbeat of Prestige. We couldn't function without her."

"We've spoken on the phone," he said. "Great organizational skills and an effective communicator. I agree, she's a great asset to your organization. It's a pleasure to put a face with a name, Ms. Morrison." He shook Skyler's hand, quick and perfunctory without holding on.

Skyler stood there, blushing, silent. In all the time they'd worked together, with all the rich, powerful men that Skyler had met, she'd never been at a loss for words.

"We were discussing the venue," Hope prompted

"Yes. The venue. Right. It's...beautiful." Skyler cleared her throat, then smoothed a hand down her slacks. "And the champagne is delightful. Dry but not pretentious."

"I'm glad you approve."

"Yes, well. Can I get you a glass? I mean, it is yours, right?"

He cut his glance toward Hope. "I'd rather your boss fetch it for me." His tone had changed. Now it was firm, an order that promised reward or punishment. "Then I'll spend a couple of minutes discussing strategy with her before I meet the first of your candidates."

A moment later, one of the servers circled the room, carrying a tray of filled flutes.

Their final guest arrived, and Skyler smiled, as if she'd won a reprieve. "I'll greet Hannah."

"Thank you." Hope fought to keep her tone even.

Skyler dipped one knee, the move suspiciously like a curtsy. Hope blinked, resisting the temptation to wring her assistant's neck.

"Ma'am?" The server offered wine.

From across the room, Hannah demanded, "You're sure he's not a sadist?"

Hope closed her eyes, praying Rafe's hearing wasn't as good as hers. His smile told her it was. Her earlier resolve to abstain from alcohol wobbled. Deciding she needed the fortification, she plucked a glass from the tray.

Rafe studied her. It was obvious he was waiting for her obedience. A dozen thoughts jammed together. He could get his own damn champagne. After all, he was as close to the server as she was. But with his studied silence, he was reminding her of last night and what they'd shared.

Had he been anyone else, she would have offered a glass without hesitation. After a long internal debate, she complied.

"Perfect." He made sure their fingers touched and a satisfied purr curled through his words.

Despite her resolve, his approving tone sent shockwaves of unwanted response through her.

"Pleasing me is painless. Isn't it, sweet Hope? Part of you finds it gratifying, even."

"Ma'am, would you like a glass?"

Jolted, Hope realized the server was still close by. Once again, Rafe had filled her entire world. "Ah... Thank you." She accepted a flute for herself.

Disconcerted by the realization that what he had said was true, even though she didn't want it to be, Hope took a much larger sip than normal. The bubbles burst through her mouth, tickling her nose. It tasted of honey and citrus and luxury.

"It's to your satisfaction?"

"I didn't think anything could be as good as the one we had last night." She should not have admitted that. "It's superb."

He touched the rim of his glass with hers. "I changed the order this morning with you in mind."

"You..." Before she could lose herself in him, she sunnily focused on the event. "So, strategy. This event is scheduled to end in two hours. I hope you'll take a chance to chat with each candidate, get to know her a little. We will keep an eye on you, and if you don't appear to be enjoying yourself, one of us will join the conversation. I think I've mentioned it before — if you like someone, we will set up another meeting on your behalf."

Rafe turned and allowed his gaze to sweep over the people in the room. "Let's get this over with. Tell me about the women anxious to become Mrs.

Sterling. Enough so that they're interested in discussing whether or not they will let me punish their misbehavior. Perhaps with my hand or even a leather flogger." He looked at her pointedly. "Speaking of that, I trust you're still following my orders?" He leaned toward her. "If you've orgasmed without permission, we'll have to excuse ourselves. I have use of the club's private rooms."

His behavior was calculated to be outrageous. She just wished she had better control over her reactions—that her face hadn't reddened, that her pussy hadn't tingled. "Business, Mr. Sterling."

"I don't see Miss Texas in the room."

That he'd followed her lead left her reeling. It took a minute before she could respond, "She's not here."

"Was she the one terrorized by the thought of being with a sadist?"

"That was Hannah."

"Ah." He scanned the room. "The woman who just arrived? The one with the voice that carries?"

Hope nodded. "Yes. She's an attorney. Well respected, with a good reputation."

"No doubt plenty of courtroom presence." He cleared his throat. "We didn't scare her off?"

"About that...she's, ah, open to a discussion."

"Did you share any of your personal experiences with her?"

Hopefully, her grip wouldn't shatter her glass stem. *"No."*

"You did have all the women fill in my

questionnaire?"

"I opted to stick to generalities and allow you to proceed how you see fit." She had no interest in knowing which of the women would hump his mattress.

He grinned, the motion so quick she might have imagined it. "Back to Hannah."

"She's thirty-one, open to the possibility of having children."

He gave a sharp nod, as if filing away the information. "Who else do we have?"

"Over near the champagne, my associate, Tony, is talking to Charlotte. Also blonde, twenty-nine, an accomplished pianist, plays with the symphony. Enjoys kayaking."

"You were listening. Impressive. And the other one? By herself, near the window?"

"That's Destiny Faulks. She's a graphic designer. Very well regarded." Hope had met her at a fashion event and had been captivated by her enthusiasm. At the moment, Destiny was sketching a picture on her cellphone screen. She hadn't been among Hope's first choices for Rafe. But when they moved on to the second tier of candidates, Hope had reconsidered. With her adventurous nature and potential interest in a BDSM relationship, Destiny had warranted an invite.

"Who does she work for?"

"Herself. She owns the company and has a couple of employees. Entrepreneurial spirit. Tireless, enthusiastic. She rides every Sunday morning on

Buffalo Bayou — a road bike. She's open to trying a mountain bike. Also willing to learn to kayak."

"Excellent."

"And the last one?"

"Norah is a financial manager."

"You've done well. They are all accomplished. Bright. Attractive. Willing to consider, if not embrace, a kinky lifestyle. How many did you ask?"

"Seventeen."

"More than twenty percent were intrigued enough to show up." With his points made, he placed his unfinished champagne on the tray of a passing waiter. "If you'll excuse me?" With confidence bordering on arrogance, he crossed the room to introduce himself to Destiny.

It wasn't until he was on the other side of the room that Hope allowed herself to exhale. God, her heart was thundering.

Tony joined her. "How's it going so far?"

She watched Destiny. The woman's head was tipped back, and she was staring at Rafe with something resembling unfettered adoration. He was smiling, basking in her attention.

Emotions in freefall, Hope pretended to be consumed with the bubbles in her glass.

"It appears we may not need another mixer if the way he's talking to Destiny is any indication."

"Yeah." She should be pleased.

"I'd high-five you, but that would be unprofessional."

Less than a minute later, Destiny was showing

him her cell phone screen. He leaned forward as if intrigued.

She swiped her finger across the screen several times, and he nodded. Then she began to draw on the face of the device again. After some discussion, he took the stylus and added a few strokes.

"I might not have invited Destiny." Tony tipped an imaginary hat. "Once again, your matchmaking skills leave me in awe."

Her attention still straying to the other pair, Hope forced a stiff laugh.

Rafe offered Destiny his business card along with a polite smile before walking over to the champagne fountain to fill another glass.

Destiny studied the card, flicked the edge, then slid it into a pocket in her cell phone cover. The window reflected her smile.

Had he invited her to call him to set up a date? Even though that was against Prestige's recommended protocol, sometimes a client proceeded at his own pace. Because Rafe's need was urgent, Hope wouldn't be surprised if he took an active role in finding a bride.

"That appears promising, right?" Tony beamed. "Let me go find out." He walked toward the window.

Skyler, evidently finding her professional demeanor and realizing that their client was on the move, intercepted him, then walked with him to where Hannah stood, her eyebrows furrowed.

Hope shook herself. She had a job to do, no

matter how challenging the assignment was. *This is why it's a bad idea to sleep with a client.* After tonight, she had to turn Rafe over to her associates. She wasn't as strong as she thought she was, and Skyler was capable of organizing and overseeing the meetings and handling the follow-up. Hope would write Skyler a nice bonus check too, for all the extra work. And maybe move her into the role of an actual matchmaker. That would mean they would need to hire a new assistant. Replacing Skyler would be a challenge.

Tony walked Destiny out while Hope and Skyler mingled with the remaining guests, chatting, making introductions. It didn't matter who Rafe was speaking with. He left his phone in his pocket and gave each person his full attention. No doubt all the candidates would agree to date him.

Rafe refilled Hannah's glass before he excused himself. Once again, Skyler joined him and made the introduction to Norah.

After Hannah had finished a piece of chocolate, she came over to say goodbye.

"Did you enjoy the event?" Hope asked.

Hannah glanced toward Rafe. "He wasn't what I expected."

"Is that a good thing or a bad thing?"

"I'm not sure." She frowned a little. "More...personable. Charming, even. Makes me nervous, but in a good way."

Since Prestige didn't discuss clients in front of potential candidates, Hope let the conversation hang.

"I'll have Skyler contact you in the morning to follow up. Thank you for coming."

Over the next half hour, the other candidates exited, leaving the Prestige Group alone with Rafe.

"If you want to go home, I'll wrap things up with Barbara," Skyler said to Hope. Then she turned to Rafe. "As we discussed, if you'll let us know who you're interested in getting to know better, Mr. Sterling, I'm happy to see if they'd like to join you for coffee or lunch. We recommend you don't have dinner or drinks until the second date. That way —"

"Thank you, but I won't be requiring anything further."

"I'm sorry?" Skyler scowled, then flicked her glance toward Hope.

As confused as Skyler, Hope took over the conversation. "Have you already made arrangements to meet with one of the candidates?"

"No."

"Then...?

Instead of responding, he sidestepped the question. "Thank you for your efforts this afternoon." He checked his classic, pricey watch.

Hope pulled back her shoulders. "I'm sorry we didn't do better for you." She took over the conversation. He should like at least one of the women. What the hell had Prestige done wrong? "I'll have Skyler contact you when we have another set of candidates for your consideration. I doubt we can arrange another mixer this week, but perhaps Monday or Tuesday."

Skyler nodded. "I'm on it."

Ignoring everyone else in the room, he addressed Hope. "That won't be necessary."

Hope frowned. "I'm afraid I don't understand."

"There's a woman I'm interested in pursuing."

Since this morning? Since he'd been with her? At a loss, she dug her fingers into her palms. "In that case, I'm not sure why we went ahead with this mixer."

"You and your team went to a lot of work, and I didn't want to cancel at the last moment."

"You wasted everyone's time."

"I don't agree. Destiny's designs are intriguing. No doubt I'll be contracting her for some work. I have a couple of friends who may want a meeting with Norah. Hannah, I'm sure, is a great legal mind who might make a good addition to the DA's office if she'd like to change sides. Public service and a judgeship could be in her future. And I secured tickets to the symphony. Meeting new people is always interesting. Skyler is a fabulous organizer. Our new executives are always looking for top-notch assistants."

"You can't have her."

Skyler stood a little taller.

"At any rate, your matchmaking services are no longer required. We will consider your agreement with my mother to be terminated as of this moment."

Even though this was what she wanted, she was gutted he'd seen another woman after everything they'd shared. "In that case, congratulations." She forced a smile. "I wish you much happiness."

Skyler's lips were set in a grim line. She didn't appear to be any happier than Hope was.

"Do let us know if you need anything further." The last word emerged as a croak, so Hope cleared her throat.

Along with Skyler and Tony, Hope turned to leave, but Rafe placed a hand on her forearm. "A moment of your time, Ms. Malloy?"

"Is it necessary? We can't handle it over the phone?" When he remained silent, she relented. "Go ahead," she said to her employees. "I'll call for a ride when I'm done here."

"You're sure?" Tony asked.

"Go ahead. I won't be far behind you."

"I'll let Barbara know we're done," Skyler said.

Both of them nodded their goodbyes before heading toward the door. Gripping the handle, Tony hesitated and turned back. "I can wait for you near the elevator."

"She's safe with me," Rafe vowed, releasing his grip, leaving her arm heated. "I promise."

Turning back to face them, Skyler swallowed hard, as if struggling for courage before saying, "I saw the way you behaved on the street this morning."

Hope wished a hole would open in the floor.

"Did you, indeed?" His voice was bland, unreadable.

"I'll send you both a text," Hope reassured her employees. She'd known they were protective of her, but until this evening, she'd had no idea just how serious they were.

After Skyler and Tony left, the atmosphere sizzled. Rafe's eyes flared with predatory intent. The music that had provided a soothing backdrop now became intimate. Even though he'd given his word that she was safe, all her feminine instincts urged her to flee. This man was as dangerous as he was powerful. Hope wrapped her arms around herself. "You wanted to talk?"

"Let's cut through the bullshit. I want you, Hope."

Her heart plummeted. His words rendered her speechless.

"This afternoon's charade?" He waved a hand, and the emeralds in his ring winked in the overhead light. "It was for your benefit. To prove a point. You have no more interest in me marrying those women than I do. You hated watching me with them."

His voice was rich, the timbre resonant, shooting shivers through her. "Mr. Sterling—"

"Rafe," he corrected. "I fucking like the way you say my name. As I've said before, Rafe or Sir is fine, as long as you know who you belong to."

No. She shook her head and the room spun. It had to be from the champagne and not her reaction to him.

"This..." She couldn't form a coherent sentence. "I can't. We can't."

"Can't? Or you don't want to?"

She tipped back her head. The amber-gold fire in

the depths of her eyes consumed her. "You need a wife."

"You like the way I command you." He captured her shoulders.

"I'm not a submissive."

"Are you not?"

Though she shifted, she didn't pull away.

"Did you masturbate today?"

She kept silent. But he outwaited her. Because she couldn't take the silence, she said, "That's an inappropriate question."

"Were you tempted?"

She glanced at the door, afraid Barbara would return.

"Answer me, please."

"No. I didn't masturbate. And I was tempted."

"Why didn't you?"

Damn him. He knew. He fucking *knew*.

He released one of her shoulders, then skimmed the shell of her ear. "Because you were trying to please me. And you did. You're perfect for me, Hope."

"I'm not. Your future is on the line here. You need a wife, not an affair."

"Remind me of the attributes I find important."

"What game are you playing?"

"Indulge me."

"Someone who kayaks." Which was not her. "And rides mountain bikes."

"Go on."

"Smart," she said.

"I prefer brilliant," he corrected.

"Independent."

"Keep going."

She desperately thought through his list. "Impeccable background."

"Not on my list."

"Blonde."

"My mother and sister said that. No doubt because Emma was a blonde." Seeing her frown, he explained, "She was my college sweetheart. Gold digger."

"You like women who are" — she searched for the words — "less curvy."

"That, my sweet Hope, is complete bullshit. I appreciate women who are athletic, who are thin, who are voluptuous. You had my cock up inside your hot cunt. Tell me I prefer someone else."

She gasped at his crudeness.

"All day, I've thought about spanking your ass," he went on, either not noticing or not caring that he'd spun her world off its axis. "Thoughts of you interfered with my work...tying you down, fucking you, putting a collar on you, calling you mine, forcing you to your knees when I meet you at home."

Each of his words seared an unforgettable picture on her imagination.

"I want to wrap my tie around your wrists and pin you down. You want that too."

"No." She'd responded too fast, the word a breathless rush. Trying again, she added, "I don't."

"You turn pink when you're not being honest."

With his index finger, he swept an arc just above her cheekbone. He leaned closer, brushed her lips, and she tasted champagne. "Lie all you want. I enjoy punishing your bad behavior, and I'm keeping a list of your offenses."

Hope brought a hand up between them and placed it on his chest in a futile attempt to keep distance between them. It wasn't him she was fighting. It was herself.

"Did you consider yourself as one of my choices?"

Maybe once, in the darkest, most private places of her imagination, had she allowed that thought to take flight... "No."

"Another lie." He leaned toward her, just a little more, stealing her oxygen. He would back off if she used a safe word. Cursing her own weak resolve, she didn't use it.

"Marry me, sweet Hope. Be my submissive. Be my bride. Be my partner."

"What?" She shook her head. His suggestion was ridiculous. Absurd. Impossible. So tempting that she wished there was a way to accept.

"I need a wife, and you have all the C's. Chemistry." He kissed her. Deep. Hard. Persuasively. "Tell me yes," he demanded after he'd left her panting and with bruised lips.

She shook her head. A thousand times no, for a million reasons. "No."

"I'm persistent when I decide what I want." A determined glint made his eyes glacial, and an answering shiver raced down her spine. "I want you, and your refusal is the starting point for our negotiation."

"Chemistry is only one of the C's." She was learning how potent it could be. If chemistry guaranteed a successful relationship, she'd have said yes. "There's also commitment. You've been clear that you don't want to get married."

"Didn't," he corrected. "I've come to accept, perhaps welcome, the inevitability."

She narrowed her eyes. "Since Monday?"

"Since my trip to see my father this morning." A few moments ago, there'd been a gentleness in his tone, along with persistence and a slight cajoling tease. Now there was a chill. "He's not returning to the business. I'll be damned if I'll allow Noah to break apart what we've spent two hundred years building."

"You need to find someone else," she protested.

"You'd be a very wealthy woman."

At what cost? She understood the allure of financial stability, but for her, the devastation of falling for a man who didn't love her wasn't worth the risk. "I'm happy with my own results. I have no interest in a marriage for your convenience."

"I wouldn't expect you to give up your career. You've built a well-respected business, and I understand that you enjoy it. There would be a stipulation that you already know about. We would need to have children. I'd promise to be involved, and we could have a nanny. Adoption is a possibility, if that was a decision we made together. But if we want to have our own, we could stop after one if you find pregnancy doesn't agree with you."

A baby? She'd never allowed herself to dream of that possibility. It would mean taking a chance on a relationship. But the idea of having a child with Rafe... Her heart clutched, as if she'd just gone over the first exhilarating downhill on a roller coaster.

"I will be talking to my attorneys about changing the archaic terms of the trust so that females can inherit. If England can change rules for the monarchy, there has to be a way." Though she wasn't giving him her full attention, she realized Rafe was still talking. "I'll admit, I wouldn't mind trying to get you pregnant." The earlier coldness had receded from his voice, leaving behind an inviting warmth that she yearned to surrender to.

In order to remain strong, she forced herself to banish the sudden image of a child with eyes as startling as Rafe's.

"Under what terms will you walk down the aisle toward me?"

"None. Rafe... No. I can't."

"Won't," he challenged.

"I agree we have chemistry." Like spark and kindling.

"And I will be devoted to you. So we've sorted out the first two C's."

"We don't know if we're compatible."

He traced the shell of her ear, igniting something deep inside her. "No?"

"This is chemistry," she protested.

"You enjoyed being with me last night, and not just the sex. The conversation at dinner, then breakfast. You're intrigued by the Titans. I've told you my family's history and the dramas, and you've already invested part of yourself in it. If you walk away this moment, which you are free to do, you would miss being part of my life."

"Arrogant, much?" His statement was true, though. Even though she didn't want it to be.

"Go with me to Louisiana. We can leave Friday at lunchtime."

She grabbed his wrist. "I've told you that I can't just walk away from Prestige on a whim."

"Do you have anything on your schedule, workwise, that Skyler and Tony can't handle?"

She scowled. "That's not the point."

"Do you?"

Their next mixer wasn't until Tuesday. Hope had a breakfast meeting on Friday morning, and she could attend it before leaving. She and Tony were scheduled to attend a charity auction Saturday night. If Skyler were available, it would be a good opportunity to try her as a recruiter. Then she seized her last possible excuse. "The Colonel. I need to take care of the Colonel."

"What about your neighbor? Caroline, was it?"

Does he remember everything?

"We can get her a nice gift card as a thank-you, for a spa day or something to recover from the trauma. Or a bottle of champagne, perhaps?"

Caroline was easily bribed. And a spa visit would do it.

"It's two nights, not forever. I want to prove to you that we are compatible." He lowered his hand, and she missed his touch. "Aren't you in the least bit interested in seeing the Parthenon? I can get us a cottage on the property."

"Not at one of your hotels?"

"We can stay at the Maison Sterling if you wish. I just thought you'd prefer to catch your own glimpse inside the wrought-iron gates."

Excitement threatened to sweep her away. Of course she wanted to see the internal workings of his secret society. "You're not playing fair."

"Do you expect me to?" Without waiting for a response, he went on, "How many other people do you know who have been invited? And I'd like to take you to dinner someplace special."

Her mind raced through the names of famous high-end restaurants in the French Quarter.

"Outside of New Orleans," he clarified. "This one is private, someplace I can show off my beautiful submissive."

Wide-eyed, she forgot to breathe. "I don't even know if I want to be your submissive."

"Even better. A weekend away will give you the chance to find out if we are compatible in all ways. You will have your safe word, and if you hate being my sub, you can discontinue the role. Then we can continue to have a nice time as associates."

He was asking a lot. Maybe too much. Hope

wasn't sure whether she wanted that, whether she was strong enough to meet his desires and constant demands, but she was tempted.

Heat flared in his eyes. "Say yes, sweet Hope. What's the worst that can happen? You'll have a weekend away, get treated like a princess, explore your most sinful desires, learn about yourself, eat some wonderful food, visit the Zeta Society's plantation. Champagne. A massage, perhaps?"

None of those things were the worst that could happen, by any means. There was much more at stake, the possibility she would become attached to Rafe, the way her mother had been to Hope's father. Then if things didn't work out, she'd be devastated. It was far safer for her not to take the risk.

"Perhaps you might even be able to convince yourself that we are not compatible, that you wouldn't fit into my lifestyle or that I would fit into yours. But you'd know for sure. Come with me, Hope. Find out for yourself."

CHAPTER TEN

Damn Rafe and his tempting suggestions.

Hope's alarm blared, and she dragged herself awake to turn it off. When blessed silence hung over the room, she flipped onto her back. She'd dreamed of walking down the aisle toward him. He wore a black tailored tuxedo. Naked or in a suit, he was delicious. But in her fantasies, in a tux? He'd swept his gaze over her, a slow, soft smile of appreciation curving his lips. How could she have doubted that marrying him was a good idea?

Exhausted from the restless night, she plumped her pillow and closed her eyes again. A nightmare pulled her under, and she was trapped in a place she didn't understand. Rafe was her whole world. Bright strobe lights flashed through her, wild and unbalancing. Then she was in a house of mirrors, her image squat in one, elongated in another. She was businesswoman in a suit, a sub on her knees, a seductress at a restaurant. The glass shattered, and she was in a room that spun with color and screams, infatuated with a man who didn't return the feeling.

She woke screaming, clenching the sheets.

The Colonel leaped onto the bed, eyes filled with condemnation.

"Sorry." Hope released her death grip. "Did I disturb you?"

The cat licked her paw, then burrowed beneath the blankets, ignoring Hope.

With a sigh, Hope pushed herself up onto her elbows and grabbed her phone. Her heart stumbled at the sight of a text from Rafe. Why, oh why, did she have to have such a powerful reaction every time he contacted her?

Have dinner with me tonight? My place. We can talk privately. Try to cover the third C.

She was pretty sure they had that covered too. Last night she hadn't wanted to admit the truth to either of them.

Phone still in hand, she dropped back against her pillow and blew out a breath as she considered his invitation. The last time she'd had a night that restless was almost two years ago, when her mother had died. Nightmares had lasted for weeks before exhaustion had cured her insomnia. Yet if she said no to Rafe, her brain would continue to feed her this horrible mix of possibility and fear. The question was, would she be as disturbed if she said yes?

It wasn't just Rafe who'd caused the difficult night. Her subconscious had needed time to process everything that had happened. Maybe if it had evolved over a week or month, it would be easier to sort through.

Since caffeine was an essential food group this morning, she grabbed her phone, then headed for the kitchen. While the coffeemaker hissed and sputtered, she texted Skyler.

I overslept. Sorry. I'll bring lattes as my penalty.

The reply she should have expected came less than thirty seconds later.

And doughnuts.

Before she could type her own answer, Skyler sent a second message.

Make mine chocolate.

Hope hadn't even managed "will do" before her phone pinged again.

With sprinkles.

Actually, make it two.

Don't forget Tony. He says he doesn't eat doughnuts, but he's a big, fat liar. He's always stealing mine. I want my own, Hope.

Hope grinned, the vestiges of the restless night losing their grip.

Since Skyler was on top of things, Hope took her time, sipping her first cup and deciding on a bath rather than a shower.

As steam wafted around her, she sank down and rested her head against the inflatable pillow. She thought about everything she'd experienced since meeting Rafe, the ways he'd challenged her and expanded her world, introducing her to unimagined carnal pleasures. As she remembered the thorn at dinner and her reaction to it, arousal unfurled. Hope shook her head to force away the dangerous, erotic thoughts. She needed to be pragmatic while she had some time to think.

Memories, desires, fears all bubbled to the surface. The part of herself that she'd always listened to urged caution. But the part that had been awakened was curious about everything he offered. Any normal human being would be interested in learning about the secret society he belonged to, and of course she was intrigued by the idea of seeing the Parthenon.

She relaxed once again, and she was able to

admit the truth to herself. Even as nervous as she was, she wanted to visit the restaurant he had mentioned. Until he'd mentioned taking her there, she hadn't believed places like that existed.

In a way, she'd had a somewhat sheltered upbringing. Her mom had rarely taken time off work, and when she had, they'd driven to Galveston to spend a couple of days at the beach. It hadn't been until after college that Hope had gone on a cruise. Her work in Texas kept her busy, and though it was close, she hadn't visited New Orleans recently. How could she say no?

It would be simpler if she wanted to say no.

Her mind more than half made up, she climbed out of the tub. She had a towel wrapped around herself when the Colonel strolled in and bellowed as if the hounds of hell had been unleashed. "Breakfast. Right. I'm on it."

The Colonel sat in the doorway, staring and continuing to meow.

"I love you too, you dictatorial fur ball."

The cat stood, turned around, flicked her tail, then headed for the kitchen. Hope followed. Too bad she hadn't thought to fill the food dish while she made coffee.

After taking care of the cat, Hope poured herself another cup of coffee.

A few minutes later the phone rang. Rafe? In expectation, her pulse slammed. When Celeste's name appeared on the caller identification screen, a confusing mix of relief and disappointment slowed her heart rate. After a third ring, emotions under control, she answered. "Morning, Celeste."

"I'd ask how you are, but I'm too nosy to waste time being polite."

Celeste's disarming honesty made Hope grin.

"How did Rafe's mixer go?" Celeste asked.

"Should I drag this out a bit longer?"

"Good God, no. Get to the point."

"He refused them all and proposed to me."

"Ah." Her mentor sighed, triumphant. "As I suspected."

"What?" Hope put her cup down so she didn't spill. "What are you saying?"

"I knew you were the one for him. That's why I recommended you to Rebecca."

"You thought…"

"Rafe needs a woman who's bright and articulate—well, most of the time, anyway." Her voice was dry. "Only you can make the decisions that are right for you. But I can vouch for Rafe. If he asked you to marry him, he meant it. He wouldn't have done so without thinking it through or believing you two could have a successful relationship."

"I'm not sure about any of it. Getting married." She paused. "Or the Zeta Society."

"Rafe's offering you an opportunity to see for yourself."

In the corner, the Colonel finished eating and started dipping one paw into her water bowl and licking the drops away. The distraction gave Hope a moment to figure out what was bothering her. "Did he suggest you call me?"

"Darling, I don't allow myself to be manipulated."

Because she trusted Celeste's answer, Hope confided her greatest fear. "I'm scared, Celeste."

"Because of your father? Your mother's inability to move on?" As always, her mentor filled in the blanks of what Hope had left out. "You are much stronger than Cynthia. I'm not one to meddle—"

Much.

"You've closed yourself off. In fact, I'm not sure you've ever allowed anyone inside your little clamshell."

As they spoke, Hope paced, and the Colonel glared at her, as if her peace were being disturbed. "There's the whole submission thing too."

"Life is filled with risks. Adapt and overcome."

Hope sighed at her mentor's signature phrase.

"Perhaps I'll see you this weekend?"

Hope gave a noncommittal answer before ending the call.

Rafe's dinner invitation was still on her phone's screen, waiting for her answer. Yet she couldn't give it.

Her phone chimed again.

Where's my latte?

Realizing she'd taken over an hour when she'd given herself thirty minutes, Hope hurried to dress and head out.

She arrived at work and jerked to a halt when she walked in the door. The biggest bouquet of flowers that she'd ever seen sat on Skyler's desk. The arrangement was so tall that Hope couldn't see her assistant behind it. "Hello?"

"Coffee!" Skyler popped up with her hand extended. Zombielike, she headed for the tray bearing the lattes.

"Wait!" Hope cautioned. If Skyler plucked out a cup, the other two might become unbalanced. In silent offering, she placed the gifts on the edge of Skyler's desk.

"Did I hear coffee?" Tony shouted.

"And doughnuts," Hope responded.

"I don't eat doughnuts." His phone rang, and he lowered his voice as he answered it.

Hope waited until Skyler had taken a few sips before asking, "Who sent you flowers?"

"They're not mine."

"Oh?"

"More for you. I'll have you know I didn't read the card. I was dying to, but I didn't."

Hope took in the colors and the size of the bouquet. It was amazing the thing didn't topple over. Her fingers itched with the need to pluck the small envelope from the plastic stem it was attached to.

Before she could decide what to do with the flowers, a second delivery arrived. "No. No, no, no."

"I need someone to sign for these."

Skyler put down her cup to accept the vase.

Hope frowned at the sight of Skyler's name on the screen of his electronic device. Perplexed, she glanced up. "Those are for you," she told her assistant.

"Me? This is my lucky day!" As if part of a conga line, she chanted out, "Nah, nah, nah, nah, nah, nah," as she danced around. Then she gave a small kick before grabbing the envelope. Rather than lift the flap, she tore off the end. "Oh my God. They're from Rafe!"

"From…?"

"It says *'Thank you for all the hard work to make the mixer successful. Prestige is lucky to have you.'*"

The bastard. When the man played to win, he didn't play fair.

The deliveryman cleared his throat. "You need to sign for them."

Jolted, she scrawled her name with the stylus. Then she reached into her kitty purse for tip money. "Thank you."

With a nod, the man left.

"They're beautiful! Aren't they? I wish all our clients were like him."

Wasn't it just a few days ago that Skyler thought he was a pain in the ass? And just yesterday that she'd confronted him, then hesitated before leaving Hope alone with him?

Tony emerged from his office. "What's all the fuss?"

"Mr. Sterling is the *best*."

Hope shook her head.

Tony crossed the reception area and reached for the one cup remaining in the tray. Then he sneezed violently.

"Are you allergic?" Hope asked in what might have been her least intelligent question ever.

"Must be the romance. He's allergic to romance," Skyler replied.

"I've never had a reaction before," he protested, eyes watering.

"I'll move mine into my office," Hope said. "Sorry."

"No problem." He sneezed again, and he had to move his cup as far away from his body as possible to prevent his coffee from spilling over.

"I'll put mine in the conference room," Skyler offered. Then she ruined it. "If I have to."

"I'll soldier on," Tony said, his watery eyes showing his fortitude. After another sneeze, he grabbed one of the doughnuts that he'd said he didn't eat, then sought refuge in his office.

Hope and Skyler exchanged shrugs. "Poor thing." Hope cast her glance toward his now closed door.

"I had no idea," Skyler responded.

Hope scooped up her bouquet and carried it to the credenza in her office.

Skyler walked into the office. "You forgot this." She held up Hope's mug. Instead of leaving, she plonked herself down in a chair.

"Do you mind?"

"I know who they're from. It was the same

delivery company." With a cheeky grin, Skyler put down Hope's cup, then settled back to sip her own.

"Fine." Hope snatched up the envelope and slid her finger under the flap. *What can dinner hurt?* "As you suspected, Rafe," she informed Skyler. "Just like yours, a thank-you for our efforts." The explanation was half right, but the lie was bitter.

"Tell me what happened after I left last night."

"Nothing."

Skyler raised one of her pencil-enhanced eyebrows. For a second, Hope considered continuing the fib. Then again, if she did go to the Parthenon, she would need Skyler's help in covering her Saturday-night fundraiser. Giving just enough information, she drew a breath and admitted, "He invited me to go away with him this weekend."

"No shit?" Her assistant leaned forward and slipped her drink onto the desk. "Are you going? Spending time with McHottie? Heir to one of the world's biggest fortunes? Oh my God." She fanned herself. "Wait. Wait, wait, wait. Wait a sainted second." She drummed her fingers on the arm of her chair.

Hope could almost see Skyler start to join the puzzle pieces together. "*You're* the woman he was talking about last night." She phrased it as a statement, rather than a question. "That's why none of the others were suitable. Damn, Hope. Are you going? You've got to go."

She was making Hope dizzy.

"I'm thinking about it."

"What the hell is there to think about?"

She laughed. Put that way, what was there to think about? "I have a ticket to an event on Saturday night. A charity dinner and silent auction fundraiser at the Ivy for a pet adoption group."

"No worries. I'll go. I had a date and the rat-fink punk canceled on me. It'll do me good to get out rather than staying home and feeling sorry for myself."

Hope saw through Skyler's brave smile. Her heart was generous, and she'd spent years taking care of others, investing herself in relationships, sometimes at great emotional cost. Hope frowned.

"I promise I would say something if it was a problem."

"I'd need to leave late Friday morning."

"Shouldn't be anything that I can't handle."

When Hope remained silent, Skyler pursed her lips. "What's really going on?"

"I'm not his type."

"Well, he must think you are if he invited you along after you spent the night at his place."

Don't remind me. "It's…complicated." She didn't have the courage to admit he'd also proposed.

"Is there a reason you don't want to?" Skyler's stared. "Oh." She tugged on her braid. "The whole BDSM thing?"

"That's part of it." When Skyler didn't fill in the silence, Hope took a drink of the coffee she still needed. "I don't fit in his world."

"Why do you say that?"

"Isn't it obvious?"

"Why would it be? You do fit his profile. What would happen if you stopped doubting yourself? Would a weekend away be so bad? I mean, you'd find out more, right? About him. About you. Then you'd have more information." Skyler nodded, as if she'd reached a decision. "Consider it a fact-finding mission. You can decide after it whether or not dating would be a good idea. It will help you decide."

The front door opened. "Delivery for Hope Malloy!"

"Again?"

"How much money is in petty cash?" Skyler asked. "I can't continue to fund your suitor's flat-out romantic assault."

"Potential suitor," Hope contradicted, more out of obligation than anything. She didn't, however, correct the romantic-assault part.

"Right." Skyler stood. "Potential suitor." She headed for the door, then glanced back. "Conference room for these?"

Since the previous day's bouquet was still there, Hope said, "Let's donate them to the doctor's office next door."

Skyler nodded. "Oh, and I'll want all the details on Monday morning."

CHAPTER ELEVEN

"May I help you, sir?"

Exhaling his gratitude, Rafe turned toward the clerk. Christ, he hoped so. "I had no idea it would be so difficult." Rafe had pictured getting out of the car, strolling into Uptown Flower Power, selecting a nice arrangement, then walking back out. Instead, the small, stuffed-to-the-ceiling store overwhelmed him. There were tulips and sunflowers and little purple blooms. Tiered circular displays held potted plants. Bamboo. Cactuses. Five-foot-tall trees.

Mylar balloons floated everywhere. *Get well. Happy birthday. Congratulations.* Then there were the characters from movies and cartoons. Superheroes and princesses.

Perplexed, he wandered to one of the multiple refrigerators filled with cut flowers in all kinds of vases — large, some shaped like baby carriages, in pink, blue, even yellow. There was a glass container shaped like a heart. The biggest refrigerator held roses. Red, yellow, white, pale pink, from a single tight bloom in a tiny vase to one holding thirty red roses in a bowl big enough that it should have fish swimming in it. For a moment he considered purchasing it. All those thorns…

"Is this your first visit to a flower shop?"

Her lime-green apron was so glaringly bright that he had trouble making out her features. "Am I that obvious?"

The clerk grinned. Instead of answering his question, she said, "Let's start with the basics. What's the occasion?"

Seduction. Convincing a woman to marry me and submit to my authority.

"Anniversary?"

He shook his head.

"Birthday?"

"No. I just want something…nice."

"How nice? Are they for an apology?"

Again, he said no. "Something nice for the table. I'm making dinner. For someone special." He continued to look around. Who the hell guessed it could be this complicated?

"Ah! Date night."

A date? Rafe didn't go on dates. "You could say

that," he allowed.

"Does she like any specific color?"

No idea. Then he thought of her handbag. "Pink." Then the shoes she'd worn to the event last night.

As if she dealt with this kind of confusion all day long, the clerk came around the counter. "Does she prefer brights or pastels?"

If he knew the answer to that, he wouldn't need help. "Yes."

She smiled. "Where are you dining? Inside? On a patio?"

He hadn't even considered the options. He'd assumed they'd eat at the kitchen island. But that wasn't romantic. "Can you excuse me a moment?"

"Uhm. Sure."

He stepped off to the side to send a message to his housekeeper, hoping she hadn't left yet, asking her to set the dining room table for two.

Sienna replied that she'd already done so.

And the outside table.

A moment later, she replied that he should consider it done.

"How about both?" he said when he returned to the clerk. His cell phone danced around in his pocket, and while he waited for her to gather all the things required, he checked the message.

And you're having chocolate cake for dessert.

With whipped cream. It goes on the cake, Mr. Sterling.

He grinned. Sienna had earned a bonus, and he made a mental note to add one to her next check.

After twenty minutes, he ended up with two custom-designed arrangements, one a bunch of yellow tulips that had shocking red stripes. They reminded him of Hope. The other hourglass-shaped vase was stuffed full with bright colors, including hot pink. The clerk had placed the bouquets in boxes so they would survive the journey to his condo, and she helped him carry them to the car.

"Good luck tonight. I'm sure she'll love them."

The thought that she might not unnerved him.

Before he drove away, he checked the time. He still had forty minutes. He'd wanted to pick Hope up from work, but she'd said she had a late meeting with a potential new client and promised to arrive no later than seven.

It had taken her hours to agree to have dinner with him. He'd given her references to women who had submitted to him at the Retreat, and he'd suggested she discuss her concerns with Celeste. He knew she'd done so, because Celeste had mentioned it in a phone call.

Rafe hadn't contacted Hope until this morning, holding off as long as he was able. He'd been awake for over two hours before he'd given in and sent a text, inviting her to a casual dinner at his home. There had been nothing casual about the nerves he faced during the interminable hours while he'd waited for her answer.

Now, in his condo, he placed the bright flower arrangement on the indoor table and the tulips outside. He stepped back. Against the iron table, they didn't stand out, so he switched the vases. Then he shrugged. Who the hell knew it was this complicated?

By the time Hope rang the bell, he had the champagne on ice, the steaks out of the refrigerator, and the flowers where they belonged.

As always, the sight of her walloped his solar plexus. Her hair floated around her shoulders, which would save him the effort of plucking out another clip. She wore a purple sheath dress that ended midthigh, and she had on cream-colored heels — pumps, he supposed they were called. Tonight she'd selected a strand of pearls that fit like a choker. Had that been deliberate? "You're stunning as always, Hope." Betraying nerves, her knuckles were white where she clutched the handles of her kitty purse. "Come in. Please." He stepped back. "A glass of champagne?" he offered after he'd closed the door and she'd placed her bag on the bench.

"Really?"

"We're not playing. At least not until much later."

"Oh." She tilted her head.

Dare he hope she was disappointed?

"In that case, yes. Please." She followed him into the dining room. "The table is pretty."

Sienna had done a superb job as usual, setting two places with beautiful china that he didn't know he owned, cloth napkins folded in the shape of crowns in the middle of the plates, filled water glasses. She'd set up a coffee service on the bar next to where he'd chilled the wine.

After removing the wire cage, he uncorked the bottle to pour them each a glass.

"I could get used to this," she confessed, accepting the drink.

He'd like that. "The evening has cooled a little. Mind coming outside while I cook the steaks?"

"Sounds wonderful."

She followed him out the door and continued walking until she reached the edge of the balcony. Remnants of the sunset inked the sky. A few intrepid people splashed in the swimming pool below and a couple was out for a power walk.

"So relaxing."

Joining her, he nodded his agreement. He could count the times he'd sat on the patio. Now he wondered why.

Rafe savored her pleasure. This wasn't about chemistry or commitment; it was the other C. Compatibility. He liked her company.

They touched the edges of their glasses and watched the remainder of the sun fade. "Are you hungry?"

"Famished. I missed lunch. And I had a latte to hold me over. It wore off a couple of hours ago."

"In that case, I'll get the steaks going and bring

out a snack. Make yourself comfortable."

He put down his glass, then ignited the flame on the barbecue. "I'll be right back." For a moment he looked at her, appreciating the way she enjoyed the evening. Shaking his head, he went back inside to grab the vegetable-and-dip plate.

When he returned, Hope faced him, propping an elbow on the railing. "I just realized you set two tables."

"I wasn't sure whether you preferred to dine inside or out."

"You think of everything."

"I wish I could take credit for it. It was all Sienna."

"Everything is perfect." Hope walked across the patio to select a carrot that she dipped into the dressing. "You'll have to tell her she did a nice job with the flowers."

Stupidly relieved, he grinned. "Those were my doing."

"*Yours?* Even the tulips?"

He couldn't tell whether or not approval laced her tone. His answer was cautious. "Yes."

"They're my favorite." She took a bite of the carrot before putting it down and narrowing her eyes. "Did you ask Skyler?"

"I promise. No." He held up a hand as if under oath. "The color and the stripes of red reminded me of your ass."

And now, with the way she blushed, her cheeks.

"They're beautiful. And thank you for thinking

of Skyler too."

"Anyone who worked that hard for me to reject the candidates deserves more than a bouquet."

"We ended up giving one of the arrangements to a doctor's office. And Tony is allergic to something, so Skyler and I had to run ours home. Then Skyler went to the drugstore for antihistamines. While we were away, he ate all the doughnuts I'd taken in, and that caused some tension in the office."

He winced.

"It also turns out the Colonel likes the baby's breath. In the time that I made a couple of phone calls, she pulled them and dragged them all over the apartment. Kitchen. Laundry room. Bedroom. Under the couch."

He winced. "Sorry."

"Will you please stop sending flowers?"

"Certainly. I don't want to distress your employees."

"Thank you."

"I'll send you sex toys instead."

Her hand trembled, and champagne splashed in the glass. "That's a joke, right?"

"Would you prefer them delivered to your home or your office?"

"I can't tell whether or not you're serious."

"The grill's ready." Whistling, he left her to put the steaks on. "Do you mind grabbing the baked potatoes from the oven? There's an oven mitt on the counter and a platter to put them on."

"Rafe... I mean it. No gifts."

"Vibrating panties are my favorite."

She fingered one of her pearls. Did she have any idea how perfect a response that was?

He flipped up the lid on the barbecue grill. "We have butter and sour cream in the refrigerator. Will you get those as well? Assuming you want to dine al fresco. If not, you can put them on the dining room table."

"Outside is fine." But she didn't move.

"How would you like your steak?"

After a few seconds, she pursed her lips. "Medium."

"Baked potatoes," he prompted.

"You're impossible." She put down her champagne, then strode from the patio, her heels thumping the tile in a way that made him think of heart-pounding sex.

Yeah. He definitely enjoyed her company. The thought made him wonder where the line between chemistry and compatibility was drawn.

Over dinner on the patio, he kept the conversation light, asking about her day.

"I got a contract from the gentleman I met with earlier this week."

He offered a toast with his glass.

"Thanks." She did a little shimmy on her chair. "It doesn't get old. I still get the same kind of rush that I did when I signed my first agreement. Skyler's already planning the mixer for next week."

"I'm curious how you became a matchmaker."

"You mean other than wanting to stick my nose

in other people's business?"

"Ouch." He winced at her thrust. She had a good memory. "That round goes to you."

She leaned toward him. "I didn't know you were keeping track."

"I'm competitive," he conceded.

"Now I'm curious. What's the score?"

"Three to one."

"I've got to know who's ahead."

"As you can see, it's rather close."

She laughed. "That has to mean I'm ahead. Otherwise you'd be gloating."

Her enthusiasm lit something inside him that he hadn't realized was dormant. "It pains me to admit you're winning."

"I'm so celebrating my victory!" She raised her glass high, cheering for herself.

"No one likes a sore winner."

"Of course they do. Everyone enjoys watching the underdog emerge victorious. See?" She shook her shoulders, and he shook his head.

"You're rubbing it in."

"Why keep score if you're not going to high-five or eat a chocolate doughnut when you win?"

"The game isn't over."

She gave a fake shudder, then grinned, despite the growled warning woven through his words. "I'm feeling pretty confident in my abilities, Mr. Sterling."

"I hope that saves you, Ms. Malloy..." Because he couldn't help himself, he pushed back his chair, stood, then cupped her elbow and guided her up.

"What are you going to do?" she asked with a mock-scandalized tone while she clutched at her pearls.

More and more, he was falling for her. "I do believe I'm going to kiss you."

"What will the neighbors say?" But she didn't check whether anyone could, indeed, see them.

"I think they will say I'm one lucky bastard." He pulled her onto her tiptoes. Rafe started the kiss with as much tenderness as he was capable of.

Within seconds, her response ignited his fire.

He forced her mouth apart, tasted the sweetness of wine on her tongue and the tang of her complete surrender. Like a pirate, he plundered deep, leaving no part of her unexplored. With a tiny shudder, she wrapped her arms around his neck, letting him support her. In this way, and many others, he wanted to do just that.

Rafe made love to her mouth. As she opened wider, he mimicked penetration, letting her know that she might win the battles, but he intended to win her.

He kissed her until neither could breathe and she became his world. "That will have to hold you until later," he said against her ear when he ended the kiss.

"I like the way you share my celebration." Her voice was dreamy, lazy.

That was not what he'd been doing at all. Rather, he'd been planning the next assault in his battle plan.

"You're pretty good at that." She ran a finger

across her lips after he released her.

"Pretty good?" He frowned. "I'm happy to practice until I rock your world."

"I suppose that's okay." She sat and fanned herself with her napkin. "Yeah, pretty good."

He wondered if she had any idea that with every passing moment, she stood less and less chance of escaping him. "Let me get dessert."

"Dessert?" Her eyebrows lifted.

"Coffee and chocolate cake. With sweet whipped cream. I'm told it goes with the cake."

"Absolutely. Cake. Whatever else could it be for?"

"Right." He imagined her gorgeous nipples slathered in the sweet stuff.

"Maybe I could stay a little longer," she teased.

"Temptation is difficult to resist." He returned her grin. "Sit tight." Rafe was anxious to get on with the evening. He began gathering the plates.

"Can I help?"

"No. You should enjoy your wine and the evening."

"But—"

"Keep arguing. And you can sit out here with a sore bottom, which may make it more difficult to relax."

"In that case, I think I'll finish the rest of my champagne." Then, with great deliberation, she added, "Sir."

Fuck. Between the kiss and the honorific, his cock was hard and throbbing. For him, tonight, everything was about Hope.

When he returned with coffee, her head was resting on the back of the chair. "I go to events almost every evening." She sat up. "When I am home, I feel the need to work or plan, even when I'm eating. So this is a real treat. You're spoiling me."

"I'm glad." He went back inside for the dessert. "Cake?" he offered, sliding a piece in front of her.

"Yum. Yes." She stuck in a fork. "I think I'm going to need some exercise later."

"I can arrange for something." He enjoyed watching her savor every bite.

"God. This is exquisite."

"I'll tell Sienna you said so."

"Is she taking new clients?"

"No. She works for me and my future wife."

"That was mean. How am I supposed to refuse you if you keep sweetening the deal?"

This time, he was the one with the triumphant grin. "I told you I intend to be the victor."

"The rules should be fair. Equitable. You know, giving both sides a chance. The side with the chocolate cake has a decided advantage."

"That sounds like extreme trickery."

"It does, doesn't it?"

Over coffee, he told her stories about his life that he'd kept secret. If she was going to marry him, she deserved to know the sordid details, or more of them than she'd already gleaned. He talked about his sister's two divorces, and how the second one had devastated her to the point that she refused to leave her apartment for over a week. He and their mother had finally gone to her place, made her shower and get dressed. They took her to lunch, and while they were gone, Sienna and a small crew had moved into action, cleaning the place, catching up the laundry, stocking the kitchen. Even though Rafe's back teeth had ached from grinding them to escape the mind-numbing boredom, they'd gone to the aquarium. He'd drawn the line at riding the Ferris wheel.

"I've always wanted to ride it at night. I think it would be a beautiful way to see the city."

"With the right company, I might find myself much more agreeable. Especially if we snuck on a flask of our favorite libation." He considered her. "And maybe a rose or two."

She gave a delightful shudder before taking a sip of her coffee. "Are interventions common in your family?"

"When my dad started pulling away, the three of us drew closer."

"Why else would you go to the aquarium?"

"Or not throw the lot of you out of my office when you show up uninvited at dawn?"

"If I remember, you did exactly that." She pushed her plate away, and they spent a few minutes chatting before clearing the dessert dishes and straightening the kitchen.

With a quick giggle, she swiped some bubbles across his nose, and that led to a slow, deep kiss. Once again, he wondered why he'd fought against a relationship for so long.

"Would you like to sit inside or out?"

"I like it out here," she admitted. "But I'm a little chilled."

He lit the outdoor heater, then arranged two of the oversize chairs near it. Then he went into his closet to fetch her one of his long-sleeved shirts. When he returned to the patio, she was curled in one of the chairs. Her shoes were crossed on the tile in a haphazard pile. He tucked the shirt around her.

Nature treated them to a cloudless night, allowing them to see twinkling stars.

He leaned forward and propped his elbows on his knees. "I'm still hoping you'll go to Louisiana with me tomorrow."

"I haven't decided." She twisted her fingers together. "I did speak with Sara, the woman you scened with."

"She must not have said anything awful."

"No. You know she didn't." She stood and paced, drawing his shirt tighter around her. "The idea of going any further with you scares me."

He wanted to go to her, reassure her. Instead, he remained where he was, giving her the freedom to sort through her doubts.

Barefoot, she returned to stand beneath the heater, keeping her distance. "I've told you about my mom, how she wasn't able to move on after my dad's death." Though he remained silent, she went on. "I don't want to be like that. I can't be obsessed about a man, that vulnerable."

"The third C is as important as the others. I will

be committed to you. I'm not like my father. If you walk down that aisle to me, you will always have my fidelity. You will be my honored, treasured wife. You will never give more than you receive in return."

She gripped her shoulders. "And the BDSM thing... I'll find out more about that this weekend?"

"That is my intention. Yes."

"Parts of it scares the hell out of me."

"Let me throw a fourth C your direction. Communication. You will always have a safe word. We will discuss everything. If something is off-limits, it's off-limits."

"You said you like to show off your subs."

The pitch of her voice had risen a bit, so Rafe sat back and propped one knee on the opposing ankle, trying to put her at ease.

"Is that negotiable?"

"Everything is. I'd want to know what made you uncomfortable. Perhaps you had conditions that would make it tolerable for you." She'd been scandalized at the Bluewater Grill when he asked her to run the rose's dangerous stem across her bared skin, but she'd done it. And there'd been a flush of excitement on her cheeks. "If you don't want to scene in a club, that's fine. We can confine our activities to private spaces. I'd invite you to visit the Retreat, or my other club, the Quarter in New Orleans. If you said no, I'd ask if it was okay for me to still attend, and we could negotiate the terms of that as well, understanding that your views might change or evolve over time."

She scowled, and an intriguing note of possession crept into her voice as she said, "I wouldn't want you playing with other women."

"Understood."

"That doesn't mean you agree."

"Perhaps you'd like to watch a demonstration live so that you have more information to judge your request?"

"If we...if we were to move forward, you would never put your hands on anyone else."

So his sweet Hope had claws. Her responses were more those of a woman who was considering a relationship than one who was thinking about it in abstract terms. "There's only you, Hope."

She exhaled. Until her shoulders rolled forward, he hadn't realized she'd been holding her breath, revealing how much his answer mattered. She'd revealed a vulnerability she'd been trying to hide. In that moment he vowed to always make her certain she was secure with him. "Come here," he invited, keeping command out of his voice. This had nothing to do with her being a sub, and everything to do with caring for the emotions of the woman he hoped to marry.

"Your chair is too small for both of us."

"That's what makes it perfect."

Still, she hesitated, even when he extended his hand.

Finally, after a long sigh, she erased the distance between them, demonstrating her trust. Rafe took it from there.

He uncrossed his legs and eased her onto his lap, pulling her against him, tucking in the borrowed shirt, cradling her body.

At first, she kept her body rigid. Though tempted to rush her, he didn't. Over the space of several heartbeats, she allowed herself to relax against him. He drew in her signature lilac scent. Then he sensed something else in her. Wistfulness, perhaps? The unfurling of trust? A slight breeze ruffled her hair, and he stroked it back. "Sweet Hope. Nothing will be more important to me than you, than the success of our relationship. Not ever. I want you as my sub. Has there been anything you hated so far?"

"Other than Tony's allergy attack?"

"Fair enough." He grinned, and her lips twitched in response.

After a minute, she inhaled before admitting, "I can't stop thinking about the things we've done, how naughty some of them were, and how much I wanted more."

More? His new favorite word. "Even the denied orgasms?"

"Those are the worst. So frustrating, so annoying. I've never crawled out of my skin, needing to come before. Which is your point, I think."

"Driving you wild is my point."

"It worked. When I did orgasm... God, Rafe, part of me can't believe I'm telling you this. No one has asked me to have a frank discussion about sex. I've just...done it, you know?"

"I do." Arrogant pride filled him. He wanted to be the one to open the world to her, change her. "When you did orgasm?" He wanted her to be comfortable discussing everything with him.

"It was powerful. So much so that one of them hurt."

At her confession, his cock responded, and Dominant urges flared. "So as much as you hated it, you want to continue with them?"

"Yes."

She was more than he'd dared dream. "And the acts of service you've performed for me?" Having her remove his cufflinks, assisting him as he dressed or undressed, soothed the savage inside him.

"To be honest, my first reaction was to tell you to do it yourself, that I'm not a servant or maid."

There were words she'd left unsaid, and he was curious. "You did it, though."

"It hadn't been on my limits list. Since I didn't have a good reason to say no, I thought I'd give it a try." She pursed her lips.

At some point in the future, he hoped she wouldn't hesitate out of a misplaced sense of embarrassment. He wanted the unvarnished truth.

"It wasn't as uncomfortable as I'd expected it to be. Part of me liked touching you, pleasing you. It made me happy. This might sound strange, but it was personal."

"Intimate."

She nodded, and he gave her time to formulate the rest of her response. "I realized it might be part of the scene, the whole submission thing, but it is so much more than that, deeper. I mean… People who care about each other do things for them. Like…okay, this is a strange example. But Skyler brought me a latte on Monday because she guessed I'd been up late on Sunday and had to get up early to prepare for our meeting."

"Ambush," he corrected.

"Ambush? Is that how you saw it?"

He shuddered anew. "A veritable army in high heels and pearls. Terrifying."

She smiled. "And here I thought you were braver than that."

"You're kidding, right? Have you ever gone against three powerful women determined to have their way?"

She shifted in his lap until she found a position she liked, one that left him decidedly uncomfortable.

"Anyway, sometimes on a Friday when we don't have events, I send Skyler home early. And I buy her and Tony lunch from time to time. I enjoy making them happy. It's not about them being my employees. It's about appreciation."

"Excellent example."

"And with you… There's a reciprocity that I haven't experienced with anyone else. You didn't have to drive me to work the other morning. We could have eaten dinner out. The flowers… My point is, in a lot of relationships, people do nice things for each other all the time. My mother told me that my dad always kept the gas tank on her car filled when he wasn't deployed. Little things. What I did for you? I liked it."

"You have my utmost appreciation."

"So how would you like to show me?"

A match flared inside him. This was the first time she'd ever initiated anything physical between them. He hadn't been planning to fuck her tonight. Or tie her up. It had been about making her comfortable, revealing parts of his personality that he'd kept hidden—maybe even from himself. That he was capable of the tenderness he wanted to show her stunned him.

"I'd like to be more comfortable together. I want to know what you'll expect from me if you're going to show me off in Louisiana. And…"

"And?"

"I'm horny," she murmured against his chest.

"No hiding." He moved her back and captured her chin.

"This is outside my comfort zone."

"Sweet Hope, I intend to destroy it. We can start by going inside. At the bottom of the stairs, you will remove your clothes and leave them near your purse. Then you are to go upstairs, find the butterfly and a blindfold. Place the vibrator against your clit, and I mean that. Touching it. Turn it on to the pulse setting. I'll expect to find you wearing a blindfold and spread-eagle on the bedspread, faceup. Do not move from that position. Pretend you are tied to the bedframe. And do not come."

"Uhm…" Her breaths came in short pants. "For

how long?"

"Until given further instructions."

"That's not—"

"Arguing is not in your best interests, Hope." He helped her to stand. She stopped to gather her shoes. "Leave them. I'll get them later."

"Yes, Rafe."

He was enjoying those words almost as much as he was hearing the term, "You have a deal."

At the bottom of the stairs, she shrugged out of his shirt, then drew her dress over her head. He took it and hung it from the newel post. This time she didn't hesitate as long before removing her clothing.

Hope stood in front of him in a matching bra and panty set, all black and wisps of lace. *She dressed for me.* Possession rocketed through him. "Tell me about the pearls." Unable to stop himself, he touched one, finding it warm from her skin. "They look like a choker."

"You mentioned collars." She dropped her gaze briefly. "I was imagining what it might be like."

He very much approved. "And what do you think?"

"I'm torn between the weight of the commitment and how sexy it might be."

"Could it be both? If I were to put a collar on you, it would tell you, me, and the world that you were mine. You'd receive all the benefits of that, including my protection." Which she had, no matter what. "In return, you would have obligations."

"Such as?"

"Not allowing other men to touch you without my permission."

"I don't want to ever be shared."

Such a sweet admission. "Good. We are in agreement." He smiled. "Now your bra and panties."

Obediently she removed her bra and handed it to him. Then she stepped out of her underwear.

Her lingerie, he placed near her purse. "Go on up." When she neared the top, he said, "Stop."

She paused to look back at him.

"When I'm showing you off, I want everyone to see how proud I am of you, how much confidence you have as a business owner, a woman, my sub. I see all of you, Hope. So much admiration for you. Now pull back your shoulders. As if you're a princess, continue on. Unclench your buttocks. Own all the parts of who you are."

"Sure," she said. "That's easy enough."

"Don't dare disobey me."

She gave a ragged exhalation, half sigh, half resignation, part determination.

You're a fucking gem, Hope.

Following his instructions without further argument, she placed her fingertips on the banister and climbed the next step, then another.

"Oh, Hope?"

She paused again. This time she raised her eyebrows when she faced him. "Yes?"

"With the other toys, you'll find a pair of leather gloves. I expect you to place them on the nightstand."

"Okay." Then she spoke again. "Yes, Rafe."

He gave her one last warning before sending her on her way. "Be careful with them."

CHAPTER TWELVE

A princess? No way did that moniker fit her. But as Hope reached the second floor, her spine was still straight, and she hadn't been squeezing her ass. Following his advice had made her much more confident, in a way not much different than acting confident had boosted her business success when she first started out

His bedroom seemed a little more intimidating without him in it, as if she were encroaching on his private retreat. Sounds of him moving around downstairs reached her. Not knowing how much time she had and nervous that he'd catch her not being obedient, she hurried into his closet.

Unaccountably, her hands were shaking as she pulled out the vibrator, then the oversize blindfold and the gloves. Except for a snap at the wrist, they appeared to be ordinary driving gloves. As she carried the load to the bedroom, one of the gloves fell to the floor. She bent to grab it, and something sharp stabbed her. "Ow. Damn it." Out of instinct, she studied her palm. There was no scratch, and she picked up the glove. When it poked her again, she turned it over. Blood drained from her face. The glove was studded with pointed metal spikes. *Oh God, no.* There was no way she could tolerate that kind of pain.

Mouth dry, she continued to the bedroom. No matter how hard she tried to keep her focus, her gaze continued to stray to the metal spikes.

Downstairs, Rafe turned on classical music, soothing and seductive. But it also disguised what he was doing and would make it impossible for her to discern his footfall on the stairs. A sense of urgency drove her onward.

She laid the gloves on the nightstand, the spikes facing one another so she didn't have to see them. Then she placed the butterfly. Surely its fluttering couldn't be as bad as she remembered. But since she was so aroused, the barest brush of the silicone against her clit made her jerk.

Making her way into the middle of the bed, she dropped the remote control near her hand before picking up the blindfold. The soft black satin was lined with a thin strip of something pliable that snugged her face, making it impossible to peek.

Hope slid the lever on the remote control. The vibrator leaped to life, making her yelp. She frantically fought to turn it to pulse, and when the pressure let off, she heaved a sigh.

Once she'd settled down, she moved her body into the position he'd ordered. That made the vibrator move a bit, and it was more irritating now. Not knowing how much time she had or whether he was inside the room watching her, she forced herself to endure the sensual assault he'd dreamed up.

The thing pulsed, enough to get her attention. Then it faded away. It stayed off long enough for her mind to drift. Then it gave another quick jolt.

Hope moved her hips, seeking more, wanting it to last longer. Her legs ached from the fight to keep them apart rather than draw them together in an attempt to find some relief for the sensations crashing through her.

Her earlier guess had been wrong. The butterfly wasn't as bad as she remembered. It was worse.

She had no idea how long he left her in position, but as the minutes passed, she started to twitch, then gyrate her hips, lifting them, trying to satiate herself every bit as much as she was trying to escape. The music faded, and the darkness of the blindfold was her companion. Nothing existed but her and the damnable sex toy.

Hope whimpered. There was no way this thing had the power to create such a harsh reaction in her. It was the most awful thing she'd ever endured.

"Beautiful."

At the sound of Rafe's voice, she froze. It sounded as if he stood at the foot of the bed, where he would have a view of her exposed, raised pussy. She should have been aware of a shift in the room when he entered, should have known from his scent that he was there. The haunting music, coupled with the fact that she couldn't see, left her trapped in a world where nothing existed but the next dreaded pulse against her pussy.

Rafe was driving her mad.

The thing vibrated again, and she cried out.

"Awful, isn't it?"

Imagining how she must look to him, she lowered her buttocks to the mattress, then writhed when the butterfly pulsed once more.

"Would you like it faster?" he asked. "Like a hum? Or at full speed?"

"No! Please, Rafe. *No.*"

"You've done an excellent job of keeping yourself in position. Thank you. Since the next part will be much more difficult, I'm going to tie you so that you remain still."

He removed her blindfold. "I want to see you suffer."

A chill—fear, dread, desire—lanced her. She flashed back to that first day in his office. *"Her tears are like dripping nectar from the gods."* Hope had talked to other submissives about sadism. There were various interpretations of the word. Rafe wasn't a strict sadist, in that he didn't seek to hurt her, but there was no doubt that he experienced joy when she was like this, overwrought with need.

"You have a safe word that I will always honor."

She nodded.

"And a slow word. You remember them both?"

Her mouth dried, leaving her unable to speak, so she nodded.

Rafe's eyes were a softer shade of blue than she'd ever seen, and he'd cloaked himself fully in his role as a Dominant. With his words and expressions, he didn't ask for her trust — he guaranteed it.

He notched the slider bar up a fraction, giving her more frequent pulses but with no more intensity.

"Ankles first," he said.

He'd placed four long straps on the bed, the black a startling contrast to the snow-white duvet cover. Rafe caught her right ankle just as her pussy was jolted, making her freeze. She whimpered.

In short order, he cuffed her, attached the metal clasp to one of the strips of leather, then affixed it to the frame of the bed.

Each time the vibrator moved, he nodded in satisfaction. He was a master at what he was doing. The sensation never lasted long enough for her to get off. Instead, it frustrated her. Ignoring her small cries, he secured her other ankle in place.

Then he tugged the vibrator back a couple of inches.

She sighed as relief shot through her. "Thank you, Rafe."

"Don't thank me. I'm making sure the fit is

correct." He dampened his first finger and teased her clit with it.

Since she was so sensitized, the pressure made her yelp. "Oh!"

"You must have done a nice job in placing it. Your clit is so red and swollen." He replaced his finger with the jumping little bit of silicone. Then he adjusted the straps around her thighs and waist so that the annoying vibrator snugged against her privates. "Your wrists next."

When he was finished attaching her in place, his straps had forced her into a position so much wider, much more vulnerable. Being stretched so far was uncomfortable, but just the right side of tolerable.

"Better," he said with approval.

Frightened, she stared as he pulled on the gloves. Hope tugged a little against her restraints, but she was held firm.

"You won't hate this." He trailed the tiny spikes over her right foot.

It didn't hurt. Instead, the sensation was light, more than a tickle, which she would have hated, but less than a prick. When he pressed against the arch of her foot, awareness rocked through her.

He moved on to her other foot and repeated the process. "What do you think of the vampire's bite, sweet Hope? Will you bring the gloves to me when I let you choose the toys for a scene?"

She pulled and twisted, liking what he was doing to her.

Next, he drew the spikes up the outsides of her

thighs. The metal didn't even leave a scratch. When he moved between her thighs, her breath caught. He used more pressure, digging in to her flesh a little. Rather than being in pain, she was turned on. She shook her legs, trying to get a more contact with the vibrator. Of course she couldn't.

He pressed a palm against her cunt. Wide-eyed, she held her breath.

"How hard do you want it?"

Her heart raced.

"Tell me."

She swallowed. "More."

He squeezed her pussy, then released it before she could even ask. Flames burst through her.

"Pain and pleasure. Same side of the coin, aren't they? Not opposites, but the same?"

She nodded.

He grabbed her again, digging in more, knocking the vibrator to one side, catching the inside of one of her labia. She screamed, so damn close to coming.

"You have permission to orgasm at any time." He moved the silicone so that it once again pressed against her clit.

She lifted her head to watch him, and tears overwhelmed her. He formed a fist and used the smooth side of the leather to turn up the vibrator speed, then pulled back her pussy lips with the spikes and held her apart while the vibrator ravished her.

"Cry, Hope. Spill those beautiful tears."

Hope sobbed. Unrelenting, he turned up the device to high.

The orgasm grabbed her womb, and she screamed as she spiraled. Over and over she came, crying, shaking, her body and mind consumed by him.

When it was finally over, he turned off the vibrator and she gasped, dropping her head back onto the pillow. She couldn't imagine a life where she didn't have the opportunity to experience this.

"You are so fucking amazing. So sweet. So trusting." Pulling off the gloves, he kissed away her tears.

Shattered, she sighed. She was certain it was over, but he said, "I'm not done with you."

"I can't take much more."

"No? Safe word?"

She was too curious for that. He picked up something from the nightstand. How had she missed the whipped cream?

"Well?"

Even though she might rue her words, she said, "Do your worst."

He chuckled and dabbed a bit on the end of her nose, just enough to drive her vision bonkers. Then he topped her nipples with small artistic swirls before licking and nibbling off the sweet cream.

Instead of letting her come, he released each of her bonds and took a few seconds to rub feeling back into her limbs before stripping and putting on a condom. "I need to be inside you."

"I need it too."

He maneuvered them both until she was atop him. His cock slid into her hot cunt, and when she was astride him, she winced.

"You okay?"

She wouldn't change anything, even if she could. She liked it all. Realizing he was waiting for her answer, she said, "Yes, Rafe."

He held her hips to control how fast she rode him. That was fine for a few minutes, but soon, restlessness gnawed at her. "Please?"

Rafe tightened his grip. "Arch your back so I can see your beautiful breasts better."

"Yes." The moment she complied, he moved her faster, pounding her deep, feeding a part of her psyche that she hadn't known was hungry. Rafe seemed to know what she needed, and he gave it to her.

Hope cried out her happiness. And in that moment, she knew she was going to Louisiana with him. She was going to swallow her reservations, her fears, and do what everyone had suggested—go and make her own decisions, even if the biggest cost was her heart.

Rafe's glance across the car's passenger compartment warmed Hope's insides. It was part promise, part invitation, and all sexy, underlying threat. She stared out the side window at the passing scenery, needing something to distract her so she could breathe again.

Everything about this trip had been surreal. From the moment she agreed to come, she'd been swept up in the whirlwind that was Rafe Sterling.

Tony had volunteered to go with Skyler to the fundraising event. Caroline had caved and agreed to watch the Colonel when Rafe offered a spa day. Rafe had made his all-out assault on Hope all the more lethal when he arrived to pick her up. The Colonel, after a few seconds of making a sound more like a growl than a hiss, had wound herself in a figure eight around his ankles. He'd crouched to give her a gift. A catnip toy.

Who the hell bought the devil's-spawn Somali a peace offering?

Then he'd topped it off by ordering his company's airplane to be stocked with the champagne Hope loved.

Although he worked during most of the flight, she'd sat back in the butterscotch-colored leather seat and sipped a couple of glasses of bubbly. From time to time, she'd taken in the view and watched the big fluffy clouds.

For a moment she'd considered that maybe, just maybe, if forced, she could get accustomed to housekeepers and jet-setting.

The drive from the airport to the Titans' estate was taking far longer than she'd anticipated. She supposed the distance gave the society a measure of privacy.

"Almost there," he said, turning onto a road that

was lined with the lushness of spring.

Magnolia trees bore blossoms as big as dinner plates. Native vegetation was a bright, verdant green. The pavement meandered, appearing to lead to nowhere, inviting people to turn back. No doubt that was on purpose.

A few miles later, a right-hand turn led to a much narrower road. There were no signs, and the vegetation was thicker, more swamplike.

After several minutes, they arrived at a sturdy metal gate with no name on it. A call box stood off to the side. Rafe opened an app in his phone and placed some sort of picture against a screen on the stand.

"High tech," she said.

"Biometrics at the next one."

He wasn't kidding.

They entered the grounds. "Is that sugar cane?"

He nodded. "Since the costs of sustaining the compound are significant, we grow sugar and pecans as cash crops."

They continued on until they reached an enormous arch that contained spiked wrought-iron gates adorned with the Zeta Society crest.

"Afternoon, Mr. Sterling." A disembodied voice greeted them.

Rafe turned his head, and light beams danced outside the car. Measuring his face?

"You're cleared through to the Grand House, sir."

"Thank you, Fitzgerald."

The gates swung inward and he accelerated

through the opening. "We'll need to get you a guest pass while we're here."

"Do I need to do all that fancy stuff?"

"No." He grinned. "That's for members. Without me, you wouldn't have gotten this far. You'll need to get a microchip implanted."

Her jaw dropped.

"That was a joke."

"Mean." She glared at him. "I didn't realize you had an evil streak."

"Yes, Ms. Malloy. I do believe we'd already settled that." The lazy reminder in his tone sent flares up and down her spine.

The road ahead was canopied by dozens and dozens of Southern live oak trees, blocking the sun and sky, making it dark. Judging by their size, they had to be hundreds of years old. It created privacy and mystique, a separation from her ordinary world.

The asphalt twisted and turned, and not long after they emerged into the cloudless daylight, a magnificent plantation home stood in the distance. "Oh my God."

"It's spectacular, isn't it?"

The white home was a mansion, with contrasting black shutters, a porch across the front with tall white rocking chairs. The second-floor gallery was adorned with black wrought-iron railing. The home appeared to have wings on each side. The most breathtaking feature, though, were the ten Grecian-style columns, complete with curlicues at the top of each. "Easy to see why it's called the

Parthenon."

"The plantation was once called One Hundred Oaks. The original owner was Ian, a second-generation British gentleman. He spared no expense with the architecture. Construction took over eight years because his wife, Julie, continually asked for changes from the architect. Her husband wanted a happy wife, so he indulged her every whim."

"Smart man."

He grinned in response. "Agreed. I think history has proven her intuition correct. The home is timeless. She had many innovations in the house. After Mr. and Mrs. Kirby passed, none of their children had an interest in the property, so they sold it off. Forty or fifty years later, it changed hands again. When the owner could no longer afford the upkeep, the Zetas purchased the house and lands. Descendants of members who contributed more than ten thousand dollars now pay substantially reduced dues."

"When was that?"

"Around eighteen seventy."

That was a lot of money back then. "So, your great-great-however-many-greats-grandfather voted to save One Hundred Oaks?"

"And contributed around fifty thousand dollars, yes. My family has always had an interest in preservation."

The grounds in front of the house were perfectly manicured. The lawn was bright green and larger than any she'd ever seen. To one side was an arched trellis covered with bougainvillea. The center of the lawn was dominated by a seven-tier water fountain and an attached oblong reflecting pond. A white-painted swing hung from a branch of a live oak. "It's postcard perfect." She reached for her cell phone. "Do you mind stopping so I can take a picture?"

"I'm afraid that's not permitted."

"Are you serious?" Was that his rule? Or a Titans rule?

"We're a secret society, remember?" His voice held traces of humor, mixed with a droll obviousness.

"Oh." The reminder left her feeling a bit foolish. In the article she'd read, the descriptions of the house had been vague, and the accompanying picture, perhaps from a drone, showed the flat roof and not much else. She dropped her phone back into her purse.

Rafe pulled to a stop beneath the porte cochère attached to the side of the house.

Valets in crisp white shirts, black bow ties, and black slacks opened the car doors, and the gentleman on Rafe's side greeted him. "Welcome back, Mr. Sterling. May we take your car and luggage?"

He thanked the man before coming around the hood of the vehicle to claim her elbow. "After we get your pass, we'll settle in. I think I'll take Ms. Malloy through the front door. We'll see ourselves in."

"Excellent, sir," the valet responded, and he keyed a microphone attached to his shirt front.

"You'll see why," Rafe told her. He guided her

up the outside steps and around the corner.

Heat and humidity clung to her, making her glad she'd taken Rafe's suggestion to wear a sleeveless dress. Though it shouldn't be possible, the air hung heavier than it had in Houston. She associated this kind of oppressiveness with midsummer rather than spring, and she wished for an old-fashioned fan to wave in front of her face.

There were two enormous, polished-wood front doors, one with a large brass knocker shaped like a magnolia blossom.

He opened one door for her, and about three feet beyond was a second set.

"Typical of these houses" — Rafe explained — "to protect against storms. The floor is original. Imported from Italy, I'm told. The Kirbys enjoyed traveling and bringing back treasures with them."

The tiny tiles were well-worn, making her marvel at the history.

Rafe pulled the door shut behind him, but instead of continuing into the house, he backed her against one of the walls. In the dark, small space, her breath shortened. This was the Rafe she expected and knew. The one who terrified her. The one who thrilled her enough to take unimaginable risks.

"I'll welcome you properly at our cottage. But this will have to hold you." When he was like this, all Dominant and determined, it spiked a potent headiness inside her, spiking her pheromones.

He kissed her.

Not that what he did could be described as a

kiss.

He took and consumed, hot and determined, thrusting his tongue into her mouth, not coaxing, but demanding her submission.

She offered it, not that she had a choice, not that she'd ever had a real choice since he walked into her office to teach her about sadism. In a relationship, Hope was beta to his alpha.

He fucked her mouth with his tongue, rocking her so hard that it took all her concentration to hold on to the handle of her purse.

When he pulled away, there was both promise and threat in his expression. She had a vague sense of disappointment that it had ended so fast.

"Shall we?"

Before she nodded, she needed a moment to take a deep breath. She didn't want to walk in disheveled, like a woman who'd been ravaged in the entryway.

He tucked in hair he'd dislodged. "Oh, sweet, sweet Hope. Soon. Fucking soon."

Once she was in control again, or as much as she could be, she nodded. He opened the door and she took a step inside, then stopped to stare at the opulence. "Oh my God. This was all Julie's design?"

"All of it. I understand the architect took a year off after finishing this. Widely regarded as his finest work, however."

Inlaid parquet flooring appeared original and unblemished by the centuries. Instead of a single staircase, there were two, each leading to the second story. They flared out, curving away from each other.

Banisters were crafted from hand-hewn wood that gleamed in the light from the magnificent chandelier.

"The Julie staircase is what we call it. Lends itself to weddings and receptions, doesn't it?"

"It's fit for heads of state. Princes and princesses."

"The Kirbys entertained often. There were grand coming-out parties for their daughters, held in the ballroom. It has a conservatory where the band would set up. We grow plants in it still."

"I'm overwhelmed."

"I wanted you to see the entire grandeur, which was why I wanted you to come in the front door."

"And I thought it was because you wanted to kiss me."

"That might have been part of my plan." He grinned before pointing to the top of the staircases. "The balcony was also Julie's idea."

It protruded in a semicircle, reminding Hope a little of box seats at the theater.

"Rumor has it that Mrs. Kirby would stand there when someone came to the door. She could come down if she was interested in receiving the visitor. She had an art studio on the third floor, so it's possible, but I'd think she spent her waking hours in the main part of the house. Makes for a good story, however. I'm inclined to believe the family used it when they had soirees. Imagine looking down at your guests and having them aware of your presence."

"Like royalty."

"Indeed. We still use it for some formal occasions. The chairperson gets the place of honor."

Toward the back of the main entryway was a gorgeous bar with a large mirror hanging behind it. From the wavy texture and silvered glass, it might have been original to the house. Numerous shelves were stocked with premium liquors.

One of the tables was occupied. A man and woman stood near a wall, wearing suits, and if she wasn't mistaken, earpieces. Bodyguards? Or Secret Service? She didn't recognize the one person she could see, but he was seated with a person who appeared to be a woman, though she was shadowed by a huge potted hibiscus. Hope thought she recognized the long blonde hair, though.

Before Hope could ask, they were greeted by a man in a dark suit. "It's nice to see you again, Mr. Sterling."

The two shook hands before the man turned to her. "You must be Ms. Malloy. I'm Fitzgerald, head of security. Welcome to the Parthenon. I'm sure it was a long journey. May I have the bar fetch you something to drink?"

"Sparkling water with fresh lime for Ms. Malloy," Rafe responded for her, making Hope wish she'd snuck some of the bubbly from the plane. "Nothing for me."

The man signaled for a waitperson, placed the order, then invited them to join him at his antique desk.

After they were seated in comfortable velvet

chairs, he asked, "May I see your driver's license, please, Ms. Malloy?"

She dug it from her kitty purse, and he swiped the back of her identification through some sort of machine, then asked her to face his computer so he could take her picture.

In less than one minute, her drink arrived, just as he slid a piece of paper toward her. "These are our guest rules. Please read them and sign the bottom."

Rafe nodded for her to continue.

The expensive linen paper had a Zeta Society watermark, and it was titled *Decorum*. The page was aimed at protecting the privacy of guests and members. Picture taking was prohibited, except for rare occasions by a hired professional. Though ideas that were discussed at the annual gathering could be spoken about in general terms outside of the membership, names were not to be mentioned.

By the time Fitzgerald handed her a pen, she needed a drink of her water. Before she'd put down her glass, he presented her with a golden-colored identification badge.

"You're welcome to keep your guest pass in your purse or in a pocket, but please keep it on you at all times. You'll need it to access your cottage if Mr. Sterling is not with you. You're free to leave the compound at any time, but Mr. Sterling will need to be with you when you return. If that's not possible, we will call for him."

Rafe's name was on the top of the card. Hers was beneath it, and her picture filled the reverse side.

Hope wondered if she'd entered an alternate universe. In a way, she supposed she had. Rafe's. Until now she hadn't thought about the needs some people had for privacy. In current social-media-hungry society, stars and politicians were often photographed or asked for selfies anytime they were in public. She offered a silent thanks that she could pop down to her building's workout room or to a coffee shop or grocery store without makeup.

"As requested, you'll be in the Magnolia cottage. Everything was prepared to your specifications." Then he smiled at Hope. "If there's anything we can do to make your stay more comfortable, there's an in-room virtual assistant. Just tell it what you need. Or you're welcome to use the in-room telephone."

Rafe stood and held her chair for her. After the two men shook hands again, Rafe placed his fingers at the small of her back and led her toward the side door. He waved off the valet and took care of her himself.

The car had been kept beneath the porte cochère, and it was turned on with the air conditioner running. "This is like being at the best five-star hotel on the planet," she said when he was seated beside her.

He checked his mirrors. "The service staff was trained at Sterling."

Why was she not surprised?

"The security was trained by a firm that Celeste works with. Hawkeye."

He drove past several buildings.

"Are people allowed to stay in the Grand House?"

"The chairman and steering committee members, yes. And others as availability permits. We'll be in the cottage farthest away." He slid her a glance. "So no one can hear your screams.

CHAPTER THIRTEEN

Rafe lived for Hope's gasps, the sharp scent of fear mixed with the tang of anticipation. He didn't terrify her—he turned her on. More than ever, he was convinced she was the woman he needed, the wife he wanted.

This weekend meant a great deal to him. She would have the opportunity to meet some of his colleagues as well as understand more about him and his obligations to the Society. She'd experience what it would be like to live with him, see what being Mrs. Sterling might demand of her. Perhaps most importantly, they would each be exploring their roles as Dominant and submissive—tonight, in public. Rafe wasn't a fool. Whatever happened this weekend would define their future relationship.

"I can't believe how big this place is."

"We can go for a walk in the morning if you like. Or a golf cart tour if you didn't bring suitable shoes."

"Can I see where you have the sacrifices?"

He smiled. "That's a bit of a myth. Sorry to disappoint you. It's a bonfire." With an effigy, he allowed. "And yes. You can see where we host our annual gathering. A lot of the meetings during the event are informal, based on member interest. Some are held on porches or at the Grand House." He braked to a stop in front of their cottage, and he asked her to wait for him.

After exiting the vehicle, he rounded the hood to assist her out. "One day it will be more natural for you to yield to my wishes."

"Will it?" After a short hesitation, she accepted his extended hand.

The front porch had two gliding Adirondack chairs and a small table for drinks.

"Makes me want a mint julep," she admitted. "Even though I have no idea what one tastes like."

"Your wish is my command."

"Are you serious?"

"Would I lie about milady's beverage of choice?"

"This place may be a small slice of heaven."

"Wait until you see the inside." In front of the door, he waited for the biometric scanner to clear their entry. The lock snicked open and he lowered the handle.

The cottage was spacious, with flowers in a beautiful vase near the door. There was a living room, bedroom, an en suite bathroom, and a kitchenette.

Both the living room and bedroom had French doors leading to a hot tub and a dipping pool that wasn't large enough for swimming, but perfect for cooling off.

"Do we ever have to leave?"

While Hope's security check-in was in process, the hospitality crew had delivered their luggage and unpacked their clothes. A bottle of champagne chilled in an acrylic ice bucket, and two flutes stood off to the side. "I can pour you a glass, or we can order those juleps."

"That seems like a lot of trouble since this is already here."

"We'll have plenty of time for the sparkling later."

"You're spoiling me."

He grinned. All part of his overarching plan. After placing the order, he removed the fruit-and-cheese tray from the refrigerator, along with a platter filled with chocolates.

"Oh God. I am so tempted."

"Don't worry about the calories, Ms. Malloy. We'll be working them off."

"In that case…" She skipped the fruit and cheese and instead selected three chocolates for her small plate.

Rafe suggested they enjoy their courtyard, and

she changed into a bathing suit and covered it with a big fluffy robe she found hanging in the bedroom closet. Rafe opted to wear nothing under his.

Within ten minutes, a room service attendant arrived, wearing a bow tie and vest. Had they sent an actual bartender?

The man crossed to a sideboard and unpacked the insulated cooler. Two silver goblets were chilling on ice. With competency and showmanship, he muddled extra-fine sugar on top of mint leaves, releasing the strong aroma into the air.

"Please go easy on the bourbon in one of the drinks," Rafe requested.

"Yes, sir." When the man was almost done, he placed very short straws in each silver goblet so that the scent would fill the senses, garnished each with a perfect piece of mint, then offered the beverages on a tray.

Rafe picked up one and handed the chilled metal glass to her. She took a delicate sip. Her mouth opened, and she sputtered. "Wow!"

"Is that good or bad?" Damn, he adored how expressive her face was.

"Alcohol just kicked through my veins. And it's…" She took another sip. "I'm not sure how this works. It either cools you off or gets you so relaxed that you no longer care."

"Either way."

Hope toyed with her straw. "I get the appeal."

"I'll set up a second serving, Mr. Sterling. You'll just need to muddle the sugar"—the man held up individual bags and the long wooden pestle — "into the leaves. There's a container with shaved ice, along with two more goblets at the bottom of the cooler."

After the man excused himself, Rafe returned to her. "Shall we?"

In the privacy of their backyard, he invited her into the dipping pool. After she complained it was too cold, he tugged her in. She splashed him, and they played until they were worn out.

For a couple of hours, they enjoyed sunning, drinks, conversation, even dozing in the lounge chairs. He hoped she was realizing what he'd known all along — they were more than compatible.

After she woke up, he sent her to the shower, then joined her in the bathroom a few minutes later.

She shrieked when he opened the glass shower door. "Rafe!"

His adorable Hope made a futile attempt to cover herself. "Hiding your body from me is prohibited." There was no teasing in his voice when he said, "Lower your hands."

"I—" She broke off. "I was just about to get out."

"I'd like you to wash me."

When she stood there, saying nothing, clearly not knowing where to start, he picked up the bar of soap she'd just used and offered it to her. "Lady's choice," he said. "You can start with my back or my front."

She clutched the bar so hard that it slipped from her grip.

He could be heroic and pick it up. But a primal

beat urged him to stay there and watch her bend over. She licked her lower lip and his cock throbbed. As unheroic as it was, this arousal was linked to her touch of nerves.

She reached for the soap, and need walloped him, clobbering rational thought. He turned her, forcing her against the back of the shower, sending the bar skittering into the corner.

"I'm going to fuck you, Hope," he promised.

"Yes…" She whimpered.

"So hard you won't be able to think."

She made a tiny, desperate sound.

"Right now," he warned, giving her a single chance to refuse.

"I'm on the pill."

"I'm clean." And he knew how long she'd been without a lover.

She ground her ass against him.

"Needy little sub." He used his left palm to imprison her head against the tile. Rafe hadn't used her like this before, and her responsive moans drove him forward. Where was the Hope he'd met such a short time ago? "Spread your legs. Act like you want it."

"I do."

He guided his cock toward her hot cunt and stuffed himself inside her. She lifted onto her tiptoes to accept him, and he pulled her right arm behind her, against her back, using it as leverage as he impaled her.

"God. Rafe!"

He leaned forward to grab her earlobe with his teeth and give it a sharp bite. She gushed all over his dick, all but dragging an orgasm from him. *Goddamn.* He adored her passion.

Once her orgasm had receded, he kept his dick where it was, not letting her escape. "Put this hand on the wall." He released her arm and indicated where he wanted her, then he wedged his first finger in front of her face. "Wet it. Get it nice and wet."

Right away, she sucked his finger into her mouth.

"Wet, I said."

After a brief hesitation, she did.

"Better." He let go of her head. "Don't you dare move."

"You're scaring me."

"Use your safe word."

She shook her head.

Good girl. "So brave." And because he did have a slight amount of compassion, he made his finger wetter before pulling apart her buttocks and pressing it into her ass.

She whimpered.

"Take it."

Hope wriggled her ass, but since he used the movement to go deeper, he didn't chastise her. He kept her cheeks spread until he was seated all the way in her. "Now you can try to get away all you want."

"God! Too full! Rafe!"

He used his chest to trap her against the wall,

Sierra Cartwright

crushing her breasts flat. "Mine." Had he told her that before? He would, a dozen times, a thousand.

Rafe hammered his cock in her pussy while he finger-fucked her ass. He wasn't kind or gentle. He was a Dominant, exerting his will. She moaned, but her screams were muffled. "You can come if you have to. I prefer you wait. I want you throbbing for the rest of the night."

Her cunt clamped down on his cock. His words alone had brought her to orgasm? He rewarded her with a kiss to the side of her neck.

Steam billowed around them as he staked his claim. Knowing it would drive her to greater heights, he wedged a second finger into her ass.

"Argh!"

"You'll feel it burning all night when you're sitting."

She nodded her misery.

Rafe moved inside her, and pressure built inside him as the orgasm gathered force in his balls.

"Yes." The word was a plea, an offering of gratitude.

He went rigid, consumed with his need for her. Then with a final jerk, he released his hot ejaculate deep inside her welcoming body. For a stupid moment, he wished she wasn't on the pill. How would she look carrying his baby?

Because the thought needed to be banished, he shook his head. But the image didn't rush away. It lingered. *What damn kind of sorcery is this?* He'd never had sex without a condom, and the actual feel of her innermost flesh made him lose his mind.

Forcing himself to focus on her instead of the stunning images of her pregnant, he withdrew his fingers from her tightest hole.

She exhaled with a shuddering sigh.

"Stay there."

"Oh, there's nowhere I can go yet, Sir."

Sassy little Hope was getting so much better at this submission thing. There might have been irony in her statement, but the honorific had slid out of her mouth without hesitation. He was sure some deep part of her recognized this was right. But would the rest of her mind catch up?

He reached for the showerhead and detached it from its holder and cleaned both of them before sliding out his cock.

She allowed her head to fall back. While she relaxed, he moved the showerhead between her legs.

"Thank you," she said.

With complete fascination, he watched his cum combine with the warm water and drizzle down the inside of her thigh.

Even if she decided submission wasn't for her, he wouldn't let her go without one hell of a fight.

Nervous, Hope pulled on the hem of the black gown he'd given her. "It's going to get me arrested for indecent exposure."

"You look beautiful."

Approval laced his words, making her stop tugging.

"Come with me."

Reluctantly, she followed him into the bathroom. He placed his hands on her shoulders and guided her to stand in front of him near a mirror. The dress was made from a stretchy material and allowed no secrets. The front plunged into a sinful V. The back fell into a swoop at her hips. He'd permitted her no lingerie.

"What do you think?"

Everything about the garment was scandalous.

"Get past that part," he snapped with impatience as if reading her mind. "See it — and yourself — in a noncritical light."

She scowled. "You don't ask for anything easy." Hope appraised the whole package, focusing on the way the dress hugged her hips and revealed her cleavage. There was no doubt he'd chosen well on her behalf. Even though she was self-conscious, she had to admit the garment's fit flattered her. Did she have the courage to be seen in public, though? Let others feast on her features the way he did?

She kept her hands at her sides, resisting the urge to tug on the bottom or draw the fabric more fully across her breasts.

"That's better." He waited for her answer.

"It's..." So different from what she'd brought. She'd thought her cocktail dress was risqué, but compared to this, it was a nun's habit. Seeing approval in his gaze, she gave him an honest answer.

"I love it."

"I imagined it would be spectacular." He squeezed her shoulders. "It's better than that." She gave a tentative smile. Through her pounding heart, she admitted her fears. "Rafe, I'm not sure I have what it takes to wear it to dinner."

"No?" He eased the straps from her shoulders to cup her breasts in his large hands.

Transfixed, she watched him squeeze her nipples, rolling each between his thumb and forefinger. Her flesh responded as it always did to him. Her knees weakened, and she laid her head back on his chest.

"You may bring a wrap. But I wanted you to see the outfit as I've imagined."

She frowned.

"Stay there for a moment."

He left her like that, giving her no choice but to stare at her full breasts, her nipples peaked and swollen. She'd spent so much time protecting herself, she'd never thought of herself as a sensual being.

Rafe returned carrying something that she couldn't see.

He stood behind her once again and moved one of his hands in front of her chest. Her pulse slammed to a stop when she realized he held a collar. And nothing delicate. This was weighty, gold, and it had a padlock. "For tonight," he said. "I want the world to see you."

He'd said those words before, but now they held a shocking power.

"Wear my collar? It's not a lifelong commitment. You can consider it an experiment."

An experiment. For one night. A fantasy. Something she could replay forever, keep with her, even when she told him it couldn't work between them.

Scared to say yes, even more scared to say no, she nodded. Her heart started again with a leap.

"I need to hear the words."

It was a struggle, but she finally managed, "Yes, Sir."

Something dark flashed through his eyes. Relief? It couldn't be. Rafe Sterling had cloaked himself in confidence, the same way he wore a suit.

"Hold this." He placed the lock in her left hand.

Since her hair was already pinned up, she remained where she was. He reached around her. The snap clicked. Cold metal snuggled her skin, making her nipples swell even more.

"I fantasized about this."

She reached up to touch the collar, and her fingers found his.

He closed his hand around hers, warm and reassuring. "This is mine." He thumbed the collar. "And so is this." He traced the column of her throat. Then, keeping her gaze captive, he stroked down and circled beneath each of her breasts.

All her emotions softened.

"The lock, please."

She unfurled her fingers. From behind her, he reached across her body, the material of his suit coat dragging across her erect nipples.

He fastened the padlock through the collar with a *click* so sharp it bounced off the walls. Then he dropped the key on the counter. The metal bounced and clattered before settling.

In the first second after it slid to a stop, she felt trapped. In the next, she was liberated.

"Let me see you." He pinched her nipples viciously, making her yelp and shooting a torrent of wicked desire through her. He lifted the straps back into place. Her nipples were visible and sexy as hell as they pressed against the fabric. "Tell me what you think."

Now that the collar was in place, the dress was somehow less revealing. It was the gold, she realized, eye catching, drawing attention. "You were right."

"Those may be my three favorite words." He smiled. Then he turned her to face him. "This means a great deal to me."

It was easy to be brave when he was so encouraging.

Before they left the bathroom, she glanced at the key. "Are you leaving it there?"

"I'd prefer to, yes. But until you are formally collared, I can carry it in my wallet."

She didn't want to give in and be a scaredy-cat. "I trust you."

"Thank you, Hope."

He did indeed have a wrap for her. As he wanted, she folded it and placed it in her purse. She could do this.

The drive to the restaurant took forty-five minutes. Again, this place wasn't easy to find. The GPS screen showed the road meandering along the Mississippi River. Lush vegetation obscured signs, and nothing indicated there was a restaurant nearby.

Hope's body was tender from his rough handling in the shower, and her ass burned in a way that ensured she'd spend the evening thinking about the reaming he'd given her. No matter how she shifted, she couldn't ease the ache.

"Problem?"

"No, Sir," she replied.

His smile called her a liar. And the smirk that followed told her he wasn't apologetic. He was happy.

The valet parked the car, and once again he instructed the doorman not to assist her. Though impatient, she waited for him. This part of submission, with him taking such exquisite care of her, was wonderful. Well, she had to admit, so far, most of it had been.

This time it was more natural to accept his help, and when he offered his elbow, she accepted. Together, they walked up the stairs toward the large building.

The owner, who Rafe introduced as Bastien Cauchon, greeted them. He rounded the stand and swooped Rafe into a brief bear hug.

"Mademoiselle"—he raised her hand to kiss it—"welcome to Vieille Rivière."

Old River. Appropriate. "Thank you, Mr.

Cauchon." Neither her dress nor her collar caused him to furrow his eyebrows.

"Your table is prepared, Rafael."

Rafe turned to her and placed his fingers against the small of her back. His touch was cool against her heated skin.

"Please." He nodded for her to follow Bastien.

When she entered the main dining room, her pulse slammed into hyperdrive. Many of the tables were full. A couple had people kneeling next to the table, one a man, another a woman. Submissives? Oh God, would he demand that of her? Frantic, she turned to him for reassurance. With tight lips, he nodded at her to continue walking.

Gulping for air, she did so.

In the middle of the room, Bastien stopped. There were plenty of empty tables around the outside, but Rafe wanted her in the center of everything?

The owner pulled back a chair for her, but Rafe said, "Thank you, Bastien. I'll see to Ms. Malloy from here."

"Most certainly, sir. Enjoy your evening."

In a nearby ice bucket, champagne chilled. Would it be inappropriate for her to just grab the bottle and drink from it?

"You're doing fine," he assured her against her ear as he scooted in her chair for her.

"I'm freaking out."

"I brought you here to be seen."

Quietly, frantically, she said, "I'm not kneeling

in public."

"Agreed. Not until you're ready."

"That's never happening."

At the back of her neck, he flicked the lock. "You have a safe word, and nothing will happen without your permission." He captured her chin. "But I will ask you this. Does anyone here appear unhappy? Are they concerned with anyone other than their dining companion? Is it possible there is joy for them in the action?"

She wouldn't admit it, but he had made excellent points, even if such behavior wasn't for her.

He dropped a kiss on her mouth. "Relax." He took the napkin from the table, shook it open, and draped it across her lap before seating himself opposite from her.

A bare-chested waiter with tight black pants bowed to Rafe and requested permission to pour the champagne.

"Thank you." Rafe sampled the vintage, then signaled for the flutes to be filled. "Give us some time to settle in, please. You can check back when our glasses are empty."

After she'd downed half a glass, he asked, "Better?"

"It's more than I expected." The decor surprised her. The walls were covered in deep red silk. Paintings, some that appeared to be the work of the masters, hung from the picture rail.

In addition to the people kneeling next to the tables, one of whom was on a leash and being fed pieces of cheese, there were bare-breasted women, one wearing a collar that appeared to be three or four inches thick. One gentleman with a slight paunch wore a leather harness along with a bow tie that matched one his companion wore. No one paid her any attention at all.

For something so extreme, it was all rather…mundane. Respectful, even. "Is everyone here a Dom and sub?"

"No. Some people enjoy dressing in fetish clothing. Many different kink lifestyles are represented. And all are welcome. Discretion is the key word here."

A group of men followed Bastien through the restaurant toward a table in the back. Each of them wore a summer-weight jacket and casual pants. They appeared to be the ones out of place here.

"The owner, he called you Rafael. And your mother did too, that first day in your office."

"My given name, yes. Named after my maternal grandfather. He was Spanish, a descendent of the first settlers in the new world."

Which explained his dark skin and the glacial blue of his breathtaking eyes.

"You have a storied background." And the obligations to go with it, a world he had invited her to be part of.

For a few minutes, she took in the atmosphere, the view of the lawns beyond, and the large berms of earth that perhaps served as a levee to keep the grand Mississippi within her banks. A woman strolled past, wearing a leash that a man held.

Rafe reached into a pocket in his jacket and pulled out something that appeared to be fabric and slid it across the table.

"If you prefer not to put them on in the dining room, you may utilize the ladies' room."

No. It couldn't be. She touched the fabric. Goose bumps raised on her arms as realization dawned. Vibrating panties.

"Rafe…"

In control, dominant, with an obvious, full expectation of her compliance, he sat back, steepled his hands in front of him, and waited.

Hope went through her usual mental gymnastics, like she had with the rose at the Bluewater Grill. She wanted to say no, but she was also intrigued. The experiences with the butterfly had been awful, yet the orgasms had been worth the aggravation. The fact that they were in public gave her pause. What if she groaned so loud that others heard her? Then again, would anyone notice?

She reached toward the panties, then dropped her hand in indecision again.

Of course, there was the word she could use as a safety net, yet the wicked part of her that he'd uncovered flicked it to the side. If she did cry out, it would reflect on him.

This time, when she reached for the garment, she did it with confidence. Then she grabbed her purse to tuck the small scrap of fabric inside.

He shook his head.

"What?"

"No hiding."

"You don't care if people know what we're doing?"

"Not in the least." The rich timbre of his voice shot through her, reminding her of the dirty things he'd said to her in the shower. "In fact, I'd prefer that they did."

With a sigh, she pushed back her chair. Like a gentleman, he stood. "One day, sweet Hope, you'll do what I ask without all this equivocation."

She doubted that. Clutching the underwear, she fled toward the restroom. And once again, no one paid any attention to her.

The bathroom was elegant, in an old-world way, with gorgeous tiling and brass fixtures. There were a number of individual rooms, each with a heavy door that reached almost to the ceiling. Grateful for the privacy, she slipped into the silky panties. Then, filled with expectation, she stood there, waiting for something to happen.

When it didn't, she pulled the chain on the overhead tank to flush the toilet, just in case anyone noticed, then shook her head at her own ridiculousness.

She paused to wash her hands at the vanity, and the sight of her reflection made her do a double take. Her eyes were more golden than ever before. Perhaps because of the collar? Hope traced it, marveling at the woman in the mirror. She was still herself, but so much more... More adventurous, more alive. Rafe had given her all that, and the more she received, the more she wanted, even when he shocked her with his requests.

A woman, a Domme, if Hope was correct, entered and nodded. Jolted from her thoughts and knowing Rafe would soon send in a search party, or worse, walk in himself, Hope turned on the faucet. After washing and drying her hands, she left the restroom.

As she entered the dining room, her panties buzzed. She froze. Not knowing what to do, she looked around for Rafe. He was studying a menu, paying no attention at all.

Suddenly the vibration stopped. She closed her eyes in relief. Pretending everything was normal, she smoothed the front of her dress, then continued on.

When she reached the table, he stood and pulled out her chair for her. As she was sitting, the panties danced again.

She wasn't sure she could endure an entire evening like this.

Mercifully, he showed some restraint. In fact, he went long stretches without activating the remote control—long enough for her to relax and forget that she was even wearing the panties. Which made it all the more disconcerting when the vibration chased through her, sometimes for a few seconds, and once for much longer.

After dinner, their server returned with coffee and the dessert Rafe had ordered—the best crème brûlée outside of Paris.

She was adding sugar to her cup when Rafe turned on the panties. Her hand shook as she dumped the crystals, but she struggled to tolerate it, knowing he'd turn off the device in a couple of seconds.

He didn't.

Instead, he drizzled cream into his cup.

She squirmed.

He picked up his dessert spoon and dipped it into the dessert. "Bite?" he offered.

Had he forgotten that he'd turned it on? She shook her head.

"Don't mind if I do." He took a mouthful. "As good as I remember. You're sure?" He lifted another spoonful.

She wasn't sure how much more she could take.

Ignoring her reactions, he continued to savor his food. Breathless, she gripped the edge of the table.

"Yours is getting cold."

Her pussy throbbed, and the burn in her ass where he'd finger-fucked her intensified.

"Another thirty seconds."

"No. No." Her damn betraying body started to dampen.

"You can." He leveled his gaze at her. "And you will. Count backward from thirty."

"It should be twenty by now." She was miserable.

"Thirty," he reasserted. "Let me know when you're ready to begin."

"Rafe!" She was losing her mind.

He was implacable. Hope knew he didn't give a damn how much attention she attracted. Perversely, she was glad that he didn't let her off the hook. His resolve was something she could count on, and she drew comfort from that.

The panties shot extra sensations into her cunt. "Oh God." She squeezed her hands tighter on the table and spread her thighs as wide as the dress permitted, desperate for the underwear's crotch area to have as little contact with her flesh as possible. "Thirty," she managed, her voice little more than a hoarse croak.

"Sorry?" He took a drink of coffee.

"Thirty, Sir."

"Very good. Continue as you're ready. If you forget where you are, or if you need a break, you will begin again."

Her attempts to dissuade him had cost her at least a minute. If she had gotten on with it, she would be done by now. "Twenty-nine." She made it to fifteen before he dialed up the remote another notch. "Fourteen, thirteen…eleven!" Ten through five were a single gasped word. She reached beneath the tablecloth, yanked up her dress, and dragged the panties away from her pussy.

"Stop."

He stood and came around to her side of the table. She almost died when he flipped back the tablecloth and removed her napkin from her lap.

"Everything okay, Mr. Sterling?" the waiter asked, hurrying over.

"Fine, thank you."

With a nod, the man left them alone.

"Put your hands on the table, sweet Hope." He devoured her defenses, seeing straight into the secrets she hid in her soul "And leave them there."

"Yes, Sir." All the while, the sensations continued.

"We'll start again at ten."

What little remained of her composure threatened to splinter.

He snugged the crotch against her pussy. "That's better." He returned to his seat.

Tears of need and subjugation flooded her.

Once he held his coffee again, she started at ten. Her voice trembled, shook, broke as she fought off an orgasm, and more, tried to please him. Hope clenched and unclenched her hands with no attempt to hide her emotions. And when she reached zero, he shut off the vibrator.

Out of breath, proud of herself, delirious with joy, she sank back.

"I appreciate your efforts. You and your tears sustain me."

"Thank you...Sir." Pleasing him fed something deep inside her as well. Was that fucked up? Or was it perfect?

"Dessert?" he suggested, moving the ramekin toward her.

CHAPTER FOURTEEN

"It's a beautiful evening. How about a stroll before we head back to the Parthenon?" Rafe suggested when they were outside on the wraparound porch.

While that sounded wonderful, she was still turned on from the incident with the panties, and she was anxious about the rest of the evening. "With these shoes, Mr. Sterling, it will have to be a short one."

"I'll carry you if you need me to." His tone was dead serious.

The image of her held in his arms made her giggle. "I think that would count as cruel and unusual punishment."

He held on to her as they descended the front steps.

When they arrived, she hadn't realized how astounding the grounds were. The privacy of the patrons was protected by miles of hedges. No one, even on the river, would be able to peek inside. In front of them was a parking area surrounded by a giant sculptured hedge. Arm in arm, she and Rafe had explored the water fountain topped with a four-foot-tall carnival mask. Four curved concrete benches framed the area, with narrow paths between each leading toward the fountain. The edge was high enough to sit on.

Beyond, closer to the road that they'd arrived on, was a maze that he vowed to take her through on a future visit. As they watched, four people approached the entrance. The man stated the three women would receive a head start. Whoever made it out before he did was safe. Whoever didn't would be flogged while the others watched.

She gasped.

"Shocked?"

Unable to answer him, Hope stubbed the front of her shoe into the ground. The truth was, she was aroused.

Two of the women giggled and headed into the maze. The third was slower and got her ass swatted. Her yelp carried across the distance as she scurried off.

After checking his watch, the man strolled into the maze.

"I'm guessing he's done this before and knows the way."

"So, he's cheating?" Hope asked.

"I prefer the phrase *playing to win*."

The enthusiastic squeals and laughs receded as she and Rafe walked toward a topiary garden. Instead of gorillas or giraffes, these bushes had been shaped like masks, handcuffs, a harlequin, all the shapes that appeared on a card deck, even a mermaid. "This is astounding."

"I thought you'd enjoy it."

"Are we allowed to take pictures here?"

"As long as they don't include people, yes. And they cannot be posted to social media."

She fished her phone from her purse. When she was going to take a selfie, he asked if she wanted him to take her picture.

"Thank you."

He instructed her to stand near the harlequin. But that wasn't enough for him. He wanted her to lean one way, prop her hand on her hip, glance sideways at the topiary. "Bossy."

He snapped dozens of pictures. Then, when she was certain he was done, he took his phone from his jacket pocket. "More cleavage, please."

Her heart accelerated as anxiety and excitement tripped through her. But she did as he asked, parting the material a little more, then tucking it under so it stayed in place.

"Even more beautiful." As he snapped and zoomed and turned the phone to different angles, he walked toward her until he was standing next to her.

He tapped an icon to the front-facing camera. Then he draped an arm around her shoulder. "Say 'spank me, Sir.'"

"Cheese!"

He dropped his hand from her shoulder, reached down, hiked up her dress in the back, then pinched her ass hard.

"Spank me, Sir!"

"I love it when you behave. Again."

The warm air wrapped around her, and she was grateful for the panties preventing her from overexposure. "Spank me, Sir!"

With a carefree grin, he pressed the button on his phone. Then he did it a second time, creating a rapid burst, filling the screen with a dozen images of them together.

He reviewed the photos. "Perfect. Let's get you back so I can give you the fucking you've earned."

Hope couldn't breathe. Emotional weight constricted her chest. Desperate to escape her relentless thoughts, she eased herself from beneath Rafe's muscular arm. He held her tight, even though he was asleep. When she was sure she hadn't disturbed him, she slipped from the bed.

She tiptoed to the bathroom and pulled out the fluffy white robe, tying the belt as she crossed into the living room. Hope checked over her shoulder, waiting for sounds that he was still asleep before opening one of the French doors that led to the patio.

Outside, she turned on the landscape lights. She found the switch for the tub's jets. Seconds later, the pump roared, and bubbles shot through the water's surface.

Just to be sure, she dipped a toe in the water to test the temperature. Finding it perfect, she slipped off the robe, tossed it over a chair, then paused on the first step to give her body time to adjust to the heat. Once she was in, she laid her head on the back of the hot tub and watched clouds play peekaboo with a sliver of moon.

Though she was trying to unwind, she couldn't shake memories of Rafe's demands.

After they'd arrived back at the cottage, he'd stripped off her panties and as she stood in the middle of the room, gotten on his knees, and delved between her legs, playing with her, eating her out. He'd rewarded her courage with a mind-destroying orgasm that left her on her knees too, holding on to him.

As if she were precious, he'd stood, scooped her up, and taken her to the bedroom, where he'd made love to her. There'd been nothing but appreciation and caring in his touch. Though their coupling had lacked the physical sensations involved in one of their scenes, it had been so much more intense than anything else they'd shared, and it was devastating to her emotional well-being. When BDSM was involved, she could surrender her body while keeping her heart shrouded.

But a couple of hours before, he'd stripped that protection from her, leaving her emotions raw.

Afterward, Rafe had removed the collar so she would be more comfortable. She hadn't been. Rather, the absence of its inflexible weight bothered her. When she admitted as much, he nodded, and she pretended everything was okay.

He'd taken her to bed, then wrapped his arms around her until they both drifted off.

Hours later, the touch had suffocated her, and she'd needed to escape.

Warm water bubbled around her, the citrusy scent of magnolia drifted on the air, and cicadas buzzed in the nearby trees, yet Hope's thoughts roiled.

Out here, under the night sky, she could no longer hide from the truth.

She was halfway in love with Rafe Sterling. He'd been clear about his determination not to ever fall in love. Which meant she was invested in their relationship in a way he wasn't. Experience had taught her that could be disastrous. A wayward part of her heart wanted to shout yes to him, his domination, his lovemaking, his proposal. Her brain zinged with warning bells. Loving him without being loved in return would destroy her.

Afraid of waking Hope, Rafe snatched up his phone

that was jumping across the kitchen counter.

He sighed when he saw Celeste's name on the screen. Rafe still expected his father to show up and do his duty.

"Judge Anderson is willing to allow you to attend the planning meeting," she said without preamble. "Be in the Grand House at ten."

"Thanks." He dumped grounds into the coffeemaker, then turned the machine on.

She didn't immediately ring off, so he waited.

"The woman you asked us to look into? One Elizabeth Martin doesn't exist."

The fuck? "What do you mean Lillibet doesn't exist?"

"We accessed human resources files. All on paper. It would've been so much easier if they had been digital."

In other words, Fallon and Associates were already guilty of breaking and entering.

"Her resumé was made up. The club doesn't require an extensive background check, just calls to former employers and supplied references, none of whom we can locate. None of her coworkers know much about her, said she didn't talk much. Didn't show up for happy hours or participate in office gossip. Her colleagues thought she was a bit too friendly with some of the older members, but there had been no complaints about her work. One day, Elizabeth didn't show up for work. Her employer tried to contact her with no luck. On the second day that she didn't show, her boss went to her home.

Which doesn't exist."

"What about her paychecks?" He paced the room. "Can we see the bank records?"

"She never cashed them."

What the hell were they dealing with?

"How much money do you want to spend on this?"

"How much are we talking?"

"We're already ten thousand in. I should have consulted you before, but I figured you'd want those results, at the least."

She was right.

"I'll need fifty thousand as a retainer."

He dug a hand through his hair. With the stakes and unanswered questions, Rafe had no choice.

"I'll need access to your dad's phone records. He was contacting Elizabeth somehow."

Rafe had no idea whether Theodore's line was on a company account. "It's possible his assistant has them. Or…better, let me contact our IT department."

"Let me know. I'll start to work on it from this end if needed."

A pit grew in his stomach.

After he ended the call, he pressed redial on his dad's number. As expected, Rafe reached voicemail. This time, instead of hanging up, he left a message. "We need to talk." He paused, not for dramatic effect, but to figure out what to say next. Accusing his father's paramour of something would further alienate him. "A package arrived for you. A contract for a house in…" Where? "Barbados. Do you want me to forward the paperwork?"

Next, Rafe sent a message to the head of IT. Then he texted his mother to ask if his father had a personal cell phone account, and if so, were there any bills at their home or did she have access to an online account?

When no response was forthcoming, he forced himself to put down his phone while he poured two cups of coffee.

He carried them to the bedroom and found Hope snuggled deep beneath the comforter, her brunette hair spilled across the pillow. This morning, the sunshine reflected off it, giving it streaks of copper. Her head was tipped back, exposing her throat, the one he'd collared yesterday. Last night had been everything he'd hoped. She wasn't just the perfect submissive. She was the perfect woman.

Since she didn't stir when he walked into the room, he left one cup on a small table, then walked across the room to stand next to her with the other. He moved a hand through the steam, wafting it her direction.

Breathing out a sigh, she curled into a tighter ball, so he continued until she flipped onto her back.

"I think I'm having a dream," she said. "I don't want to wake up to find it's not real."

He swept the scent toward her one last time, and she pushed up onto her elbows. "This is real? There's coffee in that cup?"

"Indeed."

She scooched around, sitting up without

dragging the sheet across her chest. His Hope had become emboldened.

He sat on the edge of the bed and handed it over.

"How do I make this happen every day?"

"I think you know." He smoothed tangled hair back from her forehead.

After taking a sip, she purred. Then she drew her eyebrows together in a tiny, questioning furrow. "Are you telling me that if I marry you, you'll bring me coffee every morning?"

"We can write it into the vows."

"If you had said so on Wednesday, we could have saved ourselves a lot of time."

He smiled. "I've found the way to make you mine?"

Over the rim, she grinned at him.

"My meeting starts at ten. I thought I'd see if you wanted to go for that walk I promised you. We could have breakfast at the Grand House. You can sign up with the concierge for a massage or pedicure or whatever women do to their faces. Or you can spend the morning relaxing on the grounds or in the cottage."

"Sounds good. How much time do I have?"

"Fifteen minutes?"

She nodded, and before he could grab the shower, she claimed it for herself with a short laugh. He considered getting in there and heating her ass, but he'd be late for his meeting.

After a quick wash, she stepped out, and while

he showered, she dressed in the bathroom. "You're making me horny," he said, washing his hair.

Hope lowered her mascara wand to bat her eyelashes at him.

"I'm warning you, Hope. This is your version of living dangerously."

"Is it, Sir?"

He was already anxious to get his meeting behind him.

Within the allotted time, she was ready to go, dressed in formfitting white capri pants, a bright peach shirt, and a sensible pair of athletic shoes. If he made her drop her pants and ride him, the morning would be a complete success.

Outside, the golf cart that he'd ordered earlier awaited them.

"Is this your idea of a morning walk?" she teased.

"It will get us to where we're going faster." Like a proper sub, she waited for him to help her in. "Doing what I ask of you…is it getting easier?"

"It is."

He drove her toward the amphitheater known as the Acropolis. The clearing was shrouded with majestic Southern live oaks, lending an elegant air. Over the years, the seating had been expanded and now had nine tiers, all facing the enormous stage. "The facility holds just under a thousand people. We have entertainment here, lectures, discussions."

"It's really impressive." She pointed to the stage. "So, this is where the sacrifice happens?"

"Fishing for information again?" Expecting nothing less than her full persistence, he grinned. "It's a bonfire."

"Mmm-hmm." Doubt wrinkled her nose. "You're sticking to that story?"

Because this part of the country was infamous for its heat and humidity, the seating area was covered by massive peaked canvases with fans hanging from the beams. "There's an elaborate sound system, which is in storage most of the year."

"Where does everyone stay?"

"About five thousand people show up over the course of the two weeks. Since we don't have enough lodging, we have a number of RV sites. More adventurous souls can pitch a tent under the shade trees. A lot of members stay in New Orleans, and we run a shuttle service back and forth."

"And the Maison Sterling offers discounts during that time?"

"Absolutely not." He grinned. "We charge full rate if we know we're going to sell out."

"Is it true that some of the biggest rock stars have appeared at the opening night's ceremony?"

"The press does love to speculate." He parked the golf cart under a tree. "Shall we take a walk along the river?" he asked, assisting her out.

"We're going to walk?"

"I think you might enjoy it." He held her hand as they walked up the berm that kept the mighty Mississippi at bay.

"This... Wow."

He understood. Being so close to water, seeing the vast distance across and its churning tumble toward the Gulf of Mexico was stunning.

"I've only ever seen it from the Riverwalk in New Orleans. With a to-go cup of café au lait."

"After a plateful of beignets?"

"I'm not confessing." She watched the river for a minute before shaking her head with awe. "It's so different."

The Port of New Orleans and the Riverwalk were a big commercial network, with barges, tugs, tankers, cruise ships, even paddlewheel boats that hosted dinner cruises. On this bank, they were alone for miles.

"It feels as if time has stood still," she said. "I can imagine it looked like this a hundred years ago."

"No doubt it did."

For quite a distance, they walked along the top of the bank.

"Do you do this a lot?"

"Stroll? Relax? No." He was so caught up in life, in responsibilities, that he rarely took time to enjoy the solitude. "That's unfortunate, I suppose."

A man in a small fishing boat passed by, and they watched him maneuver around a massive log bobbing along on the surface.

They walked for another ten minutes, mostly in silence, before turning back. Being unable to reach his father preyed on Rafe's mind, and now, with the unsettling information about Lillibet, something had to be done.

"Everything okay?" Hope asked.

"Sorry. Family concerns." He sighed. "Celeste discovered that Lillibet may not be who she says she is."

"What does that mean?"

"Before she applied at his club, she didn't exist."

"How can that be?" She scowled.

"That's the question."

"I'm so sorry. This can't be easy."

He appreciated having someone to discuss private matters with. He kissed her with appreciation. No matter how heavy his burdens, she lightened them. Rafe might not deserve someone as innocent as Hope, but he sure as hell appreciated her.

Hand in hand, they returned to the golf cart.

"Now I'm glad you brought it," she admitted when he was covering the distance back to the cottage.

"The grounds are vast," he agreed. For a moment, he considered skipping breakfast and showing her what she meant to him. "Hungry?" he asked.

"Famished."

In which case, sex would have to wait. After this morning's meeting, they could spend the afternoon playing together. He'd brought clamps, and he couldn't wait to see them compressing her perfect little nipples.

They changed clothing, Hope into a short dress, and he selected a shirt and tie with a lightweight blazer.

Once they reached the Grand House, the maître d' seated them at a table near the window.

After they ordered and had settled back with iced coffee, Rafe regarded her. "You got out of bed last night."

"I didn't mean to wake you."

"You don't make many moves without me being aware of them. I feel you, Hope. I want to know everything you're thinking. I considered joining you. But it looked like a party for one."

"Thank you. I needed some time to"—she paused—"sort through some things."

"Ready to talk about it?"

She picked up her long spoon and stirred her drink, although she'd already done that once. "I'm not sure it's anything worth sharing." She allowed the beverage to drain from the spoon before moving it to the napkin.

"Concerns about BDSM?"

Hope glanced around the room, at anything but him.

"No." She toyed with her napkin, revealing nothing else.

"What our marriage might be like?"

"About love."

The waiter returned with a basket filled with small pastries and rolls, and Rafe took a moment to be grateful for the interruption. "About love?" he prompted.

"What if that were important to me?"

"Affection will develop out of compatibility,

sex — "

"I'm not talking about affection." She waved her hand, forestalling anything else he had to say. "I mean deep and abiding emotion that clobbers anything else. Something that would survive without sex. The fuel that becomes commitment, because you can't imagine living your life without that person."

Hope's question took him aback. They'd discussed his Three C's on numerous occasions. He looked forward to seeing her and fantasized about introducing her into deeper elements of BDSM. He'd shown much more emotion with her than he had with any other woman. To him, that was the basis of their relationship, a much stronger foundation than mercurial whims of an untrustworthy heart. Seeing the intent way she scrutinized him, he proceeded with care. "I prefer to put my trust in commitment, things that are more tangible." *Damn*. A sheen of tears covered her eyes. The exact emotion he didn't want, and he'd thought she didn't want it either. He'd fucked up this conversation, and he didn't know how to undo it. He couldn't make wild protestations of undying love, nor did he want to upset her. Instead, he settled for, "Does that matter to you?"

"It does."

"So you're saying…?"

"I won't get married without love."

The same blinding emotion that had gotten his father into the fucking mess with Lillibet? The disastrous feelings that had led to his sister's two divorces? "Hope." Rafe drew a breath, stalling for time while he figured out what the hell to say. He hadn't offered love, wasn't sure he was capable of it. He was convinced they could have a successful relationship without it. "We need to talk about this when we're alone."

She shook her head, and one of those wrenching tears escaped the corner of her eye. "Unlike everything else in your life, this isn't negotiable."

He reached for her hand, but she snatched it away. Obviously to compose herself, she used her napkin to dab her face before extracting a tube of lipstick from her kitty bag. She repainted the color, focusing on the tiny mirror on the end of the case. "There's Celeste!"

For once, Rafe considered Celeste's timing terrible. Any chance that she would offer a small greeting and then be on her way was dashed when Hope stood to hug Celeste. Hope smiled her gratitude at the reprieve while he seethed, pissed at the interruption.

"Would you like to join us?" Hope invited, desperation punctuating her words.

"Thank you. Yes." Celeste ignored the polite tip of the head, indicating he didn't want the company.

After they were all seated, their server hurried over with a menu and to inquire if Celeste would like coffee.

"English breakfast tea," Celeste replied. "Twinings."

The server refreshed their coffee, then brought

her a porcelain teapot with matching cup and saucer.

Celeste asked Hope about her stay and what she thought of the Parthenon.

Around him, the conversation continued. Some time later, he blinked, aware of both women staring at him. Obviously, one of them had been speaking to him, and he hadn't been aware of it. "My apologies." He shook his head to clear it. "Where were we?"

"Talking about the holiday extravaganza," Celeste said.

"It's April," he protested. He hadn't recovered from the trauma of last Christmas, when his dad hadn't shown up, and neither had his sister's husband. Arianna had spent the day in tears. His mother had been stoic. The entire day had been bleak and gray. Fittingly, it had even rained. In the end, he'd gone to work.

"I was suggesting it would be an excellent place for Hope to network," Celeste said.

Noah walked into the room and Rafe scowled. "What the hell is he doing here?"

Celeste splashed milk into her tea before saying, "That's why I stopped—to let you know the judge had no choice but to also allow Noah's attendance. I'm afraid your father's lack of communication has made things difficult." She took a delicate sip. "The sooner you're married, the faster this can be sorted out."

Her words were like a rock dropped into a still pond.

Celeste pushed back her chair and excused

herself, but neither Rafe nor Hope said anything. Hope's face had drained of color and tension crawled through Rafe's shoulders. When they were alone, he began, "Listen, Hope—"

"Morning, Rafe."

He bit back a curse when Noah approached, wearing a smug smile.

"I haven't seen Uncle Theodore, and I arrived last night. No one here reports having seen him either."

Rather than answering, Rafe countered. "I don't believe you've met Hope Malloy?"

Noah smiled in her direction. "Charmed." He offered his hand.

Having no option that wouldn't be rude, Hope accepted. Noah raised her hand and gave it an old-world kiss. Fury, seething and white-hot, ripped through Rafe.

Hope extracted her hand. "Rafe, will you pass the breadbasket, please?" she asked. "There's a croissant in there, I'm sure."

He admired her poise as well as the way she'd read him and the situation. "If you'll excuse us?" Rafe said. "My omelet is getting cold."

Noah slunk off, and Rafe raised his coffee cup in her direction. "Bravo, Ms. Malloy. You're a master at the social cut."

"It was either that or watch you rip out his jugular."

After breakfast, he said, "I haven't forgotten that we need to talk."

"There's nothing much to say." She exhaled a deep, shaky breath. "Depending on what time you finish up, I'd like to go home today."

Fuck. Why were things so out of control? "I'm sure it will be late."

"That's fine."

"Give me some time," he pleaded. "Give us some time."

"So I can fall deeper?" She shook her head.

Fury and desperation were a cauldron in his gut. "This is sounding like a goddamn ultimatum."

"Call it anything you want." Hope wadded her napkin, then pushed back her chair. Without another word, she left.

CHAPTER FIFTEEN

Goddamn it.

Rafe surreptitiously extracted the vibrating phone from his pocket. His father's name filled the screen. After days of the man not answering his phone, he'd called three times in the past fifteen minutes.

"Problem, Rafe?" Noah asked, interrupting something Celeste was saying.

The Titans gathered around the conference table studied Rafe.

"I apologize." He gave a half smile. "I need to take this call."

"Something more important than the Zetas?"

Noah asked.

Ignoring his cousin, Rafe nodded toward Judge Anderson. "Excuse me, please."

By the time Rafe was in the hallway, the phone had stopped ringing. He continued to a private alcove to return the call.

His father's voice was frantic, and Rafe couldn't make out the words.

"Gone."

He shook his head. "Slow down, Dad."

"Lillibet is gone."

Rafe exhaled. This was why he didn't do love. "She left you?"

"No. She's...gone."

"Can this wait? I'm at the Zeta meeting." *Where you should be.*

"Are you listening to me? She's vanished. I can't get hold of Celeste. Something has happened to her."

Rafe dragged a hand through his hair.

"I need you here."

Which would leave Noah as the Sterling representative.

"I'm"—Theodore's voice cracked—"losing my mind, Rafe."

Having no other option, he said, "I'll be there in a few hours." By the time he hung up, his father was sobbing.

He returned to the meeting room and signaled to Celeste, who joined him in the hallway. After he explained the situation, she said, "You can take my plane if you'd like to leave yours for Hope. And I'll make a team available for you, if you'd like it."

"Yeah." He raked a hand into his hair. "Thanks."

"We will need more than the fifty thousand."

Of course.

After breakfast, he'd taken Hope back to the cottage and left the golf cart there in case she wanted to go to the spa, so he asked a valet for a ride back. When he arrived, Hope was in the living room, purse clutched in her hands. Her luggage was packed, waiting near the door.

Breath whooshed from his lungs.

"You're leaving?"

"I thought you were the bellman. The concierge arranged a ride for me to the airport." Her eyes were swollen, but her chin was set in a resolved line.

His whole life, he'd been in control, and now everything sifted through his grip. He couldn't draw a deep breath. "Without telling me?"

"There's nothing more to discuss."

He strode toward her, only to have her take a step back. He froze. "*Fuck.* Hope?"

"We shouldn't have gotten involved. I knew that. This was a mistake from the very beginning. It ends now."

She deserved his full attention. They needed time, and that was the one luxury he didn't have. "Hope..." He yanked the knot from his tie. "I need to go to Florida."

"So? Go. You don't owe me an explanation."

"You're my lover, for Christ's sake. You matter."

"Do I?"

Her words hung, doubting, challenging. "It's my dad…" He needed her to understand. "Lillibet is missing."

"I'm sorry to hear that."

Damn her and her chilled, distant words. Rafe hadn't realized how much he was counting on her feedback to sort through the mess that was his family. "I should be back tomorrow. Let's have dinner. We can sort through this."

She shook her head. Destroying him, a tear fell from the corner of her eye. His gaze was riveted on the emotional path it traveled. "If you want another mixer, you can contact Skyler."

"Fuck that, Hope," he snapped. "Stop it."

She took another step away.

What the hell was happening between them? Last night had been perfect. And now…?

A knock on the door shattered the tense silence. "Bell service, Ms. Malloy!"

Rafe snarled, then shouted, "Go away!"

She walked around him to open the door.

"Don't. Don't do this."

Instead of responding, she informed the man which bags belonged to her. She followed him out to the golf cart and left without a backward glance.

Rafe picked up a vase filled with beautiful fresh flowers and threw it against the wall, shattering it and his heart into a million shards.

333

"Rafe?"

Exhausted, he glanced over at Travers, one of Celeste's most trusted operatives. Rafe had met the man a couple of times, and each time he'd been dressed the same. Black T-shirt, pants, shoes, jacket, glasses. His stealth was legendary, and until he'd made his presence known, Rafe hadn't even known Travers had boarded the *Lunar Sea*. According to Celeste, he'd come by dinghy in order to surveil the harbor.

Hoping Travers had found something, anything, Rafe excused himself from his father. In the past ten hours, Rafe had learned little. This morning, Theodore had played a round of golf. Rather than be bored with a bunch of men, Lillibet preferred to stay aboard the boat, sunbathing and drinking champagne.

When his father had returned, Lillibet couldn't be found. That wasn't all that unusual. She could have gone to the marina or a nearby restaurant, or even be visiting another boat. He'd called her cell phone and received no answer. He'd strolled to the marina and asked around, but no one had reported seeing her. Nor had any of their friends. When he'd returned to the boat, he'd observed that a couple of her drawers were ajar. A cursory search revealed that her clothing was there, but her jewelry was missing. Then he'd discovered that his money was gone. Convinced that something horrible had happened to her, he'd contacted Celeste, then Rafe.

Given what they knew about Lillibet not being

who she appeared to be, Rafe was willing to bet she had absconded with the goods herself. Compassion had stopped him from saying so to his dad. For the first time, Rafe understood how caring about a woman could screw with a man's brain.

The entire trip here, he'd been haunted by Hope's tears and coldness when she'd left the cottage. He'd called her a couple of times, but she hadn't answered, frustrating the fuck out of him.

With a sigh, he focused on Travers. "What's up?"

"You might want to have a look at this." He shone a bright light on the starboard teak railing.

A perfect Z was carved into the wood. He glanced up. "The hell?"

Travers turned off the flashlight and moved away, leaving Rafe's thoughts tumbling. A minute later, he returned to the area where his father was sitting across from Gabriella Vaughn, another of Celeste's operatives. Sleek and smart, she had proven her talents in the depths of the Middle East, working with a Special Forces team to help earn the trust of Iraqi women. Though her abilities to be empathetic and sincere were vast, they were backed up by lethal resolve. There were situations, Celeste believed, where women were much more effective than men, and Gabriella was one of Fallon's secret weapons.

"Your father was telling me about the first night he took Lillibet out," Gabriella said.

The first of many nights that he cheated on my mother? He plucked the glass of whiskey from

Theodore's trembling hand, then dumped the contents over the side.

"I need that."

"You need your fucking head straight," he countered. It was possible that Lillibet had duped Theodore. But the appearance of the Zeta symbol complicated matters. "Let's go through this again."

"Jesus, Rafe."

"You got up at…what time?"

"I don't know. Nineish, ten. Like usual." His father repeated the events in the order he'd told them before.

"What does she know about the Society?"

Gabriella leveled her sharp gaze at Rafe.

"The Zetas?" Theodore pulled his head back. "Why would she know anything about the Zetas?"

"You never discussed it?"

"Damn, boy. You know I want nothing to do with my old life."

"Come with me." Rafe led the way to the rail where the symbol had been carved.

"Who the hell did that?" Theodore demanded. "Did those motherfuckers do something to my Lillibet?" He balled his fists at his sides.

"Dad, listen—"

"I'll kill someone."

"Can you say for certain it wasn't here yesterday? Last week?"

"I don't inspect every bit of the boat every day. But I'd have noticed that."

"You may want to sit down again." Rafe sent a

message to Celeste before joining his father.

Theodore snatched up the bottle of whiskey and drank straight from it.

Threading his hand into his hair from frustration, Rafe went through what little he knew about Lillibet not being who she said she was.

"I don't understand." His father's face fell, and Rafe felt as if he'd announced there was no fucking Santa Claus.

"It appears you were set up," Rafe said, hard and flat. The goddamn problem was, he didn't know by whom or why. Had Lillibet been working with someone from the Zetas? Or had a Zeta known who she was and made sure she wouldn't become a problem?

With the story spinning circles in his head, he returned to Travers. "Anything?"

"No. Ms. Fallon is on her way. For now, she's advised against contacting the police."

Since Lillibet was an adult and there were no overt signs of foul play, and considering she hadn't been gone long, he doubted they would do more than take a report. And they might interfere with Celeste's investigation.

"I'm going to launch a search of the water, and we're checking the security logs for the dock. Not that they are reliable. Any number of cardholders hold open the gate for others."

Rafe had witnessed exactly that. People hauled coolers, pool toys, party supplies. Holding the door was a cordial, polite thing to do. "Are there video recordings?"

"We're checking that too."

With a nod, he returned to his father.

Gabriella was leaning forward with an inviting smile. "Mr. Sterling. I appreciate that this is difficult, but we need to know everything you know about Lillibet, no matter how small. Anything she said about her childhood. Friends. How she got the job at your club."

Rafe schooled his impatience as his dad sat with a clenched jaw.

Showing her calm professionalism, Gabriella persisted. "There's a picture of you two in the aft cabin. She's very beautiful. Is that why you asked her out?"

Theodore turned his phone over and over again, as if the action could make it ring.

"Dad," Rafe snapped. "If you don't want to answer, fine. We'll pack everything up and leave you to figure it out on your own." He watched a man slip over the side of the boat without even a small splash.

"It wasn't like that. We talked when I went to the club. One evening when I was leaving, she was outside crying. Her boyfriend had broken up with her and hadn't picked her up after work."

Rafe and Gabriella exchanged glances.

"I took her for a coffee and then drove her home. Christ. The apartment was a dump, and I didn't want to leave her there."

"Apartment?" Rafe demanded. "Where? We need the address."

Theodore went through old records on his phone's GPS until he found it. Then Rafe conveyed the information to Travers. Maybe they could get a real name from the lease.

Over the next half hour, Theodore outlined how the unnamed boyfriend had abused her, how desperate she was to feel safe.

Theodore had procured an apartment for her and the two began spending more time together. Rafe could see how the relationship had been built, even though the altruistic way it had begun didn't excuse his father's behavior.

Over time, she'd confessed to not wanting to ever be apart. Rafe was surprised Theodore had fallen for it. But wasn't that what love was? Blindness? Loss of good judgment? Jesus, the drama his father had opened them all to.

Rafe stood and paced, shoving aside his annoyance. He needed to focus on solving the problem.

The diver returned to the boat. Rafe shot a glance toward Travers. He shook his head, which was both a relief and a frustration.

Rafe's thoughts turned over and over, trying to make sense of one piece of the puzzle. Why would Lillibet leave now?

If she married Theodore, she would gain tremendous wealth as well as power. The missing money and jewelry represented a fraction of what she could get her greedy little hands on in the next year or two. As much as he hated to admit it, Rafe was starting to think that maybe something untoward had happened to the woman. A small, nasty part of him didn't want to care.

Even though he thought Lillibet's story about her boyfriend was part of the insidious web she had woven around Theodore, Rafe signaled to Gabriella to check it out.

Hours later, when Celeste arrived, they were no closer to answers.

Rafe took Celeste aside to show her the Greek Z carved into the wood.

"It could be something to throw us off," she cautioned.

"Yeah," he agreed. "And it could be Noah. Or someone else who wants my dad to believe the Society was behind it." The partial moon peeked from behind a cloud. "It could be the Zetas."

"We don't do things like that, Rafe."

"Never?" Members of the Society took care of one another, as they had since the very beginning. "I have to ask…"

"Fallon and Associates had nothing to do with it." Celeste's spine was stiff, her chin firm.

Such a thing was within the scope of her work if necessary, and they both knew it. He recognized how stupid his question was. Would she admit she'd been hired to remove Lillibet from his father's life?

Around eleven, Celeste notified him that the apartment was in a man's name and that her organization was attempting to track him down. She'd ordered surveillance on the building. An hour later, Celeste left for home. Her team stayed behind, with Travers remaining on the boat with Rafe and his father.

After showering, Rafe headed for a small room containing an even smaller bed. He stretched out and tucked his hands behind his head. The day's events marched through his brain in precise reverse order, ending with saying goodbye to Hope.

He grabbed his phone to call her, then realized it was after one. For a few seconds, he debated what to do. Then he sent her a text, saying he hoped she'd made it home safe and saying he'd call when he returned to Houston.

For an hour, he scrolled through messages and took notes, killing time, hoping to hear from her. Since it was the middle of the night, he hadn't expected an answer. But that didn't stop the bitterness of disappointment from crawling up his throat.

CHAPTER SIXTEEN

"How was your weekend?"

Hope glanced up from her computer screen to give Skyler a fake smile. There was no reason for Hope's disappointment and foul mood to ruin everyone's workweek. Skyler had thoughtfully arrived with gifts, coffee, and a pastry box bearing a name Hope didn't recognize.

"After a lot of internal debate and much gnashing of teeth, I went with cupcakes," Skyler declared. "I figured if the trip was wicked awesome, we could celebrate. And if it sucked, you'd need something more than a doughnut." She walked in and placed the treasure on Hope's desk. "How did I do?"

"You're a savior."

"Does this mean it didn't go well with McHottie?" Skyler removed both coffees from their holder, then flipped up the top of the bakery box. Ooey-gooey sweetness wafted on the air, fresh with the promise of making her forget her sorrows. Hope hadn't eaten all day Sunday, and now she was ravenous.

She picked up two napkins — one to use as a plate, the other to wrap around the tallest, thickest devil's food cupcake topped with so much frosting that she didn't think it could stand up on its own. Recognizing that it would make a mess unless she corrected the geometry to make it smaller, she did the sensible thing and took an enormous bite.

Deep inside, the sugar rush hit her, firing all the neural pleasure centers. She moaned in appreciation. Saturday evening, she'd arrived back in Houston during a torrential downpour. Even after a hot shower, she'd been unable to sleep. Her phone had been in her hand when Rafe's text arrived.

She'd fought the temptation to answer. Instead, she'd blocked his number.

Sunday had dawned gray and dreary, ripe with humidity. The condensation running down her bedroom window had matched her mood.

Around noon, she'd forced herself from bed. After a cup of coffee, she'd checked her phone. There was a message from Skyler, saying the Saturday evening event had gone well. After that, Hope had morosely wandered her apartment.

Being so alone magnified her grief at leaving Rafe. Feeling as if a part of her heart had been ripped out, she'd forced herself to dress and leave the house. She'd dragged herself through the grocery store and managed her laundry through bleary eyes. Then she'd spent the afternoon on the couch, binge-watching television and shutting out the world.

After eleven, she'd hoped exhaustion would help her sleep well. Instead, she'd tossed and turned. At four a.m., she'd given up all pretext of getting any rest, worked out in her apartment building's gym, then taken a long hot shower. She'd been at the office since six thirty, but she hadn't gotten any work done. The cupcake sent her into a welcomed state of bliss. If she was lucky, she could stay there the rest of the day.

It wasn't until she'd finished her second bite that she realized Skyler was staring at her. "What?" Hope asked around a mouthful of frosting.

"I'm waiting to hear what happened," Skyler prompted.

"He's not for me. Or I'm not for him."

"What does that mean?"

"I'm more invested in him than he is in me."

"Did you fall in love with him?"

Her hand shaking, she placed the sweet on the desk so she didn't drop it.

"Oh no, Hope. He doesn't return the feeling?"

Hope blinked back tears. "Better to find out now, right?" Before she'd become one hundred percent ensnared. Hope brushed her hands together.

"He's a rat-fink prickwomble. Wait. No. He's a coward, rat-fink prickwomble."

Hope tried to summon a smile and failed. Again and again, she asked herself how she could have been so stupid to allow herself to fall for him. He'd given her dizzying sexual encounters, and he'd offered marriage, but he'd been clear there wasn't a happily ever after in her future.

"We shall crown him King of the Bastards."

"And leave him to the annals of history." Why the hell did that thought hurt so damn much? She took a drink of coffee to swallow the lump in her throat. "Damn!" Hope's pulse raced from the hit of caffeine.

"I made it a quad," Skyler confessed. "I figured the King of the Bastards would have kept you awake late at night...for good reasons and not sucky ones."

She took another drink. How had she been lucky enough to hire Skyler? She was more than an excellent employee, she was a thoughtful human being. Hope felt as if she'd won the lottery, and it was time to show her appreciation. "You know, I'm going to miss having you as an assistant."

"What?" Skyler choked on her drink, and Hope reached across to grab the cup before it tipped over. "What do you mean? Am I...?" She twisted a hand into her hair. "Did I do something wrong?"

"You're too damn good at what you do."

"Hope, you're scaring me."

Why hadn't she done this months ago? "You've

been doing a lot of the work as an associate." She paused to build the tension. "It's time you were promoted."

"What?" Skyler leaped from her chair, twirled around, then gave her butt a great big shake. "I'm going to be an associate, like Tony? I mean, I don't dress as well, but, like I get to do the magic hocus pocus by myself?"

"You do." Skyler's enthusiasm was contagious. "Unlike Tony, no purple ties required."

"He wore mauve on Saturday night. And a matching flower in his lapel. Women swooned all over him."

"Including you?" Hope narrowed her eyes. Had there been love blossoming that she hadn't seen?

"Ick. No. He's like a brother…"

Tony entered the front door and walked quietly across the reception area. In a few steps, he stood in the doorway and pressed a finger to his lips. Hope hid her smile.

"Or a cousin. Maybe a father figure. Or something. But no. No. Eww."

"Thanks a lot," Tony said, a hand over his heart. He exhaled a huge, shuddering sigh. "My soul is crushed, fair maiden. It's a good thing the engagement ring came with a thirty-day money-back guarantee."

Skyler's face drained of color. "Uhm." *Shit*, Skyler mouthed before facing him.

Enjoying herself for the first time in days, Hope sat back with her latte. Her personal life might suck, but she had the best possible colleagues.

"I'll do my best to get over you," he promised, adjusting his baby-blue tie.

"You weren't supposed to hear that."

"I gathered that."

"Really, I think you're the greatest. The best. I mean, wow. All that…baby-blue…and…pinstripes?"

Hope laughed.

"And wingtips. How debonair and old-world. Any woman would be lucky to have you."

"Except my daughter, was it? Or are you my sister? I'm confused."

She tucked a purple strand of hair behind her ear. "You're far too young to be a dad. Well, my dad, anyway."

"Thanks. I think."

Hope's mood lightened, and she invited them both to come in and grab a seat.

"Cupcake?" Skyler offered, sliding the box Tony's direction.

He sat back as if the treat were lethal. "I don't eat sweets."

"Oh. That's right, Dad," Skyler replied, reaching for her chocolate goodness again.

"I want to hear about Saturday night," Hope prompted. As she took another drink, Tony began speaking.

"My *daughter* was brilliant."

Skyler lifted her treat in a silent salute.

"I didn't need to go with her. She handled the room like a pro, talking to single ladies, collecting their cards, and she even got a special invitation. Tell her," he prompted.

"I met a producer for a local television station," Skyler said. "They have a breakfast meeting once a month where people pitch ideas for features on their morning news show." She grinned. "We got a five-minute slot on Thursday morning."

"Congratulations!" Hope lifted her cup.

"I thought you might want to handle it."

"No." Hope shook her head. "You did all the work."

"Me?" Skyler squealed.

"You can practice on me," Tony said.

"Excellent idea," Hope agreed.

"But—"

"You've listened to my elevator speech dozens of times," Hope interrupted. "You've got this."

"Swoon. You mean you think I'm ready?"

"I do." Hope grinned. "Tell Tony your news."

"Turns out I'm the newest associate at the Prestige Group." Skyler jumped up to repeat her butt wiggle. It was impressive enough for Tony to blush.

"Well deserved," he managed.

And if they kept growing, Hope may have the opportunity to open a second branch, perhaps in Dallas, or even New York City. There was nothing—and no one—stopping her from moving.

A tremor of loneliness echoed inside her. She forced herself to ignore it. She had her dreams and her business, and she took tremendous pleasure from that.

"Hope?"

Realizing the world had gone on without her, she put down her cup and refocused on Skyler. "Sorry?"

"Tony had a great night on Saturday too. We make an excellent team."

He outlined his evening's results. He'd met a gentleman who might be a potential match for one of their female clients, and he'd had a discussion with a successful career woman who was seeking a wife who wanted to be a stay-at-home mom.

Interesting. "Is she wanting to sign an agreement with us?" Hope asked.

"I wasn't sure if we can be helpful."

She nodded. "If you want to spend some time on it, that's fine, but I wouldn't invest a lot of energy into it."

"Agreed."

They all shared their schedules for the upcoming week, including a mixer for a man who'd made millions in the oil business and had three ex-wives, something they would warn their candidates about.

Hope suggested Tony take Friday off as compensation for working Saturday, and she offered Skyler a vacation day the following Monday.

"And miss all the weekend gossip and pastries? No chance. Can I keep it as a floater, maybe add it to my vacation? I'm thinking I may want to go to a sunny beach somewhere with a hot guy to peel my grapes and bring me cocktails."

"A stake through my heart," Tony said.

"Perfect," Hope replied.

Tony raised an eyebrow.

"I wasn't referring to your demolished feelings, Tony," Hope reassured him. "I meant that would give us time to hire a replacement for Skyler."

"There is no replacement for Skyler," Tony countered while Skyler shimmied a shoulder.

"Can you contact the employment agency?" Hope asked, fearing he was right. Skyler was unique. For the next fifteen minutes, they brainstormed a job description and work hours for the upcoming new hire.

"If she has bookkeeping experience, that would be a plus," Skyler added. "Save us some time with the accounting service."

"What if she's a he?" Tony asked.

Hope and Skyler blinked.

"I'm feeling like men are underrepresented here."

"True story," Skyler agreed. "Maybe someone younger than Tony, you know, less like a dad. But he needs to have a nice phone voice. Sultry, you know? Think of how he could invite intimacy when he answers the phone. Or on voicemail. *Pres-tiiiiiiige* Group."

"I think I've been insulted," Tony chimed in. "Was I insulted?"

"Not everyone does sultry well," Skyler reassured him. "Don't worry. You have many talents."

"Go ahead and let the employment agency know

that's a must have," Hope said.

The meeting broke up, leaving Hope alone once more. Spending time with her employees should have made it easier for her to get on with her day. It hadn't. Instead it reinforced how she had no one to share the intimate details of her day with. Rafe would have laughed along with her at Skyler's antics.

The thought of Rafe had Hope reaching for her phone.

But she'd removed his messages and contact information.

No matter how much she tried to make herself believe that was a good thing, she failed. His absence left her heart shattered.

Blocked?

Rafe's phone call went straight to Hope's voicemail again. She had a compassionate heart, and there was no way she would be able to swipe through every one of his relentless calls on the first ring. Which meant she must have cut herself off from him.

He alternated between anger, frustration, and despair. Goddamn it, this woman got to him to the point of obsession.

"Hey, Rafe. We might have something."

He scrubbed a hand across the stubble on his cheek. How long since he'd shaved? Showered?

Slept? What day was it? Wednesday? Thursday?

"Rafe?" Travers prompted.

"Yeah. Coming." He grabbed a cup of coffee, then went out on the deck. The sun was much higher than he'd expected, and it burned his blurry eyes. He'd spent hours last night poring through video captured by a camera outside the restaurant at the dock. He'd seen Lillibet leave about thirty minutes after Theodore. A big floppy hat had been pulled low over her forehead, shielding her face. What it hadn't hidden, oversize sunglasses had. She'd been carrying a designer tote that was big enough to hold all that cash and jewelry.

"About ten minutes ago, we intercepted a friend of Lillibet's using a set of keys to get into her apartment."

"Go on."

"Elizabeth's real name is Brianna Gibbons. They talked almost every day. But Brianna hasn't called her friend since Friday."

What fucking phone did they use?

"We've got a number and we're on it," Travers said, as if reading Rafe's mind. "Our guy went in with her. There's no sign of Brianna. We're debriefing the friend now."

He wasn't sure what his next step should be. And he wanted to bounce ideas and tactics off someone. *Hope.* He wanted Hope.

On a ridiculous impulse, he grabbed his phone and pushed redial next to her number. When her cheery voice filled the void, he slammed the device onto the railing.

"Problem?" Travers asked.

"Wondering how long I should stay here." His dad was a mess, drinking too much, sitting up all night on the deck so he could watch for Lillibet walking down the wooden planks toward him.

"Not much you can do," Travers said.

As best he could, Rafe was running Sterling Worldwide from here. But given his dad's absence, Rafe was needed in Houston. Jeanine had informed him that Noah was making himself indispensable to the employees.

Rafe went back into the galley, refilled his coffee, poured a second cup, then went up top with the offering. "I'm going home." Rafe extended the drink to his father. "You should come with me. Take your mind off this."

"I'm waiting for her."

"If she shows up, Celeste's team will notify you."

"You want me to trust them?"

They'd had this conversation a dozen times. "The police, then." Two days ago, they'd contacted the local authorities. Since there didn't seem to be foul play, they'd taken an obligatory report but not much action.

"I'm staying," Theodore insisted.

With great reluctance, Rafe nodded.

For the first time, he understood his dad's obsession with the woman he still thought of as Lillibet.

If something happened to Hope, Rafe wasn't sure he'd be able to survive. At first, he'd pursued her because he needed a wife, and she was a good fit. He wasn't sure when it had become something deeper, essential.

More than anything, he wished he were returning to her. Would there be anything sweeter than pulling her into his arms, onto his lap, reconnecting and exploring deeper?

Christ.

His soul ached from the pain of missing her.

He was wrecked, with no damn idea how to make it right. But he vowed to never stop trying.

Belowdecks, he contacted Jeanine to make arrangements for his plane and asked her to have a vehicle waiting when he arrived in Houston.

Rafe packed up the few things he'd brought with him, then spoke with his father and Travers. Within an hour, Rafe was on the way to the regional airport.

"Florida's a popular destination for your family this week, Mr. Sterling," the flight attendant noted when he was seated with coffee.

He scowled. "How so?"

"I'm sorry. I assume you knew. Mrs. Sterling was here a few days ago."

"My mother?" His blood chilled.

"No. I'm sorry, the other Mrs. Sterling. I'm afraid I don't know her first name. She always has us address her as Mrs. Sterling."

"Jessica?" She'd need Noah's signature on the paperwork to authorize the flight.

"She and her friend said they had a nice time."

"Friend?"

"A blonde woman. She slept most of the way. Too much sun, Mrs. Sterling said. I'm sure her name is on the manifest." She moved off to finish her preflight checklist.

"Laurie?"

"Sir?" She looked over her shoulder from the galley area.

"What day was that?"

"Saturday, Mr. Sterling."

"Do you know when Mrs. Sterling arrived?"

"No, sir. I wasn't on that flight."

A dozen thoughts slammed together, and he called Celeste with an update.

After he'd outlined the situation she said, "I'll procure the manifest. Anything else?"

His stomach was caught in an iron vise. "Noah and his wife are members of the club. See if that information gets someone's mouth to loosen up. I'll be back in a couple of hours." He checked his watch. "And put surveillance on Noah and Jessica."

"Consider it done."

"Have you finished the interview with Lillibet's friend?"

"Brianna, aka Elizabeth and Lillibet, was an out-of-work actress, making ends meet by taking shifts at the local coffee shop. She said she'd been hired for a gig, and all the friend knew was that Lillibet was supposed to make a—and this is a direct quote—shitpile of money for less than a month's work.

Before you ask," Celeste went on, "I've sent someone to the coffee shop to ask about Lillibet and to see if anyone saw her talking with Jessica or Noah."

He couldn't believe they were having this conversation.

Within an hour, he had the manifest. Jessica Sterling and a Ms. Mumford—whomever the hell that was, another alias, perhaps?—had been the passengers. The bill had been authorized by Noah.

Celeste had included a note that she was taking no action until she heard from Rafe.

The trip was interminable. He tried to sleep, but each time he dozed, adrenaline jolted him awake. None of this made sense.

Or it did. In a sick, bizarre way that his brain refused to piece together.

As the plane approached the runway, Rafe glanced at his phone. Nothing from Hope. *Fuck...*

Once he'd uncurled his fist, he contacted Celeste for an update. Since he'd left Tampa, his cousin's wife had played tennis with her ladies' league before stopping for an after-workout coffee. From there, she'd gone home. If she was involved in something nefarious, she didn't appear bothered by it. Noah hadn't left the office, even for lunch. "I need one more thing."

"You're in charge of the clock," she said.

"It's Hope."

Celeste was quiet for a moment. "I'm sorry?"

"I screwed things up. She's blocked my calls."

"People, relationships, are special, Rafe. They

should be treated that way."

"Fuck." He exhaled. "Is this your way of telling me you won't help me?"

"Why, yes, it is." Her voice contained a cheerful note that had been missing for days. "Ultimate happiness requires risk." She hung up.

For a long time, he stared at the phone.

After Emma, he'd decided that he didn't want drama. And the fact that his father was suffering ought to reinforce Rafe's decision. It didn't. Instead, it showed him what he'd been missing.

He loved Hope.

Love didn't distract from life. It gave it meaning. Joy and pain. And he knew he no longer wanted to be on the sidelines.

He looked up a number for Hope's office and reached Skyler.

"For you, she's not in. Not today. Not tomorrow. Not any other time."

"Even if I sent you a bottle of Dom Perignon?"

"What year?"

"Your choice. A vintage year, to be sure."

"Ah. Damn you. But no."

"Can you pass her a message?"

"No."

He winced. Skyler was no longer the president of his fan club. "I fucked up."

"You most certainly did."

"Big."

"Yep."

Why did the women he spoke to take so much

pleasure in his misery? "Will you tell her I'd like to apologize?"

"Nope."

His little balloon of optimism popped. "I'm willing to throw myself on her mercy."

She laughed. "I want to watch that. She's been busy sharpening her claws."

"Fuck. C'mon, Skyler. What the hell can I do?"

"Leave her alone."

"Will you tell her" — Rafe pondered wondered how much to say — "I care about her?" He couldn't tell Skyler that he loved Hope. Hope deserved to hear that from him.

"Care? Hell, Mr. Sterling, I love doughnuts. And you *care?* Like what does that even mean?"

"I have more to say when I speak with Hope." Silence stretched and grew.

"Mr. Sterling? With all respect, you *really* fucked up. Hope's an amazing person. You should have treated her better."

"Yeah. I know." The admission was the best he could do.

Without another word, she ended the call.

After the plane had landed, he climbed into the waiting sedan from the car service.

"The office, Mr. Sterling?"

He considered. "Yes." He wanted answers. Celeste sent a message, letting him know Jessica had indeed been seen talking with Lillibet — Brianna — a few months ago, before she had left the coffee house for a better job at the club.

At the corporate headquarters, he took the elevator to Noah's office. He banged open the outer door, told the startled receptionist to remain seated or, better yet, call security, then threw open Noah's door. "Put down the phone."

Noah, standing, ended his call. "The fuck do you want?"

"Where is she?" Rafe strode across the room to slam his hands on the desk.

"What the hell are you talking about?"

"Lillibet. Where is she?" When he got no response, Rafe circled the desk to grab Noah.

"Lisa!" Noah shouted for his receptionist.

"I've already called security, Mr. Sterling," she said from behind Rafe.

The grief and loss on his dad's face etched in his mind, Rafe banged Noah's head against the wall. "Where the fuck is Lillibet?"

"You've lost it," Noah screamed. "I don't know what the hell you're talking about."

Security arrived and stood there, waiting for instructions.

"You can talk now," Rafe said to Noah. "Or you can do it when the police get here."

"Jesus, Rafe. You're a crazy fucking bastard. How the hell would I know where she is?"

"Okay, okay," one of the guards said. "Take it easy."

"I'll ask one more time—"

"I don't know what the fuck you're talking about!"

"You chartered a goddamn plane for your wife, who went to Tampa and is the last person to have seen Lillibet."

Noah went limp as he shook his head. "No. No, no. She went shopping in New York while we were at the Parthenon."

"She was in Florida."

"It's not possible."

There was no way to fake the kind of shock that Noah exhibited.

"I want answers."

Noah slumped.

"You can go," Rafe said to the security guards and to Lisa.

"Mr. Sterling?" she asked Noah.

"It's okay."

It took the trio some time and numerous sideways glances before they left the room.

"There has to be some mistake." Noah shook as he lowered his head into his hands. "She wouldn't."

"She did." Rafe contacted Celeste to let her know he and Noah were en route to the Richardson home.

"Team is standing by. Let me know if you'd like the authorities notified."

Since he wanted answers of his own, he told her to hold off. "Let's go," he said to Noah. "I have a car waiting."

The ride took twenty minutes. Noah mumbled and fumbled with his phone. Rafe snatched it away, giving his cousin no chance to alert his wife.

As they walked up the path, Travers and

another man appeared out of nowhere.

"Keep your mouth shut," Rafe warned Noah.

"It's a mistake." But his voice lacked credibility.

They found Jessica on the patio, a martini in front of her. "Noah!" she exclaimed. "What are you doing home from work?" Then she turned toward Rafe. "Is everything okay?"

"Jessie, darling, I'm sure there's an—"

"Shut it," Rafe snapped. "Where is she?"

"Whatever are you talking about?"

"Lillibet."

"I'm sorry… Who?"

"Cut it," Rafe said. He crossed the tiles and grabbed her shoulders.

"Hands off my wife!"

Travers restrained Noah.

"We've got you meeting with her at the coffee shop. It'll be a matter of time before you're tied to getting her the job at the club. Her friend can identify you. And you were in Florida this weekend. Your name is on the manifest, and Noah authorized the expenditure. I will ask one last time." He squeezed her hard enough to leave bruises.

"Noah! He's hurting me!"

Noah struggled to get away.

"Call the police." Rafe nodded to the agent. "I will ask one last time. *Where is Lillibet?*"

"Ungrateful little bitch was going to ruin it all!"

"What?" Noah went still.

"Noah, please! This should be *ours!* Ours." Hysteria mounted in her voice. "I did it for us! For you... She was going to ruin it all! Don't you understand?"

Rafe forced himself to release her before he caused real damage.

She dropped to her knees and crawled toward her husband.

Rafe crouched in front of her, preventing her forward progress. "Where is she?"

Jessica's eyes widened. "She can't hurt us." Her high-pitched voice was gone, replaced by a haunting singsong voice. "She was going to tell. Can't tell now. Can't tell now. She loved him. Ha! I promise. It's all okay. Shh. *Shh*. No one knows." She went around Rafe, focused on Noah.

"Damn it to hell, Jessica, where is the woman?" Noah asked, voice sandpapery with disbelief and disgust.

"At peace."

"Fuck. The lake house," Noah said to Rafe. "That's where she always goes for peace. God. It has to be the lake house."

Rafe knew the couple kept a second home, but he'd never been invited. "Address?"

One of Celeste's team nodded and moved into action while the other remained in place. Rafe sent a message to Celeste with an update and letting her know they might need some assistance from the authorities. She replied right away that she would be in touch with the mayors in both jurisdictions and confirming a team and the police were on the way to the house on Lake Livingston.

"Gate code?" Rafe asked. "And you're giving the police permission to enter?"

Noah nodded his assent and rattled off the gate code as well as the ones for the alarm and front door. "And boat house." His voice cracked as he added another.

"Is she alive?" Rafe asked. "Jessica!"

She didn't respond, and she grabbed Noah's ankle and started to inch up his leg, but he shook her off. "The fuck?"

Jessica collapsed in a heap, sobbing, picking at her skin.

Noah sank into a chair, head bowed, shoulders slumped, a broken man. "That poor woman."

Rafe struggled against the rising tide of empathy. But it was there, unwelcome. Noah wasn't responsible for his wife's actions, no matter how terrible. Rafe didn't envy his cousin the road ahead.

The police arrived, and Jessica curled into a ball, crying that she'd done it all for her Noah.

"My kids." Pain ripped through Noah's words. "What am I going to tell my kids?"

While Noah and Rafe watched, the police tugged Jessica to her feet, then read her Miranda rights as they cuffed her.

"Noah! Don't!" she begged. "Please! *Please!* Don't let them do this to us! I love you, Noah. This is for us. Nothing will stand in your way."

"Take her," Rafe said to the officers.

Eyes reflecting the soul of a shattered man, Noah watched his screaming wife go limp, causing her to be forcibly removed from the room.

The front door opened, then closed. "I'm so fucking..." Noah's words were strangled. "Sorry."

In the last minutes, Noah had aged a decade, causing cracks in Rafe's anger. He had issues with Noah's ambition, and his intent to destroy Sterling Worldwide, but how much had he been pushed by Jessica and her lethal, fucked-up quest for power? "You'll need to contact a lawyer." Rafe reached to clap Noah on the shoulder, but he couldn't bring himself to do it. Lillibet was no doubt dead, and his father was going to be destroyed. That, Rafe wasn't sure he could forgive. He dropped his hand. "And maybe a friend."

Drowning in loss and devastation, Rafe strode through Noah's mausoleum-silent home, intent on having the driver take him to the Richardsons' lake house. Rafe held out hope that somehow Lillibet was alive and that this whole thing was a nightmare he could still wake up from.

He strode outdoors, then froze on the front porch, engulfed in the surreal scene. Cop cars were parked at haphazard angles, their lights whirling, bouncing off trees, freakish and macabre.

Standing beyond the chaos was Hope, eyes wide, arms open, hiding nothing.

Rafe's heart crumpled. He'd figured out he loved her, but until this very moment, he hadn't known how much he needed her.

Her beautiful lips were pressed together in a white line, as if struggling to hold back emotion.

Haunting him, her features were stark. He'd done that to her.

Hope started toward him, then paused after a few, uncertain steps. In that moment, the sun caught her brunette hair, adding highlights of burnished red. She was part mirage and all angel. He wondered if he'd conjured her image to soothe the savageness raging inside him.

"Hope," he whispered, voice hoarse. Desperate for the lifeline she was, he devoured the distance between them.

She wrapped her arms around his neck and leaned in to him, offering strength, taking his pain. "Oh, Rafe. I'm so, so sorry."

He held her, cradled her. Then, when he could breathe, he pulled back a little to capture her chin. "I love you." He drew in her fresh scent, luxuriated in her. "I screwed up."

"Don't." She pushed hair back from his forehead.

He didn't deserve her. "I hurt you."

"We have time for that later."

Urgency drove him. This was important. *She* was important. "I've asked — demanded — that you to bare yourself to me, but I didn't take care of your heart." Where were the words? "Part of me is missing. I'm begging you. Give me a second chance. I'll be a better man." In the midst of the anguish around them, he lowered himself to one knee. "The only thing I have to offer right now is my love and commitment."

"That's all I want." Her eyes filled with tears.

Until now, he would have dashed them away, held her close until her emotions passed, but now he wanted them, bled for them. "Be my bride, my mate, my submissive, my partner, my equal. Let me love you." He took her hand. "Days won't be enough for me, nor the years, nor the decades."

Her tears spilled, and his heart threatened to claw its way out of his chest. "Is that a yes? Please, please say yes. Put me out of this misery."

She squeezed his hand with both of hers. "I'm scared."

"Yeah. So am I. We don't have to get married right away, if you need time."

Tipping her head to the side, she frowned. "You need to get married."

"I know. But I'll wait as long as I need to."

"I don't understand. You'd risk your business for me?"

"Do you not understand how much you matter to me? I'd risk my *life* for you."

"Oh, Rafe." Her shoulders shook.

"For God's sake, Hope, tell me you love me."

"I love you, Rafe." She crumpled into his arms, and they were bound together, on their knees. "I love you. *I love you.*"

Her words slayed him, healed him, made him whole. From here, from love, they could build anything.

Unable to breathe, he held her tighter.

Hope hazarded a glance across the interior of the car at Rafe, the man she loved. He was lost in thought, lines furrowing across his forehead as he stared straight out the front windshield.

She checked the rearview mirror, then tightened her grip on the steering wheel as she accelerated past traffic on the way up I-45.

After they'd somehow found their senses in front of Noah's house, Rafe had helped her to her feet. Police cars left in silence, and he said he wanted to go to his cousin's lake house. She'd offered to drive.

As she'd accelerated away from the metro area, they'd held hands across the center console, and he'd shared the horrible details of Lillibet's disappearance.

But as they'd navigated through traffic near the Woodlands and the highway lined by miles of pine trees, he'd lapsed into silence.

She was grateful Skyler had put Rafe on speakerphone when he'd called the office earlier that afternoon. Hope had heard his every word, and his sincerity had been an ice pick that carved through the protection she'd wrapped around her heart.

Then Celeste insisted he was suffering, right before she'd provided an update on the Lillibet situation along with Noah's address.

When Rafe had left the house, he'd stood on the porch, crestfallen with sorrow. And then, when he saw her... Her throat had swollen. His eyes had lightened as the demons had been vanquished.

The sound of a chime, followed by the disembodied voice of the navigation system, indicated she should exit the highway.

"Sorry." Blinking, Rafe glanced her way. "I was thinking about my dad. What to tell him." He pressed his thumbs to his temples. "When to tell him."

"I can't imagine what you're going through." Words were inadequate, so she settled for brushing a finger across his knuckles.

His phone rang with an update from Celeste. The police had entered the lake house and hadn't found Lillibet. A search of the property's two acres was underway.

Without saying goodbye, he dropped the phone to the console, then reached for Hope's hand.

Within ten minutes, she braked to a stop near the Richardsons' house, across from an ambulance and several police cruisers. Rafe pocketed his phone before they exited the vehicle.

"I'll wait here," she said after he dropped a kiss on her forehead.

He brushed a fingertip across her lips. "If you change your mind, text me and I'll come get you."

Halfway across the street, he stopped and looked back. "Thank you."

She gave a half-smile, the best she could summon under the circumstances.

At the gate, he showed identification, and the police officer stationed there waved him through.

Hope remained where she was, the suffocating

heat making everything difficult, including breathing. Somehow, that seemed appropriate.

Half an hour later, a uniformed police officer began cordoning off the area with yellow tape. Shortly afterward, a white SUV bearing the words *Crime Scene Unit* braked to a stop nearby, and two technicians began unloading equipment from the back. Hope wrapped her arms around herself as her heart broke — for Rafe, his father, for a young woman who'd been a pawn in some evil game.

Hope climbed into the car then leaned forward, resting her forehead on the steering wheel.

It took another hour for Rafe to walk around from the back of the house. His steps were short and deliberate, and his shoulders were slumped. Rather than waiting, she exited the vehicle to meet him.

He embraced her, holding her tight, as if he'd never let go. "God. Damn. She loved him. At some point, for her it had stopped being a charade." His voice broke. "They were going to visit Casablanca."

Hope had a dozen questions, and she didn't ask any of them. For now, it was enough that she was here for him, that they were together. The rest could be sorted through over time.

When he pulled back, his features were strained with grief. "I need to tell my dad in person."

"Yes. Of course."

"Go with me?"

The request stunned her. "Isn't this something you'd rather do alone?"

"I don't want to be apart. At least travel to

Florida with me."

She could refuse him nothing. "I'll go."

He exhaled a shaky breath that showed her how important her answer had been to him.

Although it was after business hours, he called Jeanine and said he needed a plane and the best available suite at the Sterling hotel in St. Pete Beach.

Hope drove them back to Houston. At her apartment, she packed an overnight bag, and when she walked into the living room, she found the Colonel curled on Rafe's lap.

Hope stood there for a second, staring. *How is this even possible?* "After I feed her, we can be on our way." As Hope spoke, the Colonel glared at her. "I think she might be your cat."

"Seems that way."

It wasn't until Hope opened a can of food that the Colonel jumped down from his lap.

"Traitor," Hope said when the feline entered the kitchen. She flicked her tail, then started to eat, ignoring Hope. "I feel abandoned."

"Pets always know who's a good person."

"Uh-huh."

He picked up her bag and carried it to the car. During the drive, she asked Skyler to cover, perhaps for an extended time. Then she had Rafe ask Caroline to take care of the Colonel. Caroline was shrewd. She negotiated for another spa day, a hotel stay, dinner, and a bottle of champagne.

"You drive a tough bargain," he told her. "But yes."

Hope shook her head. Was he going to be this much of a pushover when they had kids?

In his condo, he packed, and she watched the beginnings of the sunset unfurl across the sky.

"We don't have to live here," he said, coming up behind her.

She'd been so lost in thought that his approach startled her. "I haven't said yes to marriage."

"You didn't say no to shacking up." He gave an irresistible grin.

"Shacking up?"

"Living in sin? Cohabitating? Consummating? Doing the dirty?"

"Consummating?"

"We should get started on that."

At the heat in his words, her pulse turned sluggish. "We'll have time."

"Yeah. We'll go away together as soon as we can make arrangements. After the...funeral?"

When they reached the airport, the plane was waiting. Rafe held her hand through the flight, and he dozed, the stress lines around his eyes lessening. Now that it had ebbed, she recognized the anguish he'd endured since she left.

They landed after ten p.m., and they drove down the coast until they reached the hotel. "Are you sure you don't want to go with me to see my dad?" he asked after their luggage had been brought up.

She wanted to be with him to support him, but since she hadn't met his dad, it wasn't a good idea. "I'll be here when you get back."

"It will be early morning," he warned. He dragged her against him and kissed her with the emotion he hadn't expressed before.

Her toes curled, and her insides warmed. Having this moment was worth any risk.

"I love you, Hope. I'll spend a lifetime proving it."

She kissed her first two fingers, then pressed them against his lips. "Go and be with your father."

Before leaving, he kissed her again.

She walked to the window, pulled back the heavy blackout curtain, and watched him walk toward their rental car. It didn't surprise her when he stopped, turned, then scanned the windows until he saw her.

Beneath a light, he touched his heart, then pointed at her. He made her giddy, and her knees buckled in response. He was going through something horrendous, but he had still stopped to acknowledge the connection they shared.

After his car had disappeared from the parking lot, Hope drew a bath and sank into it. With memories of Rafe filtering across her memory, she closed her eyes. This time, though, the past wasn't all there was. Images of a potential future appeared there too—a wedding? The baby he'd once mentioned? Like mist, the pictures themselves were shrouded, uncertain, but not threatening the way they once might have been.

She fell into bed wrapped in a fluffy robe for security, and she was asleep when Rafe returned.

He undressed her somehow, then wrapped his naked body around hers, holding her tight, as if he'd never let her go. Deep inside, she wanted that too.

"Morning."

As the sound of the rich masculine voice sashayed into her unconscious, Hope slogged through the many inviting layers of sleep that separated her from the real world.

"I have coffee."

The devil himself knew her weaknesses and used them to tempt her.

"It's hot."

The reality of this morning, Rafe and his promises of love and their many tomorrows, was far more inviting than her dreams. With a soft smile, she allowed her eyes to drift open.

Rafe, her man, her lover, was beside her in the bed, propped on one arm. He smelled of spice. His hair was damp, and an errant drop of water clung to his forehead. Except for a white towel wrapped around his waist, he was naked. At some point, he'd opened the blackout drapes, allowing soft sunlight to filter into the room. His eyes were cerulean, and his gaze was riveted on her.

"Should I make love to you now or after coffee?" he mused.

"Don't make me think you woke me on false pretenses."

"Coffee, instead of this?" *This* being his dick, protruding against the towel.

"Nothing is more important than your almighty cock, Mr. Sterling." She paused. "Sir."

"Fuck," he groaned. "I need you, sweet, sweet Hope. I need you. I love you." He moved her beneath him, kissing her, murmuring words of love, nipping her earlobe.

Heat and the hunger for reconnection poured through her. "Please…"

Rafe pinned her arms above her head.

"I need to touch you."

"In a moment," he promised. "First, keep your wrists together."

He was maddening, infuriating…hers.

Rafe kissed his way down the column of her throat. He was intent, filled with purpose as he cupped her breasts, imprisoning them while he sucked on each nipple in turn. She writhed, struggling to follow his orders. Not grabbing hold of him was sweet torment.

When her nipples couldn't take any more attention, he traced a finger down her torso, over her belly, then between her folds. She'd missed his touch, and her body was on fire for him.

He made tiny circles on her clit and she arched toward him. "Rafe!"

"You can manage this," he told her.

"I…" She moved her head to the side and saw he was studying her reactions.

Connection arced through her. Though he was

familiar with her body, this was as special as their first time.

He dipped his finger inside her, seeking her G-spot.

"Oh God."

"You were made for me." He found her sensitive flesh and she cried out. "Are you going to come for me, Hope?"

"If you let me...Sir."

His eyes blazed at her acknowledgment that she wanted his dominance. "This morning, yes. This afternoon, maybe not."

She shivered at his promise of more to come.

He pressed his thumb against her clit as he stimulated her insides.

Hope screamed his name. Without warning, she came with a powerful shudder. She wasn't sure anything had ripped into her like that one. It was more than physical. It was her newfound emotional response.

She expected him to enter her, but he didn't. Instead, he lowered his mouth to her pussy and teased her until she cried his name.

"Now, maybe you're ready for me."

"I'm not sure there's anything left."

He knelt between her legs. "I'm betting there is."

Every part of her—her breasts, nipples, pussy, feelings—was consumed by him. He teased her entrance with his cockhead, making her groan. "More."

"Greedy," he said, but his smile showed that he

liked her need.

He slid in a fraction of an inch, then pulled back, leaving her wet and throbbing. He went deeper with the next stroke, and each of his movements seemed calculated to ensure she fixated on them and the relationship they were building.

"You may touch me now."

Exhaling her relief, she did, trailing her fingers across his skin.

"You're so perfect for me, sweet Hope."

He filled her completely, making her scream at his girth and penetration. Hope dug her fingers into his hair and wrapped her other arm across his shoulders, using a bit of force to leverage herself up to allow him greater penetration.

"Shit, that's hot," he said.

Their tempo changed.

Passion devoured sweetness. Carnality triumphed over longing.

He fucked her, hard, marking her with his masculinity. He demanded her full participation as a partner. Holding nothing back, she gave it.

"Wrap your legs around me." He dragged a pillow over and slid it under her to support her spine as she lifted her buttocks.

Since he didn't pull out of her pussy, it took a few moves before she was able to cross her ankles.

Once again, he trapped her arms above her head, holding her wrists down with one of his strong hands. Though he used one hand to brace himself, he was so far inside her, she could no longer think.

Over and over, he filled her.

With his cock, he claimed her

Her heart thundered, and her control splintered. Her internal muscles clamped down on him, and she gyrated her hips, grinding out an orgasm. "More, Rafe. *More.*"

"Jesus." He groaned. "The way you say that, like you can't get enough of me…"

"I can't," she confessed.

"Hope." His eyes closed. "Sweet Hope…"

She wanted to feel him come in her. Hope kept her hips high, letting him take what he needed from her body. "Yes," she murmured.

He stiffened. With a loud *"Fuuuuck,"* he spilled inside her.

Lost in him, she stayed where she was.

"So damn perfect, Hope," he managed once he'd regained control. He released her wrists. "We'll have to do that again."

"Not too soon," she said. "I may need a little recovery time."

"A hot bath will have to do you. I'm not waiting long."

She grinned as she lowered her legs. Her muscles had already tightened from being held in that position for so long. In fact, most of her body was a little tender. "I might need that bath soon."

Rafe rolled onto his side and pulled her against him. "I love you, Hope. Thank you for taking a chance on us."

She reached up to stroke back a stray lock of his

dark hair. "I love you."

"To our future," he said before kissing her temple.

"To our future," she echoed, rolling on top of him.

"I have to admit, I like your version of the future."

She grinned down at him. "I thought you might, Mr. Sterling."

EPILOGUE

"Shall we?" Rafe glanced down at Hope, who was stretched out poolside on a lounger. A giant yellow umbrella kept the sun off her, and she appeared quite comfortable with her after-dinner wine on the table next to her.

She peeped at him over the top of her book. He'd made electronics off-limits except for the hour they were each allowed to check in with the office every day. After the mental and physical grind of the past three weeks, they'd needed to disconnect and spend time alone with no distractions. In an unheard-of attempt to avoid work, he'd opted not to stay at a Sterling property and instead had accepted an invite from his college roommate, Griffin Lahey, to borrow his Caribbean island for a week. It had been an excellent choice. Each afternoon, a chef arrived by boat to make them dinner and restock provisions. Other than that, they were alone with the birds, the white sandy beach, the sunshine, kayaks, paddleboards, snorkel gear, and the bondage equipment Rafe had brought with them.

"One more chapter," she promised.

"Sunset waits for no man. Or book." The damn engagement ring that the chef had delivered this afternoon was like something live in Rafe's pocket. He'd designed it the day she'd agreed to move in with him, the Colonel and all.

It had taken the jeweler some time to create a drawing from Rafe's less than elegant sketch, even longer to procure the right diamond. The man had asked what her ring size was. Since he'd he had no idea, he'd snuck one of her cocktail rings from her drawer, traced the inside, then sent the tiny circle to the man as an approximation. Rafe had wanted it to be ready within twenty-four hours, and the jeweler had scolded his impatience, saying the diamond had been in the earth millions of years. Rafe could wait a while for it to be polished to perfection.

It had taken some finessing from Skyler to get it to the island. She'd picked up the ring from the jeweler and expedited it to the chef. The whole time, Rafe had worried that it would get lost, or worse, not make it at all before they returned to the United States.

To cover his uncharacteristic nerves, Rafe shoved his hand into the pocket of his linen pants, fished around for the diamond, then pressed his pinkie into the band. The metal, warm from being next to his body, reassured him, allowing him to take a breath. "If you have energy later, you can read in the bathtub." But for now, he intended to put his ring on her finger.

"If?" she repeated.

"I have plans for you, Hope." After they returned to the house, his plans included a prayer bench that he was sure had never been inside a church.

She gave an exaggerated shiver. "We could skip the walk," she suggested.

"We could, but we won't." While they'd been at home, they hadn't had much time to scene. They'd flown to Florida to accompany his broken father back to Houston for Lillibet's funeral. Rafe had wondered if Theodore would go back to his wife, but the thought hadn't seemed to cross his mind.

He'd returned to the office in a show of stability in the aftermath of the scandal, and he'd agreed to Noah's request to transfer to Asia, where he could keep his children away from paparazzi harassment. Before Rafe had left the mainland, Theodore had said he still intended to go on his world cruise at the end of May, and he planned to visit Casablanca. After Lillibet's death, he'd watched the movie. The unhappy ending reflected his own life. Just like the Bogart character in the movie's final scene, Theodore would always have his memories.

Hope snatched up a wrap and pulled it over her swimsuit, then slipped her hand into Rafe's. More than ever, he was grateful to have the beautiful Hope in his life. She'd been strong for him and for his father, kind to his mother, a shoulder for his sister.

She'd managed to hire a new assistant, which was a good thing. Celeste had referred so much business to Prestige that Skyler and Tony were having a difficult time keeping up.

In companionable silence, he and Hope walked down the beach. As the sun made its trek toward the horizon, they stopped. She stood in front of him, and he wrapped his arms around her.

"I can't get over how it drops into the ocean."

Texas had amazing sunsets that went on forever, but this was startling in its beauty and abruptness.

When the first stars appeared in the sky, he turned her to face him. "There's nothing more beautiful than this time together."

"Thank you for this trip. It's... It's been unforgettable."

He lowered himself to one knee. When he'd asked her twice before to be his wife, he'd meant it. But this time, with the ring created from his imagination, it was different.

She gasped. Her hair surrounded her face, tossed there by the sea breeze. "Rafe?"

His heart hammered. He'd kept shoving away the fear that she'd refuse, but now that the time was here, anxiety swallowed him. "My sweet, sweet

Hope." He pulled out the ring. "Will you do me the honor of becoming my wife?"

She pressed a hand to her heart. "You know you don't have to do this."

With Noah no longer challenging the succession, there was no longer an urgency, except for the one inside him. He wanted the world to know how much he loved her. "That wasn't the answer I wanted." There was nothing in her tone other than empathy for him. "I'm asking you because I want you to be my wife. I love you, sweet Hope, with all my heart."

"I don't know what to say." Her tears spilled, and her shoulders shook.

"Say yes," he prompted, extending the ring toward her. "Say you will be my bride forever."

"Oh my God. Oh my God. *Oh my God!*"

"Is that a yes?"

"Yes!" She squealed. "A thousand times a thousand, yes. I love *you*."

He slipped the ring onto her finger. The fit was perfect. Rafe stood, and Hope launched herself into his arms.

On the cooling, hard-packed sand, he spun her around and around. The sounds of her laughter echoed in his ears.

When he put her back on her feet, she studied the ring. "It's... Stunning." She lifted it to the sky.

"You'll be able to see it better inside. It's a yellow diamond. The gold color reminded me of your eyes." The stone was a rectangular cut and had clear diamonds on either side, representing their past and their future.

"It's beautiful." She raised on her tiptoes and leaned toward him. "Thank you."

He was a man helpless, smitten. He accepted her kiss as his due. And then he demanded even more from her.

She moaned as she molded herself against him.

"I still have plans for you."

"Do you?" She laced her arms around his neck and wiggled against him.

"There's a flogger in the bedroom."

Her eyelids drifted down just a bit. "I know."

"You know?"

"I've been waiting. Wanting. Make me yours in all ways, Rafe. Sir."

He scooped her up. Practicing carrying her across the threshold, he started toward the house.

She laughed, tipped her head while the breeze played with her long hair, and she admired her ring.

"Keep still," he cautioned.

"Or else?"

"Yeah." Unable to hide his joy, his relief, he grinned down at her. "Or else." This was the start of something amazing. He intended to savor every single moment

Be sure to check out the bestselling Bonds heroes, beginning with Crave.

Have you ever wanted to be Mastered? Here's

your chance. Discover why With This Collar was a #1 best seller. Master Marcus will curl your toes and give you a very happily ever after.

Don't miss any news! Sign up for my VIP reader newsletter for updates, giveaways, bonus reads, and more.

Please connect with me on social media or drop me an email. I love hearing from you!

www.sierracartwright.com

OTHER TITLES BY SIERRA CARTWRIGHT

Titans

Sexiest Billionaire
Billionaire's Matchmaker
Billionaire's Christmas

Power

His to Claim
His to Cherish

Bonds

Crave
Claim
Command

The Donovans

Bind
Brand
Boss

Mastered

With This Collar
On His Terms
Over The Line
In His Cuffs

For The Sub
In The Den

Master Class

Initiation
Enticement

Hawkeye

Come to Me
Trust in Me
Meant for Me

Individual titles

Double Trouble
Shockwave
Bound and Determined
Three-Way Tie
Signed, Sealed, and Delivered

ABOUT SIERRA CARTWRIGHT

Sierra Cartwright was born in England, and her early childhood was spent traipsing through castles and dreaming of happily-ever afters. She was raised in the Wild West and now lives in Galveston, Texas. She loves the beach and the artistic vibe of the island.

Made in the USA
Middletown, DE
28 December 2018